A Cornish Winter's Tale

Anna Carlyle

About the Author

Anna Carlyle has wanted to write since she was first introduced to the joys of escapism with a school assignment to imagine herself as an 'Armchair Traveller'. The love of words led to a personal collection spilling out of numerous Billy bookcases into storage boxes, and it remains her ambition to have a library capable of accommodating every book, with room for more.

Anna's greatest joy when writing is when her characters tell her what they want to say and do. Sometimes they can be most insistent. Her writing is full of unashamed wish fulfillment, because really, what's the point of creating another world unless it's just that bit more fun to live in than the real one?

When not reading or writing, Anna loves walking in nature with her camera, getting her hands dirty in her garden (and feeding the visiting wildlife), dancing to music as if nobody's watching and enjoying a glass or two of wine.

Connect via:

Website: annacarlyle.net

Twitter: @AnnaRCarlyle

Instagram: @annarcarlyle

About the Book

Summer and Jonny have been friends since childhood, growing up in the same Cornish village, sharing their love of the sea and coastal adventures. However, time and the realities of life have created struggles and long periods of separation. But they've never forgotten one another and have succeeded in finding their way back to each other when winter holiday visits have allowed. As Summer returns home for a Christmas to remember, she looks back over her life and reflects on mistakes made and opportunities missed. Back in Cornwall, with a renewed determination to finally start living the life she really wants, might Summer and Jonny finally overcome the wounds of their past and find their moment?

A compelling romance that blends lightness and laughter with moving episodes of heartbreak and drama, *A Cornish Winter's Tale* tells Summer and Jonny's story over the years, as they lose one another and then find one another again, always brought back together by a soul-deep, unbreakable connection that neither of them can ever entirely escape, even when they are foolish enough to try.

.

Acknowledgements

Many thanks to everyone who provided encouragement and expressed enthusiasm for this book. I very much hope you enjoy it.

A huge and unending thank you to Melanie, who not only provided support throughout its creation, but whose work on the cover and help with the manuscript has been invaluable. You are amazing!

Contents

Part One

The Day Before Christmas Eve

T he train eased to its final stop at Newquay station's single platform, and I got up to heave my duffle bag down from the overhead shelf. Even though this was the end of the line – only another couple of hundred metres would have had us completing our journey in the sea – it was packed with people looking to enjoy their Christmas in the warm embrace of Cornwall's magic, some visiting family, others escaping it. Tomorrow was Christmas Eve and the slightly steamy carriage was lively with excitement and anticipation – and a sprinkle of festive jumpers.

My phone pinged and I pulled it out of my pocket. A text from my father: 'Car park full. Driving round. See you by post box.' I surveyed the eager crowd gathering by the doors and sent up silent thanks that I was to be saved from playing my part in the inevitable wait for a taxi. My father, Peter Lowell, retired solicitor and all-round good egg, was reliable to a fault.

The train doors were released and passengers streamed onto the platform. I followed the crowd out to the car park, chaotic with cars circling, reversing and double-parked. I turned left and made my way towards the red pillar box on the corner. A watery sun was doing its best to brighten the winter afternoon. I texted my father to tell him I'd arrived and a few minutes later his dark blue Jaguar saloon pulled into the station approach. He did a quick u-ey and came to an abrupt halt in front of me. Exiting cars immediately began to pile up behind him, and I threw my bags onto the back seat, and myself into the passenger seat, as swiftly as possible. We managed to pull away having only been tooted once.

As we waited to turn left onto the main road, my father looked over at me with a smile. "Journey okay? How was the change?"

"The train was packed, but otherwise everything was fine. No problems at Par. I even got a seat all the way."

He nodded, satisfied. We pulled out into traffic. "Your mother's looking forward to seeing you. She's been cooking for the party, of course, but she's still filled at least a couple of tins with mince pies."

I smiled. "I cannot wait. Either to see Mum, or her mince pies. Everything going okay with party prep?"

"Oh, you know your mother. She could whip an untidy military manoeuvre into shape in a jiffy."

I smiled and turned my attention to the passing buildings as we made our way out of Newquay. I lowered the window a few inches and took an inhale of the brisk, clean Cornish air I had missed so much. Relief and the comfort of familiarity washed over me, that precious feeling of homecoming which I'd been looking forward to for weeks. The anticipation had kicked into high gear as my train had pulled out of Paddington and built steadily with every mile we had travelled west. But as soon as the train had rumbled over Brunel's iron bridge across the Tamar, I'd begun to relax with the knowledge that I was almost home. This year, my usual emotions about returning to Cornwall were augmented by a simmering excitement in the pit of my stomach, and as the fields which surrounded Newquay came into view, the anticipation of what the next two weeks could bring skittered up and filled my chest.

There had been a time, a little over a decade earlier, when I had been excited to leave Cornwall for pastures new, keen to explore the big, much noisier and flashier world beyond, but as the years had passed, I'd come to long for its beauty and wild spirit more and more. This year I'd booked these days off work months ahead, at last able to secure almost two weeks of festive vacation time. Any requests to amend my dates were steadfastly refused. Absolutely nothing would be allowed to interfere with my Cornish Christmas this time.

As we left the roundabout on the edge of town and found ourselves quickly amongst fields and country lanes, I wondered, not for the first time, if I'd been mad to ever leave. My father turned right onto the road which led back towards the sea and our village. The high hedgerows were bare of leaves under the winter sky, and I hoped that this coming year I would finally see them in leaf once again. But for now, I was excited just to see them at all.

We reached the edge of Crantock, my father pointedly ignoring the recently finished new builds as we drove past. Crantock is a Cornish coastal village, home to just under a thousand souls, surrounded by pretty countryside and only minutes from both the tidal River Gannel and the highly picturesque Crantock Bay. At its heart are the ancient church of St Carantoc, dating from the time of the Normans, complete with atmospheric graveyard and charming lychgate; a couple of pubs which have been helping to quench the local thirst for a few hundred years or more; a small village shop, currently a Londis; and a village green which still boasts a traditional, red telephone box. The houses at the centre of the village are mostly old and varying degrees of chocolate box, several flaunting thatched roofs. The houses on the outskirts are newer and less chocolate box, but still highly prized for their location just minutes from beautiful, unspoilt coastline. I was born and brought up here and consequently was lucky enough to enjoy a childhood many would describe as idyllic. I wouldn't even strongly disagree with that assessment.

We squeezed between parked and oncoming cars, then turned down the lane to home. Arriving at the narrow entrance to our driveway, flanked on either side by high hedges bursting over stone walls, we pulled in and parked in front of my parents' handsome, grey stone house.

My father tooted, and a few moments later the front door opened and my mother appeared. She waited, smiling, at the top of the steps, as my father removed my duffle bag from the car. Lucy, our golden retriever, and Donald, our Yorkshire terrier and her partner in crime, were not so patient and came bounding down to greet us. I indulged in a spot of preliminary petting, before following my father up the steps to my mother. My parents' house was built into the side of a small incline, and the twelve stone steps required to reach the front door were a source of constant irritation to delivery men. The dogs hustled up behind us and powered into the house.

My mother gave me a firm hug and we exchanged hellos. I took in the beautiful silver and white decorated Christmas tree in the hallway and the identically trimmed larger version which I could spy through the living room door. There was extravagant but tasteful festive foliage entwined around the staircase balustrade and arranged over other suitable surfaces, along with a lovely be-ribboned wreath on the front door.

"The house looks beautiful, Mum."

"Thank you, darling."

I followed her into her warm, farmhouse-style kitchen. The smell of Christmas baking filled the air. Lydia Lowell was an artist, skilled cook, extreme organiser and force of nature, elegant, poised, and the same dress size at 55 as she had been at 25.

She turned towards the kettle and flicked it on. "Why don't you go upstairs and get settled, and I'll make us some tea."

"Thanks, I won't be long."

I climbed the stairs to my room, where my dad had put my bag on the chair. A pile of fresh, fluffy white towels sat on the bed. A sprightly looking poinsettia had been placed on the chest of drawers to add seasonal cheer. I walked over to admire it, noticing a faded and dusty cardboard box, about the size of an office document box, sitting next to it. On top was a yellow sticky note from my mother: *Found this when clearing out the loft. Do you want anything in it?*

As I pulled up the flaps of the box, the memory of it came back to me. After I'd been in London for a few years, and my parents had realised that my visits home were going to be few and far between, my mother had asked me to pack away as many as possible of the personal bits and pieces I'd left behind, so they could use my room as a guest room when the need arose. Much I'd just tossed, but I'd also filled a box with various things I wanted to keep, and this was that box.

I peered inside at the contents: a few books, old cards and notes, concert ticket stubs, some faded invitations. I reached in and my hand closed around an envelope. I pulled it out. The paper had stiffened and dried out over the years, but otherwise it was undamaged. I opened it and pulled out a handful of photos. I began to look through them, nostalgia flooding over me as I saw faces from childhood and my teen years I hadn't seen in reality in a decade or more, many of whom I doubted I would ever see again. But there were some who were still familiar to me, and I stopped as I came to a photo of faces I still knew well, albeit at a distance most of the time. The photo was of me, Summer Lowell, my teenage best friend, Jenna, and the male half of our little gang of four, Jonny and Mike.

Ours having been the last generation whose memories were committed to film and paper, this was no filtered digital image, but a grainy photo with its subjects exposed in all their teenage awkwardness. Both Jenna and I wore too much makeup, Jenna particularly heavy on the eyeliner. Jonny was still trying to decide what to do with his hair, his dark curls too short at the back and too long in the front, half-covering dark, intense eyes. Mike's dirty blond hair was worn in a close crop, his smile mischievous and confident. The photo had clearly been taken at night, and the memory came back to me as I turned it over to read the note I'd made in my teenage scrawl: *Youth Club Xmas Party 5th Form.*

Part Two

14 Years Ago

I looked out my bedroom window and felt a definite sulk coming on. Tonight was the area youth club Christmas dance, and it was drizzling. I smoothed my hand over hair that I'd just spent half an hour scrupulously straightening and tried to push down the dread bubbling up in my stomach that the drizzle and encroaching mist would soon render all my efforts null and void.

I heard the doorbell chime downstairs, and a minute later Jenna came charging into my room. Her golden curls flowed perfectly down her back and around her shoulders in a manner guaranteed to induce extreme jealousy on my part. My own hair was the sort of dull, uninteresting brown that had me spending hours in the Boots hair colour aisle, gazing longingly at the boxes with their promises of glorious, glossy, *interesting* colours, but requests to my mother for permission to colour my hair had been met with a dismissive, "Don't be ridiculous. There'll be plenty of time for that kind of thing when you're older." Jenna had no such longings; her naturally blonde hair was effortlessly highlighted by the sun in the summer, and by the time it needed a bit of brightening up, spring had rolled around again and the clocks were going forward.

"Ready to go?" Jenna said, not managing to hide the hint of impatience in her voice.

I cast another unhappy glance towards the window. "I suppose so." I looked at her doubtfully. "Do you think this dress looks okay? Not too frumpy?"

I'd managed to persuade my mother to shell out for a new dress for the party, but she'd insisted on supervising the purchase, so, rather than the slinky, figure-hugging number I'd had in mind, I was wearing a tasteful, silky black affair, with an empire waist embellished with black sequins, little cap sleeves and a decidedly modest scoop neckline. At least the hem was above my knees. It was definitely pretty, but pretty hadn't been my desired vibe.

"You look gorgeous, babe, and don't pretend you don't know it. What do you think of mine?" Jenna shrugged off her coat to show off the dress that I was already familiar with, as I'd been there when she'd bought it. Her mother having handed her daughter a wad of cash as she dashed out the door, along with accompanying free rein as to dress choice, Jenna had succeeded in finding the dress in Newquay most likely to have been snapped up by a passing Mariah Carey. Barely an inch of her slender body's form was left to the imagination, and as if my hair envy wasn't already annoying enough, she was totally pulling it off.

"I can already see the steam coming off the boys when they lay eyes on you." I pulled my coat out of the wardrobe. "Perhaps I should pick us up a shitty stick on the way there to be sure I can beat them off for you when it gets too much."

She laughed. "You'd do that for me?"

I grinned at her. "What are besties for?" I threw various makeup and hair helpers into my smallest handbag as she put her coat back on. "Let's go do this thing!"

We walked up the lane towards the village hall, which was to be the glamorous venue for tonight's shindig, doing our best to shelter under our small umbrellas.

"So, who've you got your eye on tonight?" Jenna asked.

"Hmmm..." I gave it some consideration. "It depends who turns up. I mean, if either of the boys from Tarrans Farm come, that might be worth putting my flirt on for."

She tossed me an impressed glance. "Chris and Terry?"

I nodded.

"I admire your ambition. Those boys are *hot.* They're also 17 and 18, so I'm not sure they'll be that interested in a couple of 15-year-olds, even if we do look smokin', if I do say so myself." She looked at me carefully. "What about Jonny?"

I scoffed. "Oh, my God, Jenna, Jonny's like my brother. I've known him since we were like nine!"

She shrugged. "Yeah, but he's not *actually* your brother, and, I don't know, I've seen him looking at you recently in a way that's distinctly *not* brotherly. And, I mean, he's not *horrible* to look at."

It was true that Jonny Rawlings had been undergoing something of a growth spurt recently, and the boy I'd grown up with was becoming positively gangly as his teen years advanced. But the kid I'd run and slid through muddy woods with, and had to pull out of the River Gannel more than once when he'd fallen in, was someone I'd very much assigned to Friend Territory.

"If you like him so much, why don't you hook up with him?"

Jenna tipped up her chin. "Maybe I will." She grinned at me and we both burst out laughing.

We reached the village hall and shook off our umbrellas by the door. I pulled off my coat and hung it up next to Jenna's. I put a tentative hand to my hair. "Gotta go find a mirror."

"I'm right behind you."

We made our way to the Ladies and joined the crowd of familiar faces at the mirrors over the sinks. We said various hellos, and there was much mutual admiring of appearances all around. But as I'd feared, the seaside drizzle had done my hair no favours. I did my best to make repairs with the Frizz Ease from my bag, but eventually, powered by Jenna's protests that "It looks *fine*, just *fine!*" I admitted defeat and followed her through the throng into the main hall. To give them their due, the organising committee had put in some significant effort to disguise the fact that we were in a 70s prefab village hall and had gone to town with gold helium balloons and red and gold shiny streamers. The usual strip lighting had been replaced by atmospheric spotlights arranged around the room. Round tables covered in red tablecloths surrounded a dance floor that at the moment was populated only by a single couple, draped over one another as they slow-danced to Justin Timberlake's 'SexyBack'. Jenna and I exchanged glances and giggled. The DJ was set up at the far end of the room, while the drinks table extended along the end closest to the door. We made our way over.

"Two vodka and tonics, my good man!" Jenna said to the boy on the other side of the table, who was Kevin from the Londis.

He rolled his eyes at her. "You can have 7 Up, Coke, orange juice, or there's punch." He gestured towards a large red glass bowl to his right.

"Alcohol in the punch?" Jenna asked, hopefully.

He gave her a look. "What do you think?"

She sighed. "Okay, we'll take two of your finest punches."

He picked up a couple of red plastic cups and ladled generous helpings of some kind of red liquid into them. He handed them over. "Enjoy!"

"Oh, I'm sure we shall." She made a toasting gesture towards him. "Cheers!"

We both took sips of the liquid as we walked away. It was fake fruity and extremely sweet. "Not too bad," I said.

Jenna nodded. "Bearable."

I was looking around sizing up seating choices when she elbowed me gently in the ribs and nodded towards the door. "Aye, aye, here's trouble."

I turned to see Mike Douglas making his way towards us, and where Mike led, Jonny was sure not to be far behind.

"Good evening, ladies!" Mike beamed at us. I looked behind him as Jonny came into view. He was now a good half a foot taller than his best friend, but that hadn't changed their dynamic one iota. Jenna and I gave them a joint hello. Mike peered at our cups. "What are you drinking?"

"The punch," Jenna said, passing him her cup. The familiarity of the gesture did not pass me by.

He took a swig. "That would be okay with a small addition to the mix." He passed the cup back to Jenna. "I'll go and get us a couple." He looked at Jonny. "Hold the fort while I'm gone."

Jonny nodded and smiled at us, slightly awkwardly. He was wearing a simple outfit of white shirt and black trousers, but they fitted well, and I had to admit he looked okay. I wouldn't be entirely embarrassed if he asked me to dance later.

"I hope you didn't get too wet on the walk here," he offered.

I smiled. "Honestly? Between the rain and these heels?" I pointed at my feet, then Jenna's. "I'm surprised we made it at all."

He laughed. "Roll on seventeenth birthday!" One of Jonny's most fervent wishes, almost since he'd known they existed, was to own a car, and, following much begging and whining, for his sixteenth birthday the previous October, Jonny's father had given him, in lieu of a present, a card, signed and dated, with a promise to buy him for his seventeenth birthday a car and driving lessons. Jonny had been entirely satisfied by the bargain. His mentioning it now was due to his having promised Jenna, me and Mike that as soon as he'd passed his test we'd never have to walk to another party or beg our parents for another lift. He was quite overly excited at the idea of becoming our free local taxi service. Anything to spend as much time as possible behind the wheel. I just hoped that when he got his wish, he'd enjoy it as much as he was sure he would.

The room was beginning to fill up. "Shall we sit down?" Jenna said.

We all nodded and followed her to one of the tables. Mike returned with two red plastic tumblers of punch for him and Jonny. As he sat down, he reached inside his jacket and drew out a rather battered-looking hip flask. "Anyone want me to add a bit of a kick?" He jiggled the flask enticingly.

"Oh, hell, yes!" Jenna thrust her cup towards him enthusiastically, and he added a shot.

"What is it?" I asked. With Mike, you were never quite sure what he'd managed to pilfer from his parents' sideboard, so it was always better to ask.

"Vodka. My mother got in three large bottles of Stoli for Christmas, so fear not, it's all good."

I shrugged and handed him my cup. "Just a small one."

He poured in a slug, but didn't overdo it. He took Jonny's cup without being asked and tipped in a generous measure.

He'd just put the flask away when Carol, the youth club's adult community organiser, appeared by our table, waving a small camera. "Group shot, guys!" she called out. We all obediently got up and huddled together to pose for our photo: Jonny, me, Jenna and Mike. The camera flashed, and I hoped that my eyes had been open for the shot. "Great! You all look fantastic! I'll get two copies of these developed, so find me next week if you want one."

Thanks were murmured and we sat back down. Then the DJ put on P!nk's 'Get the Party Started' in an effort to get things going.

"Oh, I love this!" exclaimed Jenna. She got up and took Mike's hand, tugging at him to follow her. "Come and dance with me."

He needed no further persuasion, and they made their way onto the dance floor, which was quickly becoming lively.

I narrowed my eyes as I watched them walk away. "Is there something going on with those two?" I asked Jonny.

He was watching them too as they were increasingly hidden amongst the crowd. "He hasn't said anything."

"Neither's she." We both took a beat while we pondered, before turning back to one another. "So how are things going with school?" I asked. "Do you think you'll be ready for your mocks?"

He sighed. "Some subjects are fine, others not so much. If I get more than a 'C' in maths it'll be a bloody miracle."

I smiled. "I'm sure you'll do fine. You work hard."

He shrugged. "No choice. The only thing I'm really good at is art, and as my dad says, 'Drawing doesn't pay the mortgage.'"

"Well, I think it can, if you're good enough."

He gave me a grateful smile. "Ah, but there's the problem. I'm not at all sure I *am* good enough."

"I'm sure you could be." I wasn't lying. Jonny had definite talent, although I had no clue if he had enough to make a living from it.

He looked at me in a way that I wasn't sure about, and it made me think of what Jenna had said earlier; it definitely wasn't a brotherly look. "Thanks, Summer. I really appreciate it."

We chatted a bit more about school and what our families were doing for Christmas when Jenna returned, buzzing with energy. Mike was following behind, and, I noticed, giving her bottom some very appreciative glances in the skintight dress.

"I bet you two are talking about boring school!" she said in disgust, picking up her cup and taking a large swig of her punch.

I held up my hands. "Guilty as charged!"

"Well, stop it and get on the bloody dance floor! It's a party for Chrissakes!"

Jonny stood and held out his hand to me. "We'd better do as she says or she won't stop nagging."

I rolled my eyes. "Okay, okay."

The four of us moved onto the now crowded dance floor and began to 'shake our thang' to Oakenfold's 'Ready Steady Go', a guaranteed crowd pleaser. Some techy person did something clever, and multi-coloured lights began to swirl around the room with the beat of the music. The vodka had begun to go to my head, and I found myself giving into the beat, moving my hips and waving my arms like I almost knew what I was doing. The DJ segued into JLo's 'Get Right', a song I loved, and then suddenly slender arms slipped around my waist from behind. I turned to find Jenna moving her hips in rhythm with mine, which in the moment didn't seem remotely strange. We moved together sensuously, the atmosphere growing increasingly heady, until the song ended, and we collapsed in laughter. As we came back to our senses, we turned to see Mike and Jonny gazing at us open-mouthed, which just caused us to laugh even more.

I followed Jenna back to our table to fetch our drinks and catch our breath. A couple of minutes later the boys came back with four new cups of punch, which Mike proceeded to top up from his flask. He raised his eyebrows. "Thought you both might need to cool down after that."

Jenna took one of the cups. "Much appreciated."

I caught her looking up at Mike through her lashes, and exchanged glances with Jonny, who'd also caught it. We both suppressed smirks, but neither Jenna nor Mike noticed.

Suddenly a couple of tall figures materialised by the table. I looked up and boggled slightly: Chris and Terry Raines!

"Hello, girls. Since you both so clearly know how it's done, care to show us?" Chris was wearing a tightly fitting T-shirt and snug black jeans over a body which any girl would have been crazy to say no to. Predictably, Jenna didn't.

She stood up. "Delighted," she said, and strode out onto the dance floor, with Chris following closely behind.

Terry smiled at me, clearly highly amused by the whole situation. He held out his hand. "Shall we?"

Since it would have been entirely impossible to say no without causing embarrassment all round, I stood and took his hand. He led me out onto the floor, where the DJ was giving everyone a rest to Robbie Williams' 'Angels'. Fortunately, I'd had enough vodka that any awkwardness was quickly overcome, and Terry and I swayed politely to the music, my hands on his shoulders and his on my waist, until the song was over and he returned me to our table, just as politely. I sat down and took a deep draw on my drink. I looked over happily at the boys, but Mike was looking thunderously out at the dance floor, where Jenna was now dancing with her head on Chris's shoulder, and Jonny smiled at me politely, but – Goddammit! Was that a hint of hurt in his eyes? I sighed at the shift in atmosphere. No way was I putting up with this.

I got up and marched out onto the floor, over to Jenna. I grabbed her elbow and gave it a yank. "I need to talk to you."

She gave me an exasperated look. "Can't you see I'm busy?"

"Now," I said, firmly.

She sighed. "Okay." She looked up at Chris. "Sorry. Thanks for the dance." She threw him a wink before following me, as I led her out towards the entrance hall and some sobering bright lights. I pulled her into a corner by some coats.

"What are you doing?" I said.

"What do you mean? I'm having fun. Which I'm pretty sure is the purpose of this whole exercise."

"Are you with Mike?"

She widened her eyes in surprise, not entirely convincingly. "No! I mean, not really."

I gave her a hard stare. "Well, he seems to be under the impression that you are. When I got back to the table just now and you were still dancing draped over Chris, he was looking like bloody thunder!"

Jenna blew out a sigh. "Jesus Christ! Boys! I swear to God, if I was sitting around being all keen on him, he'd be blowing me off and dancing with bloody Polly Taylor like last time."

I wasn't entirely sure what "last time" she was referring to, but I let it go. I shrugged a shoulder. "You're probably right, but I think for now he's into you. And we were having a good time, the four of us, until the Raines boys blew into town. I'd like to continue to have a nice time, if we could. So, how about we just stick with Mike and Jonny for tonight, as long as they behave, that is?"

Jenna rolled her eyes. "Fine." She lifted a finger. "But only – and I mean *only* – if they behave. Any sulking or ridiculous ownership-type bullshit and I'm done."

I raised my hands. "Totally."

"Okay."

We walked back to the table, where the boys were still waiting. I smiled brightly as we approached and was relieved to see they took my cue and smiled back. Beyonce started advising the world that she was 'Crazy In Love', and Jenna clapped.

"Oh, my God, I love this!" She grabbed Mike's hand and pulled him behind her into the heaving crowd. He followed, smiling widely.

I turned to Jonny, who was looking up at me just a bit too hopefully. I laughed and held out my hand. "Come on, then." As he followed me onto the floor, I made a mental bargain with myself that if he had a bit of a crush on me, tonight I wouldn't mind. I might even encourage him a little bit.

A couple of hours later, I was sitting at the table with a plate of half-eaten party food in front of me, the detritus of tiny sausage rolls and crumbled up crisps failing to entice me to finish them. I wasn't sure quite where the time had gone. There'd been dancing and talking, talking and dancing, more punch consumed, and by now I was feeling rather drunk, more than a little tired and very little pain. Jonny was sitting next to me, where he'd stayed all evening, watching the dance floor, which was now about half-full with couples, including Jenna and Mike, swaying to James Blunt's 'You're Beautiful'.

He turned back to me, and I caught his eye and pulled a face. "God, I hate this song!"

He laughed. "It is a bit like listening to a cat being strangled." He took a beat. "Not that I've ever actually heard a cat being strangled. I mean, if I had, I would have intervened if at all possible. So that it was no longer being strangled."

I looked at him and collapsed into giggles. After a moment, he joined in with his own laughter. When we were finally able to stop, I considered him thoughtfully. "Oh my God, when did you get to be so sweet?"

He looked mildly offended. "I'm not that sweet."

I gave him a look. "Oh, you are. I mean, looking after me all evening, getting me drinks and," I glanced at my plate, "food. And dancing with me when I wanted to dance. And sitting with me when I didn't." My voice was soft. "Very sweet."

He held my eyes, and I could swear he was blushing. "Well, we're friends, aren't we?"

I nodded. "Yes. And don't get me wrong, it's a compliment. Being sweet is a good thing."

Christ, this drinking thing had my tongue running on autopilot. I really should shut up.

The DJ started making an announcement. "Well, folks, I hope you've all had a great time tonight. The next one will be our last song, so please all take to the floor to say goodnight."

The tinkly initial bars of Mariah Carey's 'We Belong Together' filled the now rather stuffy air. Jonny stood up and offered his hand to me with a smile. I returned the smile and stood, taking his hand as he led us onto the dance floor. We'd danced enough that evening by now to be quite comfortable with the close physical proximity, and he took me properly in his arms as Mariah begged her baby to come back to her. I laid my head against his shoulder, giving in for the moment to the thrill of how tall he was. I really needed to get a grip, but I would do that later. As we moved slowly together, it just felt really comfortable and right. I liked the feeling of his slender waist under my hand, and his hand on the middle of my back. My eyes closed as we swayed, and the sensation of comfort and trust was wonderful.

The song came to an end, and I opened my eyes and looked up. He was gazing down at me with the kind of look that no one had ever given me before, and my heart expanded under its warmth. I smiled back, before stepping out of his arms, as Jenna, with Mike following closely behind, came up to us. She caught my eye with an amused, knowing grin, but did me the favour of keeping her opinion to herself for the moment.

"Well, kiddies, I hope we've all had an enjoyable evening, but I think we should get out of here pronto," she said.

I frowned. "Why the hurry?"

She gave me an admonishing look. "Babe, you know what happens after the last song at these things? They turn the lights up!" She looked with trepidation up to the ceiling, where the unused strip lights hung menacingly. "And I do *not* want to be seen under these horrors, no way, no how. So we need to shift!"

She walked quickly over to our table and gathered up my and her handbags. I followed her. "Loos, now," she said to me. She made for the exit, shouting to the boys over her shoulder. "See you outside!"

I followed her to the Ladies, which were showing the after-effects of a night's partying. Loo roll was strewn copiously around on the floor, which was a shame, as there now appeared to be only one half-full roll left between the three cubicles. Jenna helped herself to several sheets and handed the remainder of the roll to me. We peed and met back at the mirrors, where Jenna was brushing her hair. I looked with some dismay at my face, where much of my carefully applied mascara appeared to have migrated beneath my eyes. At least it had been pretty dark in there.

I fished a crumpled tissue out of my bag and began to repair the damage.

"So, Jonny's like your brother, huh?" Jenna's smile was more smug than I would have ideally liked, but I'd known this was coming. I even felt like I kind of deserved it.

"Nothing happened, we just danced. Unlike you and

Mike, might I add!" There had been definite snogging to at least two slow songs, which I had personally witnessed. "When did that start?"

"Basically now. You saw it. And don't try changing the subject. Are you going to get together with Jonny? He clearly wants to."

I sighed and powdered my face. "I don't know. I mean, it's not as awful an idea as it was at the start of the evening."

Jenna gave me a look via the mirror. "Not awful? Summer, have you even looked at him lately? He's on the road to becoming hot. You should snag him before someone else does. I mean, okay, he needs to sort out his hair, but..." Jenna paused for a moment as she contemplated the full extent of Jonny's burgeoning hotness, then gave herself a little shake. "Anyway, yeah, you should totally go for it."

I smiled at her in the mirror as I pulled a brush through my now hopelessly kinky hair. "I'll give it some consideration."

We came back out into the hallway to find Mike and Jonny waiting patiently, Mike holding Jenna's coat, and Jonny holding mine. Jenna walked up to Mike and turned to allow him to help her on with hers. "Such gentlemen!" she teased.

I allowed Jonny to help me on with my coat as well and felt a little buzz of electricity as he gently placed his hands on my arms for a moment as he settled it into place. "Thank you," I said, quietly.

We got outside and the cold night air hit me like a slap to the face. The drizzle had cleared and a bright full moon was spreading white light from behind high clouds.

Mike rubbed his hands together vigorously. "So,

where to, ladies?"

The crisp air had woken me up, but I wasn't at all sure that my bed wasn't beckoning me. "Er, home?" I said.

Jenna threw me a disgusted look. "You've got two full weeks coming up to enjoy the comforts of home. We need to make the most of tonight's freedom."

"How about the beach?" Mike offered.

Jenna shook her head firmly. "Uh-uh, no way. Not in this get-up. Sand will get everywhere."

"There's a bench in the churchyard?" Mike said.

"Oh my God, so cold!" Jenna wailed.

Mike grinned and pulled her against him, rubbing the tops of her arms vigorously. "I'll keep you warm."

She rolled her eyes at him. "Okay, just for a little while."

We began to make our way along the road and down towards the church, Jenna and Mike leading the way, arms tight around one another, Jonny and I following behind, walking separately but close together.

The brisk air hadn't only woken me up, it had sobered me up considerably, and along with sobriety had come a renewed sense of distance between us. I wasn't at all sure I liked it. "Thank you for a lovely evening," I said.

I felt him look down at me, but I didn't look up to meet his gaze. "You're welcome, of course. Thank you for not going off and conquering one of the Raines brothers."

I laughed. "As if! They would have got bored with me in about five minutes." I sensed the sliver of hurt cut through the air from him to me, and I bit my tongue. "God, sorry! I didn't mean it like that. I mean, I had a much nicer time with you than I'm sure I would've had with either of them." I couldn't resist teasing him and slid my eyes up towards his. "Even though they are super hot."

He caught my eyes and grinned. "Fair enough. I shall consider myself even more honoured that you stuck with little old me."

I gave him my warmest smile, and as we walked along, he settled his hand lightly on the back of my waist and I let him.

We reached the churchyard and made our way to where the bench sat amongst the ancient, worn gravestones. The moon provided just enough light for us to see where we were going. We packed ourselves tightly onto the bench: Mike then Jenna then me then Jonny. The tight squeeze allowed for the sharing of body heat, which was fortunate in the circumstances. Jonny pulled his arm out and laid it along the back of the bench to give us more room.

"I used to think this place was so spooky," Jenna said, "but now I find it really peaceful. These people found a good place for their final sleep. I'd like to be buried here."

I turned to her in surprise. "Jenna! I had no idea you thought about stuff like that!"

She tipped up her chin. "Hey, I can think deeply from time to time. I have hidden depths!"

I nodded, impressed. "Clearly."

"You know, I know what you mean," Jonny said. "I did some drawing and painting here last summer, and the place has got a really good vibe about it when you sit quietly. Like the people buried here are watching you. But in a good way, not in a scary, stalkery kind of way. Like they're looking out for you, if you know what I mean."

I laid my head against his shoulder, and he moved his arm lightly around me. I realised that Jonny having something meaningful to say about this place didn't surprise me in the least, and I really liked that.

To my right, I noticed Mike turning his head and nuzzling into Jenna's neck, and she turned her head towards him encouragingly. Four was beginning to feel distinctly like a crowd. I looked up at Jonny. "Walk me home?"

"Of course," he said.

Jenna slipped her arm through mine. "You don't have to go."

I looked at her then Mike then back again. "I think I do. Anyway, I'm insanely tired." I looked at my watch. "Mum told me to be back by eleven and it's coming up to half-past, so if I don't get back soon she's going to send out a search party."

Jenna sighed but nodded. "Okay." She raised her eyebrows to me. "Talk tomorrow?"

"Definitely."

I got up, and Jonny followed. We said our goodnights and walked out through the churchyard gates. To our left, light was still spilling out of the Albion pub, but inside it was empty and quiet. As we walked up the lane in the direction of the centre of the village, Jonny put his arm around my shoulders and I leaned into him, putting my arm around his waist. We walked along in a comfortable silence, just enjoying the moment.

We reached the driveway of my house but stayed standing in the lane. No one would be driving down here at this time of night.

I looked up at him, my heartbeat kicking up a notch. "Thanks for walking me home."

He smiled, but I could make out uncertainty in his eyes. Fortunately I was still drunk enough to have the necessary courage, and I tipped my head back slightly and closed my eyes. He took my cue and leaned down to kiss me on the mouth. His lips were soft and smooth against mine, and I leaned into him, sliding my arms around his waist. He pulled me more firmly against him and I opened my mouth a little. Our tongues met, and a streak of electricity ran through my body. We kissed for a few moments more before I pulled gently away.

I smiled up at him, but he wasn't smiling back, rather looking down at me with an intensity that I didn't quite know what to do with.

"Goodnight, then," I said.

"Goodnight, Summer," he replied, softly.

I turned and walked towards my house and up the steps to the front door. When I reached it, and had found my key in my bag, I turned to see him still watching me from the lane. I waved, and he waved back. Then I let myself into the house, called out my return to my mother and climbed upstairs to bed.

Part Three

Present Day

The Day Before Christmas Eve

I was putting the photos back in their envelope when a soft, golden muzzle appeared around the door, followed by Lucy's body. She came up to me, her tail wagging gently, and nuzzled my thigh.

"Okay, girl," I said, caressing the top of her head, "I'm coming."

I went to the bathroom and did the necessary. I returned to my room and changed my top from the sweater I'd travelled in to a long sleeve T-shirt more suitable for the warmth of my mother's kitchen. I brushed my hair (still long, still brown, a significantly better cut), re-tied my ponytail and made my way back downstairs.

I found my parents in the kitchen, my mother sitting at the table with the teapot, its accompanying paraphernalia and a seriously delicious-looking plate of mince pies. My father was keeping her company, standing with his butt against the counter, a glass of whisky in his hand.

"Have everything you need?" my mother asked.

"Yes, thank you." I sat down with her, poured myself a cup of tea and helped myself to a mince pie. "I found the box from the loft. I'll go through it properly when I've got a minute." I bit into sweet, crumbly pastry and suddenly it was really Christmas. "All on track for the party tomorrow night?"

My mother's Christmas Eve party was a village tradition, and friendships could be begun or ended on the basis of an invitation, or lack thereof.

"All under control," she said, breezily.

"How many people have you got coming?"

"The usual crowd, about sixty or so. I wasn't in the mood to expand the invitation list much this year, but I did add Richard Schofield, who just finished building that big new house at the back of the dunes." She caught my father's eye. "Your father does not approve."

"Bloody new money, building a fucking monstrosity, ruining the area for everyone else!" he said in disgust.

"But!" my mother said, a finger held in the air, "Loaded. It would be very useful if he decided to become a proper member of the community. There's always something that needs donations." She took a beat. "And it wouldn't hurt if he wanted to buy one or two of my paintings. I could do with some pocket money."

My mother painted tasteful watercolours of the local countryside and coastline. They weren't going to win any awards, but they were pretty good and appealed to tourists and lovers of the area wanting a reminder of their time here. She sold them online and via galleries in Newquay and Perranporth and did quite well.

I gave her a look. "Shameless."

She raised an eyebrow. "Nothing wrong with a bit of entrepreneurial spirit. Anyway," she continued, "I'd be grateful if you could be ready from seven tomorrow evening to pitch in with final preparations. I've got a couple of girls from the village coming to help out, but there are never enough hands, and there always seems to be some kind of last-minute emergency, however much I plan." She popped a piece of mince pie in her mouth. "Have you invited any of your old friends?"

"Jenna," I said. "We're in touch online, and we've managed to fit in the occasional phone call this year, but I haven't seen her since last Christmas and I'm dying to catch up with her. Her Instagram feed lately has been mostly posts of elaborate nail jobs from her salon and 'How To' guides for attaching false eyelashes, so I'm looking forward to a proper catch-up."

"I expect she'll have plenty of outrageous stories," my mother said.

I shot her a grin. "Hope so."

"Anyone else?" my mother asked.

I allowed myself a little smile. "Jonny."

My mother took that news with satisfaction. "Good. I bumped into Barbara in the shop yesterday and she mentioned he was going to be staying with them for Christmas, so I was wondering if you'd invited him."

"I did."

My father, whether by coincidence or due to some sort of 'spidey sense', decided to make himself scarce. "Just going to watch *Pointless*," he said and took his whisky into the living room.

"So, how are you two getting along at the moment?" My mother's voice was wary.

"Fine. We've stayed in touch while I've been sorting things out."

"And have you made your decision?"

"I think so, but I need to spend some time with him and talk some things through while I'm here. I've promised him my final answer by the stroke of midnight on New Year's Eve."

"How very dramatic of you."

I gave her a smile. "I thought you'd like it."

"Well, I hope whatever you decide, you can finally be happy, Summer. These past years have been quite the roller coaster."

"Me too, Mum," I said.

Part Four

Present Day

Christmas Eve

The following morning, I was sitting on my bedroom floor in my PJs wrapping the presents I'd had delivered to the house pre-arrival (Thank you, Internet!), when Jenna returned my text from the night before with an actual phone call.

"*Baaaaaaaaaaabe!*" she screamed down the phone at me.

I laughed. "Oh, my God! It's so good to talk to you! It's been much too long."

"Well, whose fault is that? *Some people* could visit more than once a year. Those of us stuck down here at the edge of the map would appreciate it."

"You know you have a standing invitation to come up and stay with me in London any time, so don't give me that," I said. "Anyway, you'd better be coming tonight."

"What? Miss your mum's delicious party food and bottomless supply of quality booze? Are you kidding? I will be there at curtain up!"

I grinned down the phone. "Excellent."

"A little bird tells me that a certain Jonny Rawlings

will also be attending."

"He will," I laughed. "I was going to tell you, of course, but who's this little bird of whom you speak?"

"I saw Mike in the pub a couple of nights ago, and he mentioned that Jonny had told him."

"Ah, okay."

"So, everything good there?"

"You mean with Jonny?"

"Of course I mean with Jonny."

"I think so. I mean, he's been giving me space to sort things out this year, but we've been talking on the phone and things have been moving in the right direction. I just need to be able to spend some quality time with him so we can make a final decision about how we move forward."

"'Quality time' with Jonny sounds very promising," Jenna said.

The knot of excitement in my stomach tightened with a hint of nervousness. I very much needed the next few days to go well. "I really hope we can sort everything out."

"Well, I'm crossing fingers and toes for you, obviously. It is *way* past time for you two to get your shit together."

She wasn't wrong. "Agreed."

"I do have something I wanted to ask you about, not Jonny-related…"

"Go on…"

"Well, when Mike heard about both Jonny and me coming to your party…"

"My parents' party," I corrected her.

"Yes, sorry, your parents' party, well… I got the distinct impression that he'd quite like an invite. He was talking about how he hadn't seen all of us together in years."

I thought about it. "He has a point. It's gotta be, what...? Ten years?"

"You know, I think it might be longer."

"God, I've no idea where the time goes."

"Anyway, I'm sure he's got a bunch of other things to go to. Don't feel pressured to invite him."

I thought back to the photo I'd found in the box, and the memories it had stirred up. "You know what, ask him if he wants to come along. Is he still with... What was her name?"

"Briony."

"Yes, her."

"No, they split last spring."

"Damn. Didn't they have a little girl?"

"Yes. It's kind of messy. But he's supporting Claire – who's almost one – and is on decent terms with Briony. He's dating people, but I don't think he's with anyone serious at the moment. How about I tell him he can bring himself if he's okay coming solo, but that's it because otherwise it's adding too many people to the guest list?"

"That's fine. Just make sure he knows it's black tie. If he can't swing that, he should just get as close as possible. And let me know what he says so I can tell my mother if I'm adding to the numbers. I mean, she always has too much of everything, but I should make her aware."

"Of course." There was a brief pause while I heard Jenna talk to someone in the background. "Sorry, hon, I've got to go. Some kind of eyebrow emergency. The place is rammed this morning. I'll see you this evening. Shall I come early?"

"Oh my God, would you? It'd be great to catch up before the party starts and I get roped in to passing out nibbles and refilling glasses. Can you come around six? You can finish getting ready here."

"Well, we don't close until five, but I'll be there as soon after six as I can, okay?"

"Brilliant."

"Love you!" She disconnected before I could return the endearment, leaving me with that sensation of warmth and excitement that was part and parcel of our friendship. I was beaming as I put down the phone.

I finished wrapping my presents and decided it was time to get dressed and go out for some fresh air. I was dying to see the sea again. I threw on jeans and an old thick jumper that was still in the wardrobe from years back, put my hair up into a messy topknot without even brushing it and went downstairs. I found my mother in the kitchen rolling out pastry for a quiche.

"I'm going to take the dogs out," I said.

"Oh, good. I haven't had the time to walk them, and they'll have much too much energy this evening if they don't get plenty of exercise today. And of course your father has some kind of essential, impossible crossword to complete before he'll agree to leave the house. Can you walk them round to Polly Joke?"

"No problem. I'll even take them the long way."

"Perfect. But make sure they don't disappear down any holes. There's been more subsidence along the cliff path."

"Noted."

"And could you pick me up a couple of things from the shop?" She handed me a small list and a £10 note.

"Sure."

I went into the kitchen vestibule by the back door and removed my mother's old Barbour from one of the pegs and checked for gloves in the pocket. I put on the jacket and removed the dogs' leads from their hooks, stuffing them in a pocket in case I needed to leash them at any point. The action brought them immediately to their feet, and then mine.

"Come on, then," I said, opening the door and gesturing them out. In the lane, we turned to walk towards the beach. I zipped the jacket all the way up and pulled on the gloves. The cold was as brutal as any I'd ever experienced in Cornwall. The weather forecast was for potential snow tonight, which was basically unheard for this area at Christmas. I still had extreme doubts it would actually materialise, but it was certainly cold enough. Fortunately, the dogs didn't seem to mind, having the time of their lives exploring the various tempting smells of the hedgerows.

We reached the National Trust Crantock Beach car park, which was unseasonably busy with the cars of dog walkers and coastal ramblers. We walked about halfway down, then through the gate up to the dunes and the coastal path. We made our way across the sand and grasses, buffeted by the wind. And then, finally, we rounded one of the huge dunes cliffed onto Crantock Beach and there was the sea. I stopped to take in the view and breathe in the pristine air and the spectacular beauty of this place, and my heart soared, as it always did when I returned here. The tide was almost all the way out, and the beach was huge and beautifully patterned from the artistic endeavours of the ebbing waves. The shallows of the mouth of the River Gannel snaked across the sand. Tiny people braved the stiff breeze to walk their dogs across the beach, bodies hunched against the wind, hands stuffed deep into pockets.

I let out a heavy breath, letting go of as many as

possible of the stresses and worries from London that I'd brought down here with me. I called to the dogs, and we set off along the coast path towards West Pentire.

Once we reached the headland, as I'd promised my mother we took the long way round, following the path that skirted the cliffs rather than cutting across the fields. The tide was still out when we reached the cliffs above Polly Joke cove, and children and dogs were running back and forth across the wet sand below, splashing in the pools which had been left by the receding waters.

Following the cliff edge path brought me to a bench I knew well, where you could sit and admire the views from a perfect vantage point. I checked to make sure the dogs were safely exploring and sat down. I thought back over the many times I'd stopped here before, taking a time out on one of my countless coastal explorations. One particular memory emerged and elbowed its way to the forefront of my mind: a time I'd sat here with Jonny. I furrowed my brow, remembering. It must have been a decade ago. We'd had our whole lives ahead of us, and very little idea what to do with the coming years. I remembered the bittersweetness of sitting here with him, and my heart ached to remember it, but I let the memories come all the same.

Part Five

10 Years Ago

I ducked out of the cold into the warmth of the Old Albion pub, which was generously bedecked with festive decorations suitable for the season. Red berries, green fir branches and tasteful Christmas toys were tucked along beams and ledges. The Albion being hundreds of years old, and rich in dark oak beams, real fires and leather Chesterfield sofas, there was little more one could want from a place to meet friends for a Christmas reunion.

It took me only a few seconds to spot Jenna, curled up in a huge Chesterfield armchair, with what I could safely assume to be a vodka and tonic on the coffee table in front of her. Mike was in the matching armchair next to her, his hand around a pint of bitter, and the sofa opposite was handily empty. She waved furiously as soon as she saw me and beckoned me over.

I looked behind me to where my boyfriend, Charlie, had followed me in. We walked over, and I did the introductions. I'd told Jenna about Charlie via Facebook message, but I didn't know how much she'd told Mike, with whom she was now just friends, so I filled him in. "Charlie's at uni at Leeds with me, but he's doing something useful, namely Economics." I ignored Jenna looking unimpressed out of Charlie's eyeline, and we sat down on the sofa.

"So you two couldn't bear to be apart over the Christmas holidays?" Mike asked, clearly amused by our naïve level of devotion to one another.

"Nope!" I smiled and squeezed Charlie's hand. "But him being here is also something to do with his parents being in Australia at the moment and him not wanting to make such a long trip between terms. So, my good luck, obviously." I turned to beam at him.

"Yeah, really kind of Summer's parents to ask me to stay. Otherwise it would have been a bottle of red and a ready meal on my tod in front of the Queen, Christmas Day." He raised his eyebrows to me. "Drink?"

"Yes, please. White wine."

"Okay." He got up to go to the bar.

"So, how's uni going?" Jenna asked. "I check your Facebook, but I'm not sure I've seen remotely enough pics of debauched parties and traffic cones on top of statues. I'm afraid you're letting the side down when it comes to living a properly fulfilling student life."

I laughed. "You're probably going to way more debauched parties than I am. I have to spend much too much time in the library keeping up with my workload. Anyone who thinks an English degree is an easy option is sadly mistaken."

Jenna stuck out her bottom lip in mock sympathy. "Cry me a freaking river! At least you're out in the big, wide world seeing and doing interesting shit. Me and Mikey are still stuck here endeavouring not to be swallowed up by the threat of out of season unemployment and dead-end jobs."

I immediately felt guilty. Jenna's lack of a university education was a very sore subject with her. She'd always been quite clever enough to go, but her parents' messy divorce in her final year of A-levels had brought chaos to Jenna's life and her parents' finances. So the offered place at Manchester had not been taken up, and she'd been kicking around Newquay, taking various jobs in bars and shops as they became available. Mike, never having had any aspirations towards college, was quite content working as a lifeguard in the high season and signing on in the low season. As long as he had money for beer and weed, and a bed at his parents' house in Perranporth, he was happy.

"I'm sorry, Jen," I said. "I will shut the fuck up and count my many blessings."

Charlie returned with a white wine for me and a gin and tonic for himself. I caught Mike eyeing Charlie's girly drink with suspicion, but he kept his thoughts to himself.

I looked around. "Wasn't Jonny supposed to be joining us?"

Jenna shrugged in a way which put me on alert that all was not entirely to her liking on that score. "He said he'd try and make it, but he wasn't sure if he'd be able to. Apparently his parents – by which I think he means Barbara – are being very demanding on his time as he's away so much in Bristol."

Jonny had finally triumphed over his father's distrust of art degrees and was taking a BA in Fine Art at the Bristol School of Art. I hadn't seen him since the summer after we'd left high school. I came back from Leeds in the holidays, but he hardly ever seemed to be down here from Bristol, even outside of term time. A part of me I didn't really want to admit to wondered if his avoidance of Cornwall had anything to do with me.

After our kiss the night of the Christmas party, during our GSCEs year, I'd woken up the following morning wondering what on earth had come over me the night before. I really liked Jonny, but only as a friend. I wasn't even looking for a boyfriend. I had far too much on my plate with exams, and the thought of trying to satisfy the needs of those serious brown eyes terrified me. I just wanted everything to go back to the way it had been before. Good friends. No, great friends. A friend I could talk to about anything – well, almost anything. I'd enjoyed our kiss and our little romantic interlude, but... no, just, no.

He'd called me the day after the party, and I'd agreed to meet him to go for a walk. But as soon as I saw him, I knew that we were on totally different pages as to the status of our friendship. He was hoping – expecting, even – to pick up where we'd left off the night before. A hope I appreciated was completely reasonable, but not one I could share in. I'd tried to tell him this as gently as possible, and of course he'd accepted what I was asking for and even made an admirable stab at pretending he was fine with it. But I could see that he wasn't, and I felt horrible about it.

As we were friends with the same people, we still saw one another often until we left school, but things were never the same again, and the loss of our proper friendship, now barely more than politeness much of the time, never failed to make my heart ache.

Jenna had been absolutely furious with me. I'd related to her the full details of our kiss after the party, and of my feelings the next day, and she'd told me in no uncertain terms that I was a bloody idiot, along with berating me for leading Jonny on at the party and then afterwards. I couldn't argue with her. I was pretty disgusted with myself so didn't hold it remotely against her that she was disgusted with me too.

Always, over the following years, she'd try to do what she could to mend Jonny's and my friendship, bringing us together when she was able. Telling us news about one another which we otherwise wouldn't know. Trying to keep us in touch as best she could. I'd asked her once why she did it. Why was she so invested in us as a couple when it would never be? But she'd just shrugged and said again that she thought I was a bloody idiot who didn't know what was good for me.

I'd followed Jonny on Facebook, and he'd been gracious enough to follow me back, but he hardly posted, so I had very little idea of what was going on with him. Then a few weeks ago, coming up to the Christmas holidays during my second year at Leeds, Jenna had emailed me to confirm this little get together, a few days before Christmas, saying she'd finally managed to pull together a date when our original gang of four could meet up. She and Mike would even come to Crantock, so Jonny and I would have to venture only steps from our doors. There would be no room for any excuses from anyone.

Except... here was Jonny making his excuses. I hated how narcissistic it made me sound, even to myself, but I couldn't help but wonder if this had anything to do with my email to Jenna the week before, asking if it was okay for me to bring Charlie along to our little reunion, as he'd now be staying with my family over Christmas, and it would seem rude to go out to meet friends without him. Jenna's atypical one-line reply to my email had simply read: 'Sure, see you then. x'. Had she passed on to Jonny that I now wouldn't be coming alone? Was that why he was a no show? Was I being too spectacularly obnoxious for words to even consider that what I did still mattered so much to him?

But Jenna had been fine when we'd come in, her usual warm and bubbly self, so I wasn't sure what was going on. I hoped enlightenment would shortly be forthcoming. But I appreciated that may well only happen in the absence of Charlie.

Our little group chatted away for an hour or so, small talk on all sides, until too many moments of silence made it clear that it was time to finish things up. I realised now that bringing Charlie had been a mistake. I should have made my excuses, told him he'd be bored and left him at home. He'd have been perfectly happy hanging out with my dad over mince pies and a game of chess. Jenna was right; I was an idiot.

I finished my second glass of wine and got up. "Just going to the Ladies. Jenna? Keep me company?"

"Sure." She got up and followed me.

As soon as we'd made it to the loos, and I'd checked the stalls for occupants, I turned to her. "I'm so sorry! I shouldn't have brought Charlie. I didn't think he'd be such a... damper on things."

Jenna raised an eyebrow. "Did you not?"

I shook my head. "No, honestly, I didn't. I guess I've been away too long. He fits in with my crowd at uni. I didn't think it through properly, I'm sorry."

Jenna crossed her arms in front of her. "So, he fits in fine with your la-di-da friends up there, but not with your common-as-muck friends down here?"

I looked at her, shocked. "Jen, you can't possibly believe that's what I think? Honestly, you're making it so I couldn't win. I did bring him, and he wasn't your and Mike's sort, so things were awkward, but if I hadn't brought him, you'd have said I was ashamed of you. I just wanted to have a nice time and catch up with you and Mike and Jonny. It was so cool of you to arrange it, and now it's been spoiled." A flush prickled my cheeks. "What the hell happened to Jonny? Why didn't he come? Be honest with me."

She sighed and uncrossed her arms. "You're right about you not being able to win. I'm sorry, that was mean of me. As to Jonny, I really don't know. What I told you is what he told me. I haven't spoken to him. We were only emailing, like I was with you." She shook her head. "It's true he backed off definitely coming after I told him you were bringing Charlie, but Summer, I had to. I couldn't risk having him blindsided when you walked in with a new boyfriend. That wouldn't have been fair."

I looked at her, frowning. "You think it would still bother him? It's been so long."

Jenna gave me an exasperated look. "I think there's a good chance it would still bother him, yes. I realise it's been a long time, but you really did a number on him, Summer. First love cuts the deepest and all that."

My voice was quiet. "I didn't mean to. If I could have taken back what happened that night, I would have."

Jenna rubbed my arm. "I know you didn't mean to. But honestly? Even if it hadn't gone to hell that night, it would have happened sooner or later. He loved you more than you loved him, and that never ends well."

I looked at her. "That's the thing, I don't even think he did love me more than I loved him, he just loved me differently. I missed him so much after things changed. I lost a best friend."

"Oh, Summer, you really don't have a clue, do you? Have you seriously never been in love?" I looked towards the door, but she scoffed. "Don't you even dare to think that's what you have with Charlie boy out there, cos, just... no."

I pulled myself up. "What makes you so sure I'm not in love with him?"

She fixed me with a hard stare. "Well, are you?"

"I don't know..."

"Well, there you go, because if you were you would definitely know it."

I rolled my eyes at her. "You're such a hopeless romantic."

"Don't knock it until you've tried it. Anyway, Jonny was in love with you, and he definitely knew it. Until you've been there, you can't understand what it's like to be in love with someone who doesn't love you back in the same way. So, don't judge him for whatever he's done to protect his heart from you. And unfortunately, the loss of a best friend is the price you had to pay. Which is less than the price he paid, trust me."

I gawked at her. "Crikey, when did you become so wise?"

"Girl! You know I've always been a queen of wisdom!"

I tipped my head. She was right.

"So, what should I do about Jonny? His parents only live five minutes from mine. Should I go and knock on his door? *Without* Charlie, obviously."

Jenna considered. "Would this visit be for you or for him?"

I thought about it. If I were honest with myself, it would be for me, because I wanted to see him. "God, I'm such a selfish bitch."

"You're not, but honestly? I think it would be kinder to leave him be. If he wanted to see you, he'd be here.

We are literally only a few hundred metres from his door. Unless he's trapped under something heavy, he could've popped in for ten minutes."

I nodded. "Okay."

She swung an arm around my shoulders. "Before I leave you for now, my love, tell me I'm still invited to your parents' Christmas Eve party."

"Of course! I'm so happy you still want to come!"

She smiled widely. "Wouldn't bloody miss it. But I have a cheeky request, to ask if I can bring a guest of my own?"

"I'm sure that'll be fine. Who is it?"

"Guy named Paul. He's a lifeguard in the summer, so I met him through Mike. Hot as…!"

I laughed. "I'll tell my mother you're bringing a 'plus one'."

"Thank you kindly. Now, we'd better get back to the boys or they'll think we've fallen in."

The three main days of Christmas passed happily enough. Food was eaten, presents were exchanged, and at least two bottles of Baileys were consumed amongst the four residents of the Lowell household alone (although, it has to be admitted, the imbibers were mainly me and my mother). My mother was slightly confused about my willingness to take out the dogs, Ernest the lab and Kitty the Jack Russell, twice a day without complaint, but she didn't question my enthusiasm for the task too closely. But by the fifth day of this, I was no longer trying to hide from myself that I was doing it for any reason other than that I was hoping to bump into Jonny during our walk through the village. By the time we got to the day after Boxing Day, I had no idea if he was even still in Crantock. He could well have gone back to Bristol. But still I looked for him whenever I was out of the house. And still I didn't see him.

Then, that afternoon, I was coming out of the Londis after an emergency mission to buy crisps, milk and chocolate digestives, and I literally almost bumped into him on his way in. I looked up at him and actually felt my mouth drop open. The burgeoning hotness that Jenna had identified in high school had solidified since I'd last seen him into full-on smokin' deliciousness. He was now at his full height, which I estimated to be at least a couple of inches above six foot, and the lankiness of a teenage boy had filled out into what I could tell, even from limited opportunity to investigate, was the lean muscle of a pretty devastatingly attractive man. His dark, curly hair had grown out into a very Heathcliff mass of soft curls which the breeze blew around his face, so that he had to keep pushing it back with long, artistic fingers.

I succeeded in closing my mouth before any insects flew in, and before Mills and Boon-worthy descriptions could turn my mind completely to mush, I said, "Wow! Hello!"

He looked down at me and I saw that there was something about him that most definitely had not changed: the intensity of those dark brown eyes.

He managed a smile. "Hello, Summer."

Someone was trying to get into the shop around us, so we moved to the side of the doorway so as not to block the pavement. "I missed you the other day at Jenna's get-together," I said.

He did me the favour of looking a bit awkward. "Yeah, sorry about that. I haven't been down here for ages and my mum kept coming up with things for me to do."

So, he was sticking with that excuse. I nodded. "Sure,

I understand she wouldn't want to share you when she hasn't seen you for a long time." Those weren't just words; I really did understand.

I looked away under the intensity of his gaze. Something told me that if I met his eyes for more than a moment, I'd end up begging him to... what? I wasn't even sure anymore.

He paused for a moment, evidently thinking, but then he decided to take pity on me. "But I'm not going back to Bristol for a couple more days if you want to catch up? We could meet for a drink?" He took a beat. "Or go for a walk? I know how you love to walk by the sea."

My heart cracked a little; he really was the only one who knew how much I loved to walk the coastal path and spend time by the ocean. Before things had been spoiled between us, we would meet up often, to explore the cliffs, or along the banks of the Gannel. I'd continued to walk our routes by myself afterwards, but it had never been the same as when I'd walked with him, sharing my love of the beauty of the scenery, and the sky, and the nature all around us.

I lifted my eyes to his and met his gaze. "I would like that. Very much."

He smiled. "How about tomorrow morning? Nine o'clock? If you don't mind it being that early? I need to take the dog out anyway."

My smile broadened. "So do I. Take our dogs out, I mean." This was the perfect arrangement. As I'd be taking the dogs for their walk anyway, no one would bat an eyelid when I stuck to my usual routine. It wasn't as if meeting up with Jonny was some dirty little secret, I just didn't want anyone else to know. No Charlie to misunderstand, or my mother to have an opinion.

"I'll see you tomorrow, then. Meet by the church gate?"

I nodded, smiling. "Yes, see you then."

I watched him go into the shop, and I made my way home with my purchases, feeling like I was walking on air.

The following morning, I was awake by six and couldn't get back to sleep, my chest full of excitement, my stomach full of butterflies. I finally got up at half seven and went to take a shower and wash my hair. I crept back across the landing in my towel, desperately trying to avoid the creaky spots, keen not to wake any other members of the household. Enquiries as to why I'd showered and hair-washed *before* taking the dogs out would not be welcome.

As I sat in front of the dressing table mirror with my hair in rollers, carefully applying makeup, I pondered how to get out of the house without being seen. Because questions as to why I, who usually made no more effort to enhance my appearance in the morning than slapping on sunscreen, was going out in full makeup and a cloud of hairspray, would be even less welcome.

A little before a quarter to nine, I poked my head out of my bedroom door to check the coast was clear. I could hear the shower running in the bathroom, which would be Charlie, following his usual routine. My father would be reading the news in bed. The real danger was my mother, who could be in bed with a cup of tea, in the living room watching BBC Breakfast, at the kitchen table listening to Radio Four, or secreted in a cupboard waiting to jump out at me as I passed by. I would put nothing past her.

I'd done my best to conceal the extent of my non-date preparations by pulling on my new cashmere bobble hat (Christmas present from Charlie, so of course I absolutely did not feel remotely guilty putting it to use on this occasion), lightly covering my curls by wrapping my pashmina loosely around my neck, and already having my coat on over my favourite grey cashmere polo neck sweater (which, to be clear, I never usually wore on anything but special occasions – I didn't want to admit to myself what it meant that I was now risking it ending up smelling of dog). I completed the outfit with my favourite jeans. My walking boots were by the back door.

I made for the stairs and crept down as lightly as possible. The living room door was slightly ajar, and I could hear the sounds of morning television drifting out into the hallway. Result! I turned towards the kitchen, relieved I should be able to get out of the house unseen, when I sensed my mother come out of the living room behind me. I carried on walking.

"Just taking the dogs out!" I called, without turning around.

"Hang on a minute!" my mother called back. "I've a list to give you so you can pick me up a few things from the shop on your way back."

"No need to disturb yourself!" I replied. "Just tell me where the list is." I looked slightly frantically along the kitchen counters, where my mother would usually have left a shopping list. But it was no good; there she was beside me, reaching into one of the kitchen drawers. She drew out a notepad and tore off the front sheet. She handed it to me along with a £20 note. I kept my head down as I took it from her and headed towards the back porch to put my boots on. The dogs were now weaving around my feet expectantly.

I was thinking I might get away with it when I heard her say, "You look nice."

I stopped. Damn! Busted! I didn't turn around. "Thanks."

"Meeting somebody?"

I continued walking towards the back door. "Just thought I'd make a bit of an effort, it being a lovely sunny morning and all."

"Summer."

I stopped, huffed out a sigh and turned around. "Fine. I bumped into Jonny yesterday at the shop and we're going to walk the dogs together this morning. That's it. Happy?"

My mother's satisfied smile indicated that she very much was. "That sounds nice. Have a lovely time, darling."

I sat down on the bench by the door and pushed my feet into my boots. "Thanks," I said, tightening the laces.

"I won't mention it to Charlie."

I shot her a look which I was quite sure she would understand, before finishing tying my boots. I stood up to take the dogs' leads from their hooks and let myself, Ernest and Kitty out into the brisk morning air.

When I reached the church just as it was coming up to nine, Jonny was already there, sheltering from the stiff breeze underneath the lychgate. Bertie, his parents' stunningly gorgeous Dalmatian, was sitting obediently at his feet but got up and came forward to greet Ernest and Kitty with a wagging tail as we approached.

I'd rearranged my pashmina on the way down the lane to display my curls to best effect, and I was pleased to see that my appearance provoked a suitably gratifying expression of admiration on Jonny's face as we met.

"Good morning," he said.

"Hi," I beamed. I looked up at the cloudless blue sky. "Looks like we've been blessed by the Cornish weather gods."

He laughed. "Yes, those most fickle of deities."

Without discussion, we turned down the lane which would take us towards Beach Road, the dogs trotting ahead of us, patrolling for smells and animal activity.

"Did you have a nice Christmas?" I enquired.

He nodded. "Yeah, actually. It was good to be back down here. I've missed it."

"You don't get down here much?" I hoped he would pick up on the implicit 'why' of my question, which he did.

"No. Obviously I can't during term time, and I work most of the time during the holidays. Turns out a Fine Art degree is insanely costly in terms of all the materials you need, and, given that Dad wasn't very keen on me studying art anyway, I don't feel like I can ask him for any more money than he's already giving me. The course and accommodation are expensive, and, of course, Bristol isn't cheap if you want to have any kind of social life."

I nodded. "And you're finding it okay to get work when you need it?"

"Yeah, I pick up bar work easy enough."

I glanced over at him. I didn't doubt it for a second. If I managed a bar, I couldn't imagine a better way to get girls through the door.

We reached Beach Road, and I called the dogs to heel. Cars could come too fast down here at any time of the year, and I didn't want the day spoiled by squashed canine.

"Did you have a good Christmas?" he said. I could feel

his eyes on me as he asked, but I didn't turn to meet his gaze.

"Yes. It's always lovely to be back here. And my mother really pulls the stops out."

He smiled. "I recall."

I suddenly realised something. "Oh, God! Did you get an invite to her Christmas Eve party? I'm so sorry, I should have made sure she invited you."

"No worries. She did tell Mum to ask me, but I didn't feel up to it. I was so busy fielding party goers at the bar the couple of weeks before I came down here, I just wanted a quiet Christmas. I hope that's okay."

"Of course. I totally understand you wanting peace and quiet." I decided to take him at his word and not imagine that he'd been in any way avoiding me. He was being perfectly friendly and normal with me right now, so my previous fears must have been a result of my over-active and egotistical imagination.

"Jenna mentioned you'd brought a guest down with you from uni. A new boyfriend?"

I looked up at him. If he was remotely bothered by this, he was doing an absolutely excellent job of hiding it. *So much for him still being hung up on you, Summer!* I made a mental note to give Jenna a hard time about encouraging my delusions on that front.

"Er, yes." I was slightly horrified to realise that it was me, not him, uncomfortable with the introduction of Charlie into the conversation. "Charlie. He's doing Economics."

Jonny raised an eyebrow. "So his artistic tendencies are deeply hidden? Or non-existent?"

A slight flush crept up my neck, and I struggled to keep the defensiveness out of my voice. "I don't know. We seem to find plenty to talk about, whatever."

We reached the beach car park and slowed our pace. "River or sea?" Jonny asked, pointing right and then left.

"Sea," I said and led the way to the gate to the coastal path.

Once we'd reached the top of the steps and were walking through the dunes, he spoke again. "Sorry about just now. I didn't mean to sound critical. It's only... you've always been so artistic, such a lover of nature and its poetry, I thought maybe someone studying something as sensible as Economics might not share that with you." He paused. "Not that it's any of my business, of course. As long as he makes you happy."

I felt my heart squeeze. How on earth could he talk to me like this, just *getting* me so perfectly even though we'd hardly talked in years? It was simultaneously exhilarating and infuriating.

His brutal honesty made it impossible for me to respond with anything less. "I wouldn't say he 'makes me happy' as such. I mean, he doesn't make me cry. But we get along. We have lots of the same friends, and we enjoy being together. And he treats me really nicely."

"I'm glad."

I chewed on my lip, unsure of the wisdom of my next question, but somehow unable to stop myself asking it. "What about you? Do you have a girlfriend?"

I should have been prepared for the pain that sliced through me at his response, but I wasn't. "Yeah." His eyes lit up far too brightly for my liking as he described her. "Felicity. She's taking a degree in Art History, so we have lots to talk about."

Images of Jonny and Felicity standing in front of old masters, heads together, excitedly discussing their history and the painters' techniques, flashed through my mind and I felt a bit sick. "That sounds perfect."

He nodded, smiling at the thought of this girl that I would be happy never to hear mentioned again. "Yeah. It's great to have a partner you really have a lot in common with, you know?"

I didn't, but I nodded anyway.

"She really gets what I'm trying to do with my art, and she has lots of great suggestions and feedback. Her support means a lot."

At this point, my preferred next update on Felicity was that she'd run away to the other side of the world, never to be heard from again. "Sounds wonderful. How long have you been together?" Apparently, I was intent on going full-on masochist this morning.

"Um… about nine months? Yeah, about that. We met last spring."

I nodded. "Well, I'm really happy you've found someone great." I looked up at him. "No one deserves it more." I really meant it and was pleased to see that he seemed to pick up on my sincerity.

"Thanks, Summer."

We reached the point on the path where the sand dunes gave way to a panorama of the bay. The tide was in, and the crystal blue waters sparkled under the rays of the sun. We stopped to admire the view. I took a deep inhale. "It never gets less beautiful," I said.

"It really doesn't."

We started walking west along the edge of the bay, and I considered it was now reasonable to move on to other topics. "So how are you enjoying your course?"

He smiled widely, his eyes alight with enthusiasm. "I love it. We studied printmaking last term, which was fantastic, and sculpture is on the agenda for next term, which I'm really looking forward to as I've never done it. Well, unless you count making clay pots at school as 'sculpture', which I don't, so..." He looked at me. "How are you getting on with your English course?"

"Well. I have to admit, it's harder work than I thought it would be, but I'm learning a lot. We studied the Romantic poets last term, and I'm now officially in love with Keats."

He raised an eyebrow. "Not Byron?"

I shook my head firmly. "Too much of a selfish bastard."

He laughed. "Fair enough."

We stopped to watch a small fishing boat chugging along near the coast. I called to Ernest to come back from the cliff edge. Kitty, with her usual defiant independence, was nowhere to be seen. Bertie was obediently sniffing around only a few yards away.

"Your dog is much better trained than my pair."

Jonny looked fondly at the Dalmatian. "That's my mother. She brooks no nonsense."

I chuckled. "I remember."

His face took on one of his intense looks as he turned his attention back to me, and I looked away towards the horizon. "Do you think you'll come back here to live? After university, I mean."

I crossed my arms and tucked my hands in under them to warm my fingers. "I don't know. Probably not. I mean, it seems like it would be a waste of time going to the trouble of getting a degree and then coming back here. I'm not sure the career opportunities are that great." I squinted up at him in the sunlight. "How about you?"

He shrugged. "No idea. I'm just trying to live in the

moment and enjoy what I'm doing right now. Thinking about making a living with an art degree is a guaranteed way to induce extreme anxiety, so I attempt to avoid it as much as possible."

"Fair enough."

We nodded greetings to a couple of walkers coming the other way along the path and set off again towards West Pentire. We turned the conversation to the birds and nature we passed as we walked, and it felt for the moment as if our friendship had never come under strain. I couldn't remember being happier. By the time we reached the headland above Polly Joke cove, I was feeling thoroughly relaxed and like all the cares of the world were a million miles away. We came to a bench perfectly positioned between the path and the cliffs and sat down to admire the view. The tide was receding, and several dogs were playing in the shallows on the beach below. A girl played fetch with them, tossing a ball far enough with a throwing tool that it took whichever one chose to chase it at least a minute or so to bring it back.

"I wish I'd brought my camera," Jonny said. "I'd love to have taken some preparatory shots for a painting. The studio space at college enables us to work on much bigger canvases than I've ever been able to before. It costs a fortune in oils, of course, but it's worth it."

"I'd love to see your work someday," I said. Looking at him now, exhilarated at the thought of his plans for his art, he really was incredibly attractive. I pushed down the thought that listening to Charlie enthusiastically discuss the benefits of monetarist versus Keynesian economics just didn't have the same pull. I could feel the safety of my carefully constructed world shifting beneath my feet.

I took a deep breath and stood up. "Shall we walk

back?" I didn't say that I also didn't want to be gone too long unless it raised awkward questions from Charlie about where I'd been, questions that I wouldn't want to answer.

He looked up at me, and I detected a hint of disappointment in his eyes that I was cutting our walk short. We would once have walked all the way to Holywell Bay without a second thought, and it was possible he'd been expecting to do that this morning. But he got up without resistance and gave me a smile. "Sure."

We walked back through the fields that were full of poppies in the summer and rejoined the coastal path via the hamlet of West Pentire. We walked back around the bay and through the dunes, mostly in contemplative silence. I wondered if he was dreading our impending parting as much as I was. God only knows when we would see one another again. As we walked back up Beach Road towards the village I didn't trust myself to speak, the ache in my chest was so intense. I risked a glance over at him, but he didn't meet my gaze. We walked past the church and the Old Albion in silence and up to the centre of the village, until we came to where he would turn left down the lane to his house.

We both came to a stop. "Well, I guess this is me," he said.

I nodded and lifted a limp arm to my right. "I have to get some bits from the shop for my mum."

He settled his eyes on me, and I gathered my courage and met them with my own. "It was lovely seeing you again," he said.

I bit the inside of my lip to resist threatening tears. "You too. I hope it won't be so long until next time." I swallowed. "Have a fantastic time in Bristol."

"And you in Leeds. Say hello to your mum for me."

"I will."

We stood for another few moments, neither of us wanting to be the first to walk away. Suddenly he bent down and pressed a soft, gentle kiss to my cheek. I put my hand up and squeezed his arm.

"Take care, Summer."

And without another word, he turned and walked away. I watched him until he rounded the corner out of sight, but he didn't look back.

Part Six

Present Day

Christmas Eve

I walked the dogs back from Polly Joke in a thoughtful mood. I couldn't wait to see Jonny again tonight, but all the reminiscing I'd been doing over the past twenty-four hours had me wrangling with a few too many regrets about time wasted. Jenna was right; we needed to get our shit together.

I followed an excitedly sniffing Donald up the little lane towards the St Carantoc church gate, with Lucy, tired by this point, walking along much more sedately at my heels. We passed the Old Albion pub and started to walk up toward the Londis so that I could pick up my mother's shopping. I was just approaching the old red telephone box when I saw a tall, familiar figure walking towards me from the opposite direction, and I gave a little scream. I broke into a run and unashamedly threw myself into his arms, wrapping my legs around him as he lifted me off the ground. I started kissing his face with wild enthusiasm, burying my hands in his hair. A passing car tooted us even though we weren't remotely in its way, and I finally drew breath and smiled into his happy laughter.

"Well, that is quite the greeting!" Jonny said, setting me down as I unwrapped my legs from around his body.

"You'd rather something a little more dignified?" I took a step backwards and held out my hand for a formal handshake.

He laughed, took my offered hand and pulled me to him, curling his arm around my waist and treating me to a soft, deep kiss.

"Phew!" I said, fanning myself when he finally let me go. "Save some of that sugar for later. I am going to require many, many kisses this evening."

He smiled at me wickedly and gave me a playful salute. "Aye, aye, cap'n!"

I took the chance to look at him properly. I hadn't seen him in almost a year, and the sight of him was like warm honey sliding over a sore throat. His hair was a little shorter than I'd seen it in a long time, and I wondered if he'd had a trim in honour of tonight's party, but it was still long, the dark curls wild and untamed. And he had a two-day-old beard. But other than that, he was the usual beautiful, crazy-sexy Jonny.

"And you remembered it's black tie? I know it's a pain, but my mother loves it, and it gives everyone a chance to dress up."

"I remembered. And I even have a recently dry-cleaned dinner jacket ready to go."

I made an impressed face. "Excellent." I took another beat to admire him. "By the way, if you choose not to shave before tonight, that would be perfectly okay by me."

He treated me to a heated look. "Noted."

Lucy nudged me a little impatiently, and I bent down to stroke her under the chin. "I think that's my cue." I stood up and gave him another quick kiss. "I'll see you tonight."

"Tonight," he said.

I backed away, watching him as he turned up the lane to his parents' house, until he disappeared around the corner and I resumed my mission to Londis.

I toed off my boots by the back door, hung up my mother's jacket and was relieved to get inside to the warm embrace of the toasty kitchen. The dogs trotted in at my heels. Delicious savoury smells filled the air. My mother was cutting up a length of rolled pastry in preparation for putting party-sized sausage rolls in the oven. She looked up as I came in, and I held up my purchases from the shop.

"Thank you, darling. Just put them over there, would you?" She indicated the counter next to the fridge. I did as I was asked.

She gave me a perceptive glance. "You look happy."

"I bumped into Jonny in the village," I said, smiling like a loon. "I may have been pleased to see him."

"And he was happy to see you?"

"Yes, he was." I switched on the kettle and took a mug out of the cupboard. "You really don't have to worry, Mum. I think it's actually going to be okay this time."

"Well, let's hope so."

I couldn't blame my mother for her scepticism. Jonny and I definitely had a history of making things difficult for ourselves. I spooned coffee into my mug. "Can I get you anything?"

"No, thank you, I'm fine. Just busy. Pass me that egg mix?"

I passed it, and she began to brush extra egg on a few of the mini sausage rolls.

I heard a phone bing from the back porch and remembered I'd left mine in the Barbour pocket. I went over and fished it out. A text from Jenna: 'Mike says thank you very much he'd love to come to the party. See you tonight. *Spanish Woman Dancing* emoji, *Christmas tree* emoji'. I was entirely sure Mike hadn't actually said, "Thank you very much," but I smiled all the same.

I walked back into the kitchen and poured hot water into my mug. I took the milk out of the fridge. "Is it okay if Mike comes tonight as well? Sorry, I forgot to ask you. I told Jenna she could invite him."

My mother crinkled her brow. "Mike? 'Mike from school' Mike?"

I nodded. "Yes. Jenna and I were talking about how the four of us hadn't been able to get together in donkey's years, and I thought it would be nice if we could. And as Jenna and Jonny were already coming tonight…"

Her sigh was only a small one. "Okay, that's fine." She gave me a look. "Did you remember to tell her to tell him it's black tie?"

I removed a chocolate from an open box of Godiva on the counter. My mother, God love her, liked to keep a supply in the house at Christmas. "Yes, I did. I can't promise he'll go the whole hog, but I'm sure he'll make a sufficient effort."

"Very well." My mother noticed me eyeing up another chocolate. "Before you finish all my Godiva, can you go and check on your father? He's supposed to be setting up the coat rack in the hall and making sure we have enough hangers."

"Okay, I'll go and chivvy things along."

I pinched another chocolate anyway, picked up my coffee and headed for the stairs in search of my father, who would undoubtedly have become distracted by something entirely non-Christmas-related in the loft. My whole body was alive with excitement for this evening. Fortunately, I was sure that my mother would find plenty of tasks for me to keep me occupied until then.

Jenna turned up just after six. She hustled into my room laden with bags and packages, dumped them on the bed and hung a garment bag on the back of the door. I'd already showered, put my hair in rollers and made a start on my makeup. I got up from the stool in front of the dressing table, and we both gave a little scream and fell into a tight hug.

"Oh. My. God!" I said. "It's so awesome to see you!"

Jenna grinned. "You too, my love."

I pulled a bottle of Pinot Grigio out of an ice bucket and poured us two large glasses. I handed one to her and raised mine. "Cheers!"

She returned the gesture, and we both took substantial sips.

"Oh, that's good!" she said, running her tongue over her lips. "I've been on my feet all day, and I am *parched!*"

"I thought you might be in need."

She shot me a mischievous grin. "You know me so well." She put one of her bags on the bed and rooted through it, drawing out a silky dressing gown. She shook it out with a flourish and toed off her black suede trainers. Jenna might be on her feet all day, but she still took her footwear choices seriously. She began to undress, and I sat back down at the dressing table.

"So, Jonny still coming?" she asked, casually.

I turned to her, treating her to something of an eye roll. "Yes! Will you stop fretting, you and my mother both! We've learned our lessons. Or at least I have."

"Okay, okay," she said, taking another drink of her wine.

"In fact…" I said, "I already saw him today."

She boggled at me. "Way to bury the lead! How were the first words out of your mouth when I came through the door not 'I saw Jonny today'?"

"I'm attempting to mature as I age."

"Pfft!" Jenna scoffed. "You're not even thirty. You don't have to even *start* maturing until you're forty."

"Well, I'm very close to thirty," I said, grimly. "And I've made entirely enough stupid mistakes in my life so far that I'm thinking I should move up the timetable on the maturing thing."

"Well, if you must. Anyway… Jonny?"

"Yes, I bumped into him in the village. Our reunion was *fond*, if brief."

"I'm relieved to hear it. So, it's all still on, then?"

I let out a heavy breath. "I hope so. I have to talk some things over with him while I'm down here, but I've arranged not to go back to London until after the New Year, so we've got time."

"But you've decided you definitely want him?"

I nodded. "Yep."

"And he knows that?"

"He has a pretty good idea of my feelings on the subject. We've been talking on the phone. But I told him I'd give him a final answer once we've talked everything through while I'm here, and definitely by New Year's Eve."

"God, I *really* hope nothing happens to make things go to hell this time."

I looked at her in the dressing table mirror. "You and me both."

She gathered up her long, blonde hair into a high ponytail and secured it deftly into a messy bun. "Okay to use the bathroom?"

"Of course." I hesitated. "Before you go, though, Jen... I've a favour to ask."

"Yes?"

"I'm feeling the urge to go max glam tonight, so what do you think about helping me turbocharge my makeup?"

She walked over to one of the bags she'd brought with her – a weekend-sized duffle – picked it up and carried it over to the bed. She unzipped it and pulled it wide to reveal an Aladdin's Cave of makeup and assorted tools and accessories. "You know I've been waiting my whole life for you to say those words to me, right?"

We grinned at one another.

I picked up my phone. "Right, you go and do what you have to do in the bathroom, and I'll work on music selections for when you return. Let's get this party started!"

Half an hour later, Jenna had worked her magic on me and was starting on her own party face. We'd swapped so that she sat at the dressing table and I was sitting on the bed. I was blinking under the weight of carefully applied false eyelashes. I'd never worn them before, and I was still getting used to them, but I had to admit they certainly bestowed on me the highly glamorous vibe I'd been aiming for.

I scrolled through the upcoming songs on my playlist, seeing if anything needed adjusting. "So, are you seeing anyone at the moment?" I asked her.

She shrugged. "I can find a date if I want one, but no one serious. The pickings around here have been seriously slim of late."

I picked up my phone and opened Instagram, going to Jenna's page. "What about Brian the Hot Barman?" I said, reviewing a photo from a couple of months ago of her wrapped around a good-looking man with a dark crew cut and a serious five o'clock shadow.

"Ended up being more interested in Barry the Other Hot Barman than me."

I hooted with laughter. "No!"

She nodded, unable to bite back her smile. "Yep! And while you've got IG open… Did you see that photo Jonny posted last summer, the one from Tuscany?"

I knew exactly the photo she meant. Last August, Jonny had torn himself away from his Cornish seascapes to broaden his horizons with a visit to an artists' retreat near Florence, and the villa where the retreat had been held had had a swimming pool. He rarely posted shots of himself on his feed, but apparently he'd been unable to resist sharing this one. It was of him having just pulled himself out of the pool, dripping wet, his shorts clinging to his body, leaving nothing – and I mean *nothing* – to the imagination. Glistening chest and belly hair was on show, adorning suitably toned torso and flat stomach, and he was laughing, displaying perfect white teeth, towards whoever was taking the photo. He looked like a god.

The caption read, 'Great time in Tuscany *sun* emoji, *sunglasses face* emoji, *orange heart* emoji'. I'd shown what I considered admirable restraint in my response, simply 'liking' the post and commenting with three *red heart* emojis, but at least a dozen other girls had taken a different approach, and the post had enjoyed a significant number of thirsty comments. Jonny's follower count had also jumped by at least fifty due to some enthusiastic sharing. I figured at least now he knew what to do if he ever wanted to become an Influencer.

I located the post in question and held it up towards Jenna. She nodded. "That's the one. Honestly, I'm kind of surprised your phone isn't self-combusting right now. It's demonstrating admirable self-control."

I giggled. "I'll keep a close eye on it in case I need to drop it in the ice bucket."

She nodded approvingly. "Very wise."

She gave her face a final spruce with the powder brush and turned to me. "What do you think?"

I made an enthusiastic chef's kiss and aimed it in her direction.

"Excellent." She got up and fetched the garment bag off the back of the door. She unzipped it and pulled out a gorgeous dress in a deep red velvet. She held it up against herself. "Thoughts?"

It was V-neck, sleeveless and clearly cut to fit, but otherwise it was one of the most sophisticated evening dresses I'd ever seen Jenna choose.

I gave her a thumbs up. "Let's see it on then!"

She took off her silky robe and did the necessary to slide herself into the dress. She turned around for me to zip it up and gave me a twirl. The shade of red suited her hair and skin tone perfectly, and although the dress skimmed her curves, it wasn't too tight or revealing. It was the perfect Christmas party dress. "Yes?"

"I love it," I said.

"Sure?"

I nodded firmly. "Yes."

She beamed at me. "Now you," she said, giving me a little 'hurry up' gesture.

While she put on her heels and accessorised her outfit, I pulled my little black dress for the evening out of the wardrobe. I'd tried it on in the shop and then ordered it online so that it had arrived here brand new and only mildly crumpled. I'd steamed it and tried it on this morning, and all was fortunately in order. I just hoped it would have the desired effect, because my credit card had taken a serious hit in purchasing it. It was V-neck and sleeveless like Jenna's, but that was where the similarities ended. The bust was fitted silk, enhancing my boobs in what I hoped was a charming and alluring manner, then it had an empire waist, trimmed in black silk ribbon, and below that skirts of black chiffon which ended mid-thigh. The desired effect was sexy but sophisticated, with a side of pretty and a big dose of *Wow!*

I stepped into it and pulled it up for Jenna to zip up the back. Before I asked her opinion, I removed new black silk grosgrain stilettos from their box and put them on. I stood up. "Good enough?"

She treated me to a huge grin. "You look fantastic! I'll make sure I have the fire extinguisher on standby for when Jonny sees you."

I smiled happily. "Thanks, Jen."

"One thing, though." She walked over to me and smoothed a hand lightly over my hair. "This outfit cries out for an updo. To hammer the final nail in Jonny boy's coffin, we should properly show off your neck."

I looked at her doubtfully. Apart from pulling my hair up into a topknot when feeling lazy, I had no experience of creating updos. "I have no clue how."

She patted my arm. "That's what your Aunty Jenna is here for."

Twenty minutes later we both came downstairs. My hair had been pinned up in a natural style which belied the amount of pins and spray that had been employed in its creation, and I was wearing a single-drop strand of crystals in each ear as my only adornment other than the dress, borrowed from Jenna's dizzying collection of costume jewellery. Having taken in my final appearance in the full-length mirror before leaving my room, I was pretty sure I couldn't do better. All my stops had been pulled out.

Jenna had left her long golden hair down around her shoulders, adding a simple red ribbon around her neck and diamante studs in her ears. I was a bit sorry that the guest list didn't include any men more worthy of the vision that she presented, but I was familiar with almost everyone coming from years past and my hopes weren't high. Still, if anyone could find a way to have a good time under the circumstances, it was Jenna.

My father came out of the living room as we reached the bottom of the stairs. He was dressed as instructed in black tie and dinner jacket. "Wow, girls! You both look super!"

I could see that he meant it, and I gave him a quick squeeze. "Thanks, Dad! Everything okay down here?"

He looked around, doing a mental check of assigned tasks. "I think so, I think so. Better go and check with your mother, though."

I brushed my cheek against his to avoid transferring lipstick and walked through to the kitchen, Jenna following behind. "All okay in here, Mum?"

My mother was standing at the counter checking her 'To Do' list, while two girls from the village, who I guessed to be about 16 years old, stood to attention nearby, neatly attired in white shirts, black skirts and low-heeled black court shoes. She turned to us as we came in and gave us an approving smile. "Lovely," she said.

She was wearing a slim-fitting black velvet dress, with long sleeves and pearls at her ears and throat. Her pale blonde hair was elegantly and classically coiffed, and her makeup was understated but perfect. I had to admit, I'd be pretty happy to look as good once I reached her age.

She opened the fridge and pulled out a bottle of Lanson champagne. She uncorked it expertly and poured it carefully into four flutes which had been standing on the counter. She gave us each a glass and toasted us with her own. "Merry Christmas, beautiful girls." She fixed an eye on me. "May you get everything you desire this festive season."

We raised our glasses in return and took a sip. The bubbles dissolved on my tongue and the cool, crisp liquid slid down my throat. Excitement was sizzling and buzzing in every cell of my body.

I looked around. "Where are the dogs?"

My mother let out a small huff of impatience. "They wouldn't settle and were getting under our feet, so I took them next door to Linda. She said they can keep company with Ginny until tomorrow morning." Ginny was Linda's Pomeranian. My mother handed the remaining glass of champagne to me. "Take this through to your father and ask him to pour out eight glasses of red wine to be ready for when people start arriving. I thought you girls could handle the music, if that's okay? Can you do something fancy with your phone so that it plays through the new speakers?"

I nodded. "We can do that."

"Just keep it classic, at least to start things off. Sinatra and Christmas standards, that sort of thing. You know the drill. We'll see how the evening's going if we want to liven things up later."

I gave her a playful salute, and we took our champagne through to the front of the house and delivered his glass and instructions to my father. I fetched my phone from my room, and Jenna and I set about creating a suitable playlist.

Around eight, the doorbell rang, and the first of my parents' guests arrived. My father took their coats and one of the waitresses offered them a tray with a choice of red wine, white wine or champagne. My mother made water and orange juice available, but they were tucked at the back of the drinks table and had to be specially requested; she didn't welcome the idea of sober guests at her parties. Most people either walked or came by taxi anyway, as parking in the narrow lane outside our house was highly discouraged.

I was doing my best not to clock-watch while waiting for Jonny to arrive, but by this point I'd been drinking wine of some description for well over an hour, so the edge had been safely shaved off any potential anxiety.

The biggest surprise of the evening to that point occurred with the arrival of my father's nemesis, Richard Schofield, although by the warm way he greeted his guest, you'd never have known. I'd been expecting some stodgy old middle-aged man, retiring to Cornwall having made his millions, but Richard was much younger than I'd expected – he couldn't have been older than his mid- to late-thirties – and *much* more attractive. In fact, when Jonny turned up, he'd be the only man at the party who was better looking. Richard had taken my mother's invitation note of 'Black Tie' seriously, and he was wearing a beautiful tux that looked worthy of a Tom Ford fashion layout. He also arrived pleasingly alone, no wife or girlfriend in sight.

My father thrust a glass of champagne into his hand and led him over to me and Jenna, where we'd taken refuge from assigned tasks in the living room. "My daughter, Summer, and her friend, Jenna," he said, positively bursting with pride. "This is Richard Schofield."

"Oh!" I failed completely to keep the surprise from my voice at the vision before me. "Hello!" There were smiles and handshakes all round. He smiled at me politely, but then he turned to Jenna and sparks immediately started flying.

She smiled at him almost shyly, and I noticed that he held her hand a little too long before releasing it. I looked from Jenna to him and back again. They couldn't tear their eyes from one another.

Richard finally collected himself and turned his attention to both of us equally. "Well," he looked around the room, admiring the decor and festive decorations, "I must admit I feel privileged to have been included on this guest list when I've only just moved to the village. I'm reliably informed this is the invitation of the season."

I laughed. "Oh, please do say exactly that to my mother as soon as you get the chance. You'll have a friend for life."

He smiled. "Will do." He looked around. "Where is the lovely Lydia?"

Oh, he was all charm, this one. "I think she's popped into the kitchen for a minute. I'm sure she'll be back out here soon." I looked at Jenna again, whose eyes were still on Richard. "You know, I should go and check she doesn't need me for anything. Excuse me."

I gave Jenna's elbow a quick squeeze to indicate she should stay put and went to see if I was needed. My mother had already settled things in the kitchen and was supervising the pouring of wine in the dining room. I picked up a fresh glass of champagne from the relevant table and sidled up to her.

I leaned in and spoke low in her ear. "You didn't tell

me Richard Schofield was so attractive."

She looked amused. "You didn't ask."

I rolled my eyes. "No wonder you added him to the guest list. I'm assuming he's going to be at the top of every worthwhile invitation list in the area going forward."

"Possibly. As long as he behaves himself."

I snorted. "And even more so if he doesn't."

She shot me a half-amused, half-admonishing look.

I gave in to temptation and checked the clock on the mantelpiece for the time. It was coming up to half-past eight. I was aware that Jonny would consider himself beholden to his parents' timetable, and Barbara was not known for punctuality, but I was getting really quite anxious to see him.

There was yet another ring of the doorbell, and I watched my father open the front door to Barbara Rawlings, model-like in her elegance and height. She accepted a light kiss in the general area of her cheek as she stepped over the threshold. She was wearing a silver grey shearling coat that I was pretty sure cost almost my entire monthly salary, and her dark curly hair, a feature she had gifted to her son, was piled on top of her head. Harry Rawlings, Jonny's father, followed close behind, handing my father a bottle of something with a festive gold bow on it. My father took Barbara's coat and shook hands with Harry. My heart was in my throat as I waited for Jonny to join them.

Then, there he was in the hallway. Gorgeous, taller than anyone else here, and already looking around for me. His eyes met mine, and I knew immediately, with absolute certainty, that everything was going to be alright.

I smiled and made my way towards him; I reached him as he was handing his coat to one of the waitresses.

As promised, he was wearing a dinner jacket and black tie, and he'd taken my hint not to shave since I'd seen him that morning. He looked breathtakingly sexy and beautiful. My heart felt like it would fly right out of my chest.

"Hello," I said, beaming up at him.

"Hi." He bent down and kissed me on the cheek. Then he stood and looked down at me with love and a hint of amusement in his eyes. "Looking to make an appearance in the society pages?" he said, taking in my ultra glam look.

I raised an eyebrow. "Mayyyybe." I patted my hair. "Do you not like it?"

His eyes softened. "No, I love it. You look beautiful."

A thrill ran through me. "Thank you. So do you."

He treated me to a slightly bashful eyelash dip, which of course just added to his charm.

I took his hand and pulled him through into the dining room. "Champagne?" I said, handing him a glass. He took it and made a toasting gesture towards me, which I returned with my glass, and we both took sips.

He looked around. "Wow, the place looks amazing. Like something out of a magazine."

I smiled. "You should see the tree in the living room. I think my mother bought the entire bauble stock of The White Company."

He laughed. "I have no idea what that is, but I'm sure it's expensive and tasteful."

I took another sip of champagne. "Very." I decided it was time to show him off. "Come and say hello to Jenna. I know she'll want to see you."

He followed me as we squeezed and 'Excuse me'd our way through the now crowded dining room and hallway, until I found Jenna, not far from where I'd left her. I'd been wondering if she would have made any progress with Richard, but he was nowhere to be seen. Instead, she was standing by the bookshelves which housed one of the new Bluetooth speakers, scrolling through the music streaming app on my phone. Mike had apparently arrived at some point while I was in the dining room with Jonny, because he was standing behind her, looking over her shoulder. Somehow or other he'd procured himself a glass of lager.

I put a hand on each of their backs and leaned in. "Hi, guys!"

Mike, smiling widely, turned and gave me a peck on the cheek. "Happy Christmas, and thanks for the invitation, Summer. Extremely decent of you."

I beamed at him. It really did feel good to have the four of us finally together again after so many years. "You're quite welcome." I smiled at him with approval. He hadn't quite managed the full black-tie thing, but he'd put in a definite effort. He was wearing a nicely cut black suit, white shirt and black silk tie. "Very smart," I said.

He grinned. "I don't look like I'm going to a funeral?"

"Context is everything."

He looked past me to Jonny and moved his grin to his friend. "Mate!" he said.

I moved so they could bump shoulders and clap one another on the arm in greeting.

Jenna gawked at Jonny. "Wow, look at James Bond here!"

He smiled, amused. "Good evening, Jenna."

"Seriously," she said, "how on earth did you have that in your wardrobe?"

"It's no big deal. I got it back when I was at uni for our graduation ball. My mother insisted it was necessary.

It's been sitting in a wardrobe at my parents' house ever since." He looked down at himself. "Fortunately it still fits."

"Hell, yeah, it does!" said Jenna, fanning herself comically.

He laughed. "Why, thank you."

"Any time, babe." She threw him a wink. She looked at my phone in her hand. "You know what we need to do while the night is still young and we all still look hot? Photos!"

There was a general murmur of agreement to the suggestion.

She gestured to me and Jonny to pose together and directed us to go and stand by the Christmas tree for an appropriately festive background. We did as we were told. Jonny put his hand around my waist, pulling me close to him, and I put my hand on his back. Jenna took a few shots, until she professed herself happy with the results. Then I took the phone from her, and she posed with Mike while I took photos of them by the tree.

My father appeared behind me. "Can I take one of the four of you together?"

"That would be great, Dad!"

I fiddled with the camera app until I was satisfied that all he would need to do would be to press the shutter button once we were all posed together, and I went to join the other three, who'd lined up in front of the tree. Jenna beckoned me to squeeze in to stand next to her, which I did. Jonny took up position on the other side of me, placing a cheeky hand on my bottom. I looked up at him and saw his lips twitch in amusement while he refused to meet my eye. I gave a little wiggle of my butt for his benefit and turned to smile at the camera. Mike put his hand on Jenna's back and leaned in on her other side.

"Ready?" my father said.

We all nodded.

"Okay, say 'Cheese!'"

"*Cheeeese!*" we all yelled obediently.

"One more for luck!" he said. We posed for another, and he declared himself satisfied. I took the phone from him and checked the results. In the first one, Mike had his eyes half-closed, but the second one was perfect. We all looked happy and beautiful and like nothing was less than perfect in our worlds. I made a mental note to have this one printed properly on photo paper; maybe I'd find it again in ten years and it would have the same magical effect in bringing us all back together as the one I'd found yesterday.

I spotted my mother beckoning to me from the doorway. I handed the phone to Jenna and walked over.

"Do you have five minutes to help us lay out the buffet?" she asked.

"Of course."

I followed her into the kitchen where she led me to the fridge. She opened it to take out a huge dish of smoked salmon and put it on the table to remove the plastic wrap which had been covering it. "Can you take this into the dining room? The girls should have cleared enough space on the table by now."

I picked up the heavy plate and manoeuvred myself through the throng in the hallway, managing to get the salmon to its destination without disaster. I added it to the buffet spread, and I was surveying the set up so far to see if anything needed attention when Richard Schofield materialised behind me.

I checked his wine glass, which was almost empty.

"Top up?" I said, fetching the relevant bottle of white wine out of its ice bucket.

"Thank you," he said, as I poured. "Tell me," he paused, evidently not entirely sure of his ground, "is your friend, Jenna, single?"

I smiled. "As far as I'm aware."

He nodded thoughtfully. "Okay, well, thank you for that information. I didn't want to step on any toes."

"Always better to be safe than sorry."

"Indeed."

I popped the wine bottle back in its ice. "Excuse me, would you? I just need to check on something."

He made a gesture to let me go. "Of course."

I scooted out of the dining room and back to Jenna in the living room, where she was chatting happily with Mike on one side of her and Jonny on the other. I stepped behind Jonny and slipped my hand through the crook of Jenna's elbow. "A word," I said, low into her ear.

She followed me over to the other side of the room, her eyebrows raised questioningly.

"Richard Schofield just asked me if you're single," I stage whispered.

Her eyebrows shot up even higher. "*Reeeally?*"

"Yep." I examined her face. "Are you interested?"

She thought about it for no more than a moment. "Definitely."

"I thought so." I grinned at her. "I thought I saw sparks fly when you were introduced. I was actually a bit surprised to find him gone when I came back with Jonny."

She shrugged. "Your father came over and introduced him to some other neighbours. I think he was just doing his duty as a host."

I pursed my lips. But then my dad had always been

oblivious to the nuances of human interaction; expertise on that front was my mother's territory. "Do you want me to take you back to him? He's in the dining room."

She looked at me slightly doubtfully. "Wouldn't that be a bit obvious?"

I expressed mock shock. "Excuse me? Where's the real Jenna Paley and what have you done with her?"

She rolled her eyes at me. "Fair enough." She gestured with her arm towards the door. "Lead the way, Miss Cupid!"

I led her back into the dining room, where Richard was standing with a plate in his hand, surveying the now heaving buffet table.

"Look who I found!" I said, brightly. "Jenna, you said you were hungry, so, please, do tuck in."

I handed her a plate and napkin from the pile, returned her slightly scolding look with a grin of my own and left her to it. I was confident that Jenna could handle the situation quite ably without me.

I returned to the living room, turning the dimmer switch lower as I passed the door. It was time for a bit more atmosphere in this joint. Mike had taken charge of my phone and was perusing music options. He was sitting on the arm of one of the armchairs, where Jonny was lounging, his long legs stretched out in front of him. I went over and greeted them.

"Can you take a look at this playlist?" Mike said, handing me the phone. "Jenna had been working on it before you took her away, and I've added some extras. We were hoping it might be okay to drag the evening's soundtrack out of the Stone Age." He gave me a cheeky grin.

I took the phone from him and scrolled through their suggestions. The list was highly sensible given the crowd:

Roxy Music, George Michael, Adele, Coldplay, some Stevie Wonder. Everything melodic, nothing too noisy or brash.

"This looks fine," I said. I pressed play on the first track, and Will Young's 'Changes' started streaming through the speakers.

"Thanks, babe," Mike beamed at me. He got to his feet and raised his empty glass in my direction. "Just gonna get a refill," he said and disappeared through the doorway, quickly swallowed by the crowd.

I looked down at Jonny, making himself comfortable in the armchair, and met his warm smile and warmer eyes. I couldn't resist. I dropped into his lap and slid an arm around his shoulders, placing my free hand on his chest. I could feel his flesh, warm beneath the cotton of his shirt. My fingers itched to undo the buttons and slip my hand inside. But instead, I smoothed my hand over the soft fabric and leaned in to nuzzle his cheek with my nose.

He put his hand up to cover mine with his own, picking it up briefly to kiss my fingers, before settling it back on his chest. "Enjoying the party?" he asked. I could hear his amusement at my public display of affection in his voice.

I sat up and looked down at him. "Yes, I am, thank you very much. I feel confident in saying that my enjoyment of it has been substantially increased by your presence, so thank you for coming."

He laughed. "Well, thank you for inviting me."

I looked at his mouth, then met his eyes and wondered what on earth I'd been thinking during those times I'd let him go. He stroked the back of my hand softly and I felt almost dizzy with desire. I pressed my nose into his hair, and he turned to breathe in the skin of my neck.

The beat of Roxy Music's 'Same Old Scene' began to play, and I moved to get up. "Dance with me?"

He edged forward in the chair, helping me to stand. On my feet, I began to move towards the back of the room, where an area had been cleared for dancing. I moved and jived to the music as I walked, sensing him following behind me. I turned to him, taking his hands to pull him towards me, and he moved in, slipping a hand around my waist, the other taking my hand in his. He began to lead, moving his hips in time to the music, twirling me and pulling me back to him. I followed almost breathlessly. This was a level of expertise galaxies away from the boy I'd danced with at the village hall all those Christmases ago. Another couple joined us on the floor but didn't attempt any complicated moves.

The soundtrack segued into George Michael's 'Careless Whisper', and we moved into a slow dance. He held me close, his hand on the back of my waist, firm but not restrictive: the perfect amount of pressure. I looked up at him, met his gaze, and he smiled at me, and I saw something in his eyes that I'd never seen before: He was sure of me.

I reached up and caressed his cheekbone with my thumb. "I love you," I said.

His eyes widened for a moment in surprise, then he treated me to his bottomless look of love. He didn't reply to my declaration, but he didn't need to. His answer was in his eyes. With Jonny, everything was always in his eyes.

The song ended, and I realised I really needed to cool down. I pulled open the French windows and stepped out onto the patio, the frigid night air immediately freshening my senses. I took a deep breath.

Four tall gas heaters had been set up, one at each corner of the paved area, along with fringed blankets draped over the wicker sofa and chairs. (My mother really did have this whole party thing down to an art form at this point.) The heaters were having only limited success in their battle against the cold, but I wanted to stay out here for a few minutes anyway. I thought I probably needed to get at least some semblance of a grip.

I picked up a blanket, wrapped it around me and sat down on the sofa. Jonny closed the glass door behind us and came and sat down with me. I settled half of the blanket around his shoulders and snuggled into him. He turned to me and put his arms around me, pulling me to him. I nuzzled my nose into his neck.

"Christ! It's cold!" he said.

I nodded against his skin. "They said it might snow. I'm doubtful. I can't remember seeing it snow in Cornwall."

"It can happen."

I turned further towards him and hooked a leg over his. He gave me an amused look, and I giggled. "It's important to share body heat in the face of extreme cold," I said, seriously.

"One should always pay attention to the science," he replied.

I shifted myself further up his body until my eyes were level with his. His eyes moved from mine to my mouth and back again. I moved in and pressed my lips to his. He responded immediately, kissing me back and opening his mouth. Our tongues touched and electricity scorched through me. Clearly that getting a grip thing was going to have to wait.

Things were prevented from getting entirely out of hand by the French doors opening and a man stepping out onto the patio, cigarette and lighter in hand.

Jonny and I drew apart, attempting not to appear flustered.

"Don't mind me," the man said, who I recognised as one of my dad's friends from the parish council. "Just dying for a fag. Didn't mean to disturb."

I disentangled myself from Jonny and managed to get to my feet. "It's okay," I said. "We were going in anyway. It's absolutely freezing out here."

The man took a deep drag on his cigarette. "You're not joking."

Jonny and I stepped back inside, straightening ourselves up as we did so. The room was now absolutely packed. The livened-up playlist seemed to have succeeded in kicking the party into a higher gear, and at least four middle-aged couples were dancing affectionately in the designated area.

I turned to Jonny. "I'd better go and check with my mother I'm not required for any reason. Are you okay looking after yourself for a few minutes?"

He nodded. "Of course."

In the hallway, I passed Mike being happily chatted up by a couple of my mother's friends from her book club. I made for the stairs; I needed to repair my appearance before I faced my mother again. I reached the upstairs landing as Jenna was coming out of the bathroom. Our eyes met, and I raised an eyebrow. "So? How goes it with Richard?"

She took in my slightly dishevelled appearance. "Not quite as well as it's evidently going with you and Jonny, sadly, but things are definitely looking promising."

"Ooh! Do tell!" I went into my bedroom with her following. I sat down on the dressing table stool, and she took up her spot on the bed.

"Well, we had this really adult conversation about *business*, if you can believe it! He asked me what I did for a living, and I was telling him about managing the salon, and he was asking me a load of follow-up questions, as if he was really interested, and I told him about the market for our services in Newquay, and…" she paused for effect, "get this! He says he might want to set me up with my own salon! He'd provide the investment capital, and I'd get shares too for setting up and managing things. But I wouldn't have to put in any money myself – which is just as well, as I don't have any. But we'd split the profits." She waved a hand. "I mean, all those details would have to be worked out, but… Can you believe it?" She stopped, examining my face. "Does it sound too good to be true?" Her face fell slightly. "It sounds too good to be true."

"No, no!" No way I was raining on her parade tonight; this was a night for wishes to be granted and miracles to be distributed liberally. Anyway, for all I knew, Richard could be entirely serious. He'd made his money somehow. "I mean, you know what you're talking about, right?"

She nodded.

"And you could definitely run the kind of salon you're talking about at a profit?"

She nodded again.

"Then it's entirely possible he can see that and wants to make money going into business with you."

"Well, he did say that now he's going to be living down here, he wants to support local businesses and invest in the area."

"There you are, then. I mean, it may not work out. But it might do. I don't think there's any harm in proceeding as if he means what he says." I paused. "Except…"

"Yes?"

"Maybe don't sleep with him right away."

She rolled her eyes at me and pulled herself up in mock indignation. "Honestly, what kind of a trollop do you think I am, exactly?"

I gave her a hard stare, and we both giggled.

"Fine, fine. I'll try to be sensible. But, Summer, he's *hot*, don't you think? I mean, I'd never imagined myself going for an older man, but I guess it depends on the older man."

"I don't think he's that old," I said. "Definitely not more than forty." I considered her. "It would be good for you to spend some time with a man who knows how to treat a woman properly, and he looks like he might know how to do that."

"Hands off!" she laughed.

I held mine up. "I would never!"

Jenna grinned at me. "Not now you wouldn't. Seriously, when's the wedding? I will cut a bitch if you don't make me maid of honour."

I laughed but tossed her the biggest eye roll I could manage. "Cool your jets. We're miles from that."

"But you'd say yes?"

I took a moment to pretend to consider, even though there wasn't much to think about. "I think I would."

She clapped her hands together in glee. "Oh, thank God, Summer! I'm so relieved. For you, and for him." She gave me the eye. "But mostly for him. That poor boy was going to have his life ruined if you hadn't come to your senses."

"Well, I did, thank God."

I turned towards the dressing table mirror, taking in my flushed face, slightly mussed updo and kissed-off lipstick. I pointed at my head. "Can you help me fix this?"

Jenna stood and cracked her knuckles. "Emergency assistance incoming!"

I came downstairs about fifteen minutes later with my appearance fully repaired. I left Jenna to go and locate Richard and went in search of my mother. I found her in the kitchen, supervising the girls rinsing plates and stacking the dishwasher.

"Oh, thank God, Summer!" she said when she saw me. "I wondered where on earth you'd got to." She pointed at a large trifle on the table. "Can you take that through to the dining room? We seem to have got really behind tonight. Everyone took ages to eat their main meal, and now it's almost too late for desserts."

I picked up the heavy glass bowl. "I'm sure it'll be absolutely fine, Mum. Everyone is having a whale of a time out there." I looked at her seriously. "I hope you're finding some chance to enjoy your own party."

She waved a hand. "Well, it's not really about that. But don't you worry about me. I'm having a fine old time." She settled me with an amused, penetrating look. "As are you, I think?"

I smiled happily. "Yes, I am. I'm having a wonderful time."

"Then I am too."

I felt my heart expand. "Awww! Mum!"

I put down the trifle and went over to give her a hug. She accepted the embrace but patted my back slightly impatiently. "Yes, yes. Now, the trifle?"

I gave her one of my faux salutes and took the delicious-looking pudding through to the dining room. People were already making inroads into the desserts that had been laid out earlier. My stomach grumbled, and I realised I hadn't eaten a thing since a sandwich at lunch-time. I was starving. I helped myself to a slice of chocolate gateau and put another onto a plate for Jonny. I picked up napkins and forks and made my way back into the living room.

Jonny was standing by the fireplace, holding court be-fore three of my mother's most glamorous friends, who were clearly entranced. I put his piece of gateau down on a table and stood back to enjoy the show, while forking cake into my mouth.

"So the gallery in St Ives always has some of your work showing?" one of them said, looking at him through her lashes.

He nodded. "Yes. But if you don't see anything you like there, I'd be happy to show you additional paintings in my studio. It's in Gwithian, so same sort of area."

The three of them twittered excitedly at that sugges-tion.

"What size canvases do you produce?" another asked, this with an air of some authority on the subject.

"To the larger end of the scale," Jonny said. "Probably three feet by three is the smallest I work on. But I can go much larger. I prefer six by six. I think that allows me to produce my best work."

"Hmmm… That size would be perfect for our place near Rock," the second woman said.

Jonny spotted me standing back listening, and our eyes met; his twinkled as if we were sharing a secret. He turned his attention back to his audience, and he reached into his jacket. He pulled out some business cards and handed one to each of the women.

"My number, email, and website address are on there," he said. "Please do take a look at my site, and if you see anything you like, or just like my style, please let me know and I'll be happy to show you what I have available. I also take commissions if you're looking for something particular, either subject-wise or to fill a particular space."

There were general murmurs of approval, and the cards were secreted safely into handbags.

"Now, if you'll excuse me, ladies. It's been lovely to meet you." He touched the woman to his right lightly on the elbow, causing an additional flutter, and moved away from them towards me.

I finished my cake and set down my plate as he reached me. I indicated that I'd brought him a piece if he wanted it. "Not that you're not clearly quite sweet enough already," I said, my eyes dancing with amusement.

He grinned at me. "I hope you don't mind me doing a bit of self-promotion at your party."

"Of course not! And it's my parents' party, not mine, but I'm sure they wouldn't mind either. In fact, I think they would positively approve. I bet those ladies will be all abuzz tomorrow about the wonderful artist they met at the Lowells' on Christmas Eve." I looked over to where they were still chatting as a threesome. "I hope you get at least a sale or two from them." I looked at him, impressed. "Your sales pitch was extremely professional."

Another grin. "I'm not just a pretty face, you know."

"Clearly." I gave him a look of heartfelt appreciation. "Although your face *is* very, very pretty."

A charming little blush and lowered eyes, before he lifted them to mine again. "I love you," he said.

My heart filled at his words.

"I didn't say it earlier, when you said it to me. But you know I do, of course. I always have."

I felt like my heart would not be held in my chest by

my ribcage. What the hell had I been doing the past ten years, letting him live without me? Bloody idiot. "I know," I said. "And whatever it may have seemed like sometimes over the years, I've always loved you too."

He didn't argue with me, taking my declaration as it was intended. He leaned down and gave me a soft kiss on the mouth, before turning his attention to the untouched plate of gateau on the table next to us. "So that's for me?"

"It is."

"Thank God! I'm starving!"

Coming up to a quarter to midnight, and our little gang of four had somehow all made it to the dance floor. I was dancing with Jonny, languidly leaning against him, my arms looped around his neck, largely relying on him to keep me standing by this point. Jenna was dancing with Richard in a very lady-like manner, one hand on his shoulder, the other in his, his hand resting gently at her waist. But they were clearly quite wrapped up in one another, their attention not wandering elsewhere. Mike was dancing with one of my mother's younger friends, a gorgeous divorcee in her early forties who lived a few houses down from ours. She looked thoroughly happy to have hit the jackpot and be ending her evening with a good-looking man a little over ten years her junior.

Wham!'s 'Last Christmas' started playing over the speakers, and even a few couples who'd resisted dancing so far decided to join in.

"Poor George," I said, as the lyrics made their way into my tired brain. "Always so much heartbreak."

Jonny pulled me tighter against him. "I feel his pain."

I looked up at him. "Not anymore. And never again, if I can help it."

He smiled down at me.

I reached up and gave a tug on his bow tie. The silk knot slid apart, and with a little more work from my fingers it was loose around his neck. I stood back and undid the top three buttons of his shirt, easing it gently apart to display a smattering of dark chest hair.

I smiled, pleased with my handy work. "More comfy?"

He chuckled. "Much."

I bit my lip, not managing to suppress a mischievous smile. "Good. I've been dying to do that all night."

He gave me a teasing look. "And you're happy to stop there?"

I let out a regretful little sigh. "Better had for now."

My father appeared next to us and touched me on the back lightly. "Can I ask you a favour?" He shot Jonny an apologetic glance.

"Of course, Dad."

"Would you fetch your mother's bouquet from the garage? She wants me to help hand out the crackers for the midnight toast, and I'm afraid I won't be able to get it in time."

"Of course. I'll go get it now and put it outside on the patio so it's right there when you want it."

"Thanks, love."

He bustled off to take on his assigned task.

I stepped outside and immediately picked up the blanket I'd used earlier and wrapped it around me. If anything, it was even colder than before. Jonny came out with me.

"What are we doing?" he said.

I started walking quickly across the garden towards the garage, him following.

"Every year, my father gives my mother a Christmas bouquet at midnight, to thank her for all her work organising the party. And every year, he hides it from her so that it's a 'surprise', even though he does it every year, and she totally expects it. But it's a tradition now, and so, well, here we are."

"That's so sweet."

I turned to him and smiled. "It kind of is."

We reached the side door to the garage, and I pushed it open. I found the light switch by the door and flicked it on. Sitting on the bench, just inside, was a large, beautiful bouquet: red and white roses interspersed with red berries and seasonal foliage. The flowers were wrapped in red paper, and the arrangement was secured with white satin ribbon. I picked it up and headed back out. Jonny switched the light off and closed the door behind us. We scuttled back over the lawn to the patio, and I rested the bouquet on one of the sofa cushions. I dropped my blanket next to it, and we scooted back inside out of the cold.

People were helping themselves to Christmas crackers from large baskets being handed around, and there was much hooting of laughter as they pulled them and told one another the bad jokes and balanced the paper hats on their heads. Smaller baskets containing party poppers and party horns were also making the rounds. People were helping themselves, but not using them yet, the majority of the crowd being well enough acquainted with tradition to know to wait for midnight.

Jonny and I did our bit, although neither of us were able to get the paper hats to stay on our heads over our hair, so we gave up on that.

The two waitresses, by this time looking dead on their feet, were carrying around trays, offering everyone small glasses of champagne for the midnight toast.

At about five minutes to, my father came over. "Would

you fetch in the flowers and hold on to them while I make my speech?"

I gave him a little two-fingered salute and went to do as requested. I stood at the back of the room by the French windows, holding the bouquet, and Jonny came over to keep me company. My father took up position in front of the Christmas tree and clinked a dessert spoon against his glass to get everyone's attention.

"Thank you, thank you!" he announced. The crowd obediently quieted down to hear him speak. "Thank you once again to so many of our dear friends for joining us this evening for our annual Christmas celebration." There was a murmur of 'Thank you's uttered in reply and a smattering of polite applause. "As you all know, this event would not be possible without a quite staggeringly large amount of work from my beautiful wife, Lydia."

My mother, who had been standing near the doorway, put her hand to her chest in a gesture of gratitude for his words, and there was more enthusiastic applause, several cries of "Hear, hear!" and even a jolly "Fantastic job!" from the other end of the room.

"So, as we come up to midnight, I'd ask you all to join with me in thanking our hostess for yet another phenomenal party."

Everyone shouted out 'Thank you's at varying volumes, and there was a hearty round of applause.

This was my cue, and I squeezed through the crowd to my father, who came forward to collect the flowers from me. He met my mother as she walked up to the Christmas tree and handed her the bouquet. They kissed one another on the cheek, and she took the flowers, giving little waves and nods of appreciation to her audience.

"Right then," my father looked at the silver clock on

the mantelpiece, "I'd say it's about time for the count-down." He raised his arms to encourage everyone to join in and started counting backwards, along with most of the rest of the crowd. "Ten!... Nine!... Eight!..."

Jonny leaned in with his hand on the small of my back and whispered in my ear. "Merry Christmas, Summer."

I looked up at him, my eyes shining. "Merry Christmas, Jonny."

He kissed me as the crowd erupted with an almost deafening, "*Meeerrry Christmassss!*" and poppers and blowers started going off all around us. I turned to him and pressed myself against him as he took me in his arms, and we had our first, deep – and only just the safe side of indecent – Christmas Eve kiss.

Jenna had found my phone again – which was impressive, as I had no idea where it was at this point – and was responsible for Slade's 'Merry Christmas Everybody' starting to blare out of the speakers immediately the countdown was over. There was much joining in, and as Jonny and I broke from our kiss, our eyes met and we burst out laughing.

"This is a *great* party!" he shouted at me over the noise. "Best Christmas party I've ever been to, bar none."

I laughed, thinking of the amount of it we'd spent entwined. "I should damn well hope so!"

He grinned at me, as we were briefly joined by Mike, his hand still holding the divorcee's. "Awesome party, Jenna! Thanks again for the invite!"

"Please do make sure to say exactly that to my parents as soon as you get a chance!"

"Will do!"

Slade finished and Black Lace's 'Do The Conga' started pouring out of the speakers. A conga line formed and someone opened the French doors so that it could sway and jig its way out into the garden. I exchanged looks with Jonny. "I need to find that goddamn phone right now!"

I was searching the living room surfaces for my errant mobile, when the conga line burst back into the living room. I wasn't remotely surprised to see Jenna at the head of it, Richard behind her with a firm hold on her waist. I looked around for my parents, to check if any lines were being crossed, but my mother was nowhere to be seen. I guessed she would be in the kitchen putting her flowers in water. My father was chatting to one of his golf buddies, seemingly completely unfazed by the turn of events.

Jenna waved to me as she danced past. "Fantastic party, Sum!"

I shook my head at her in mock exasperation. "Where's my bloody phone?" I yelled.

"Wouldn't you like to know!"

I gave up and went back over to Jonny, who was languishing against the wall by one of the front windows, observing proceedings with a cool, quietly amused, spectacularly sexy detachment.

I took the glass of ice water he'd somehow found from him and took a long drink. "I'd say let's get out of here, but I can't leave. *Halp!*" I said, feigning panic.

He pulled my back against his body and draped his arm across my collarbone so that we could watch the show. The conga finished, and Mariah Carey started singing 'All I Want for Christmas Is Yoooouuuu!'

I turned in Jonny's arms. "At last, a song I can get behind." I reached up to kiss him again, and Jenna appeared behind me, Richard still in tow.

"Oh, my God! Will you two lovebirds give it a rest! You're making everyone else feel inadequate."

I turned to her. "Tell you what. We'll give it a rest if you'll give me my phone."

She rolled her eyes at me. "Deal." She held out her hand to Richard, who fished my phone out of the inside of his jacket and handed it to Jenna, who handed it to me. "Now, come and get a drink with me. Do you have any Baileys?"

"I think I need coffee and/or water right about now," I said.

She gave me a disgusted look. "Lightweight."

"But I can find some Baileys somewhere for you."

I set up my phone to play the earlier, more civilised playlist and made my way to the kitchen, with Jenna, Jonny and Richard following. The room was astonishingly tidy and organised. A veritable oasis of calm amidst the chaos. As I'd suspected, my mother had already put her flowers in water, and she was handing a generous amount of cash to the village girls who'd worked so hard throughout the evening.

They pocketed their money and went into the kitchen vestibule to fetch their coats. "Thanks so much!" I shouted through to them.

"Yes, thanks!" the others shouted behind me.

The girls raised weary arms in reply and let themselves out into the freezing night.

I found the open bottle of Baileys in a cupboard for Jenna and poured her a large measure. I filled and switched on the kettle for anyone who wanted tea or coffee and retrieved a jug of cold water from the fridge. I poured myself a large glass and sat down at the table, suddenly completely exhausted.

Jonny moved about making teas and coffees, in coordination with my mother, while Jenna stood by the counter drinking her Baileys, in quiet conversation with Richard. I'd finished almost the entire glass of water when Jonny put a mug of coffee in front of me.

"Decaf," he said. "Do you still take it the same way?"

I nodded. "Thank you."

He took his jacket off for the first time that evening and hung it on the back of the chair. I took the opportunity to admire his long, slender body in the slim-fitting shirt. He sat down next to me, and we sipped from our mugs in companionable silence. Things had quietened down a lot at the front of the house, and my mother disappeared out into the hallway to join my father saying goodnight to people. Mike ducked his head into the kitchen and waved goodnight to everyone, before leaving with the divorcee.

"Does your mother want any help clearing up?" Jonny asked.

I shook my head. "No, she pays a small fortune to a couple of cleaners to come in before dawn tomorrow to clean up the other rooms." I caught his raised eyebrows. "Yep. My father has adopted a 'Don't Ask, Don't Tell' approach to the cost of that on Christmas morning, which is the best approach, trust me."

He sat back in his chair, stretched and yawned. I wanted so badly to drag him upstairs to my bed and just go to sleep snuggled up with him, there were no words.

He turned to me. "Am I going to see you tomorrow?"

I perked up. "I'm sure that can be arranged. Are you going to church in the morning?"

"What time's the service?"

I thought about it. "Not sure. Ten?"

"No way my parents would be making that, but I can if you want?"

I smiled. My parents always wanted to go, and it was pleasantly festive, but I would enjoy it much more with Jonny there. "Can I text you early to confirm the time?"

"Sure. And maybe a walk in the afternoon? Weather permitting?"

I turned and looped my arms around his shoulders, nuzzling into his neck. "I would love that."

Jenna sat down on the other side of the table. "Is it okay if I crash here tonight? My car's in your driveway, and I don't think I'm in any condition to drive home."

"Of course. Help yourself to the spare bedroom."

"Thanks, babe." She got up to walk Richard out to the front door. His house wasn't far, but I didn't envy him his ten-minute dash through the cold.

I looked at Jonny. "You came in a thick coat, right? And you have gloves? And a scarf?"

His mouth twitched in amusement. "Yes, yes and no. Sorry, no scarf."

I dragged myself to my feet and went into the vestibule. I found one of my father's woollen scarves hanging on a hook and brought it into the kitchen. I handed it to him. "I don't want you getting cold."

He took it and grinned up at me. "Aw, look at you looking after me!"

I leaned down and kissed him on the mouth deeply, enjoying the fact that we were alone at last. "Better get used to it." I pulled away as my mother came back into the room. "Everyone gone?" I asked.

She nodded. "Yes."

"Jenna's taking the spare guest room," I reported.

"Yes, she asked just now. She's already gone up. Your father and I are going up now too. Are you okay to lock up?"

I sat down. "Of course."

She looked from me to Jonny and back again. "Don't be too late."

"We won't be." "It's okay, Mrs Lowell, I'm just leaving." We both spoke at the same time.

My mother smiled at Jonny indulgently. "No need to hurry. And I think you can call me 'Lydia' now, don't you?" Jonny and I exchanged glances. "Goodnight, both of you."

"Goodnight!" we both said.

My father's head appeared briefly around the door. "Night, all."

"Night!"

And finally, we were alone in a quiet house.

I rested my head on Jonny's shoulder and stroked his back, enjoying the feeling of his muscles under his shirt. He caressed the top of my arm with gentle fingers.

"I guess I'd better get going," he said, making no effort to move.

"I guess you had."

We sat there for another few minutes, bathing in the quiet and one another's company. Finally he managed to stir himself, and he got to his feet and put on his jacket. I followed him out to the hallway, where his coat hung alone on the rack. He put it on, did it up all the way and pulled on his gloves. He bent his head to allow me to wrap the scarf around his neck a couple of times until I was satisfied that he was sufficiently bundled.

He leaned down and gave me a tender kiss. "Goodnight, Summer. See you tomorrow."

I curled my fingers into the lapels of his coat and stood on tiptoes to kiss him again. "Goodnight, my love."

He treated me to a final, longing look, as I opened the door and let him out into the freezing night. I pushed the door to as much as I could to keep out the cold while allowing me to still watch him as he walked down the steps and out onto the lane. When he reached the road, he turned and waved before disappearing behind the hedge. As I went to close the door, I looked up and a few fluffy snowflakes started to drift down from a cloudy sky.

I wanted to watch a little longer to see if the snow would continue to fall, but it was too cold, so I pushed the door shut and turned the key on the deadbolt. I trudged into the living room to check that someone had locked the French doors, which they had (I was guessing my father on that one), and then into the kitchen to lock the back door.

The house safely secured for the night, I dragged weary limbs upstairs. I opened my bedroom door wide so that I could turn on the bedside lamp using the available light from the landing. No way I wanted to deal with the 60-watt overhead right now. I was relieved to see that Jenna had moved her stuff off my bed.

I pulled off my shoes, enjoying the blissful relief of the transfer from heels to carpet, and wrangled my way out of my dress, laying it carefully over the chair. I stripped off tights and underwear, wrapped my robe around me, and padded into the bathroom, where I peed, removed my various eye gunk and brushed my teeth. That would have to do for tonight.

Just before I hit the sheets, I peeked out the window; snowflakes were still falling, but there was no sign of them settling yet. I crawled into bed, enjoying the cool of the pillow against my skin. In spite of exhaustion, my body was still buzzing with excitement from the evening. Even in my dreams I hadn't expected things to go quite so well, quite so quickly, with Jonny. But once we'd seen one another again, the power of our indefinable, undeniable connection took over, and at long last we were in a place where we were able to allow ourselves to be swept along by it. I could hardly believe that things might finally work out for us. I could still feel his mouth on mine, his hands on my body. Things had *better* work out now, because I didn't know how I'd be able to live without him if they didn't.

I turned over and pulled the duvet a little tighter around me. I thought back to the first time we'd kissed like that, that grey, rainy Christmas after I'd left university and was living in London, so hard up my father had had to send me the train fare for my Christmas visit. We'd both been in such different places in our lives back then, but the memory of that time had held me in its thrall for years afterwards. My weary brain tried to recollect how many years ago it had been.

Part Seven

6 Years Ago

I walked down the lane towards the Old Albion, my hood up and head down against an incessant drizzle that didn't seem to have stopped since I'd arrived home three days ago on a cold, grey, miserable Christmas Eve. The few days of Christmas with my parents had been fine, although I was not in the best of moods at the moment, and, finding me on edge, they'd wisely chosen to leave me mostly alone. Now, finally free of all Christmas responsibilities, I was making my way to the pub to meet Jonny Rawlings. I hadn't seen him in a long time, not since our brief reunion dog walk four years ago. Since then, we'd both graduated from our respective university courses, and I'd moved to London while he'd stayed in Bristol.

I'd kept vaguely in touch with him, emailing every December to see if he would be back in Cornwall to get together at some point over Christmas time, but he never had been, always replying that he was staying in Bristol for the holidays, never relaying much by way of details about his life there. Until this year, finally, I received a response to my enquiry saying that he was going to be in Crantock at Christmas time, and indicating that he'd be willing to meet up. I'd suggested today, the 27th, know-ing that I wouldn't have to participate in any festive fam-ily activities I couldn't easily be excused from, and he'd replied that the date suited him too. So now, here I was, walking through the rain to meet him, wondering if I'd find him much changed since the last time I'd seen him, curious to hear his news, somewhat trepidatious about what I had to report about my own life.

I stepped into the pub and peered about. The usual festive decorations were in evidence, but the place was quiet. The lunch crowd had mostly left, and only a few parties with drinks or coffees in front of them were scat-tered about. I was just wondering if he was running late, or had ditched me altogether, when a man stood up from one of the tables furthest from the door and waved at me.

I realised from his height and movements that it was Jonny but felt I could be excused for taking a moment to recognise him, because the clean-shaven boy I'd always known was now sporting a beard! I reached him, and he bent down to kiss me on the cheek, clearly amused by my evident surprise at his new look.

I took off my coat and did a circling motion towards my own chin. "When did this happen?"

He laughed. "At least a couple of years ago now."

I examined him. The beard was natural, not long and straggly nor overly trimmed, but, as was to be expected from his general body hair situation, the hair was thick and dark. It suited him. Same as last time I'd seen him, his hair was long, although now possibly grown out even longer and thicker; he looked almost absurdly sexy. I swallowed.

He returned my examination. "And I see I'm not alone in changing things up a bit." He raised his eyebrows towards my head, and I touched my hair.

"Oh! Yes! I went red." A year or so ago, I'd finally followed through on all my years of longing looks in hair colour aisles and had dyed my boring brown locks a dark, hennaed red. I liked how it looked most of the time, but the upkeep was a chore, and I wasn't sure I'd keep it. Still, when I'd washed and conditioned and styled the long layers with rollers, as I'd done this morning, it could look pretty good, not too far off the 'Julia Roberts in *Pretty Woman*' vibe I was going for. I regarded Jonny, wondering if my crowning glory would have the desired effect on him. But his expression was guarded.

"So, what do you think?" I said.

He gave me a small smile. "Yeah, it looks nice."

Gee, thanks. I put my coat on the back of the nearest chair. "Are we sitting?"

"Of course. Would you like a drink?"

"Vodka and tonic, please."

He nodded and made his way over to the bar. He returned a couple of minutes later with my V&T, putting a pint of bitter on the table in front of his chair, before sitting down opposite me. We both took quiet sips.

I realised I was going to have to start things off. "So, tell me all your news. Leave nothing out, no detail too small."

He chuckled. "Not even the time last summer I had to have a rear molar filled?"

I shook my head firmly. "Not even that."

He grinned, meeting my eyes, and the years fell away. "Well, quick recap. I graduated from uni a... year and a half, I guess...? After I last saw you?"

I nodded, agreeing with the timeline.

"I decided to stay in Bristol to see about jobs because

it's still a city, you know, but not as expensive as London. But, turns out my dad was right, and an art degree really doesn't pay the mortgage. Or even the rent, as it turns out. I did bar and restaurant work to make money for canvases and paints, but I couldn't sell much, and I'm not even sure that wasn't fair. After I left college, I just couldn't seem to get inspired. Too much concern about what might sell, maybe. And, of course, when you worry about that, you're finished before you've even begun."

I met his eyes, and I hoped that mine conveyed my sympathy and understanding for what he was telling me. "What degree did you get?" I fully expected to receive good news on that front, but he puffed out a sigh.

"2.1. I just couldn't get excited about the written side of things. I was warned it would compromise my final grade, but, well, you know me and written course work."

I tipped my head. "Still, a 2.1 is great."

He shrugged. "Sure. It's fine. And hey, at least I have a 'BA (Hons)' in something, right? So my life so far hasn't been a total failure."

I was slightly shocked by his downbeat tone. "Of course not!"

"Anyway," he continued, "after a couple of years in Bristol doing dead-end jobs, getting nowhere with my art and achieving nothing more than getting further and further into debt, I admitted defeat and came back here to Crantock. So, I've been living at home since last summer, and, given that my dad just spent thousands of pounds for me to be 24 and back living under his roof with few prospects for a decent career, you can imagine how much fun that's been!"

I reached across the table towards him. "Christ, Jonny! I'm sorry!"

He turned his hand over and took my fingers in his own. "Thanks, Summer." He met my eyes. "And sorry to be such a whiner. I just needed to off-load."

I turned my hand and squeezed his fingers. "Of course."

"Anyway," he moved his hand to settle around his pint, "give me your update. Mike heard from Jenna that you'd graduated from Leeds and were living in London, is that right?"

I nodded. "Yes. Although, while I did manage to get a job, it's not exactly my dream career either."

"What degree did you get?"

"2.1 as well." I smiled at him. "Although that was because I wasn't clever enough for a First, so I'm perfectly happy with it."

He returned my smile. "Good. That you're happy with it, I mean."

"Anyway, I applied for jobs in publishing and TV and film production, but no dice. So, I am..." I mimed a drum roll, "an events organiser!"

He looked at me uncertainly. "And that is... good? Bad? Honestly, you're gonna have to help me out here because that sounds fine to me. Isn't that basically like being a party planner on steroids?"

I laughed. "Not quite. And mostly not remotely as fun. I do corporate work, so it's largely conferences and trade fairs, that kind of thing. There's the occasional party thrown in, but mostly then the client knows what they want, so it's just making sure the venue has the right orders for drinks and food, and that it all goes smoothly. And when it doesn't, it's all high drama and our fault, even when it's not."

"So, quite a lot of people being a pain in the arse,

then?"

I nodded. "Exactly. And at my level the pay *suuuuucks!* I think we're supposed to be grateful for the 'training' or something. The only people in the company who seem to make decent money are the managers, who don't actually do any of the day-to-day work but focus on getting and keeping clients. They get bonuses based on a percentage of how much gross revenue we make, which, trust me, is *a lot!* But we foot soldiers don't see any of that. I'm spending most of my salary on rent for a house share in Ealing, which is a ridiculous forty-five minutes into central London. I'm so bloody broke my dad had to send me the money for train fare down here this Christmas. It's embarrassing! And I'm not even sure if I want to keep doing this." I couldn't hide wry amusement as I looked up at him. "How's that for a whine? Feeling in good company now?"

He gave me a warm smile. "I feel considerably better, thank you. Although I would point out that living in London with a job is still a definite step up from living with your parents without one. So I think we should admit right here and now that my right to a decent slice of self pity is greater than yours."

I tipped my head, considering. "Okay, I'll give you that. But only by a slim margin. And," I fixed him with a serious look, "at least you have a real *talent*, a calling. I'm still sure you'll make it, even if it takes a little while to sort yourself out."

He looked at me, his eyes filled with the kind of affection and admiration I realised I'd really missed from him. "Thank you, Summer," he said quietly. "That means a lot."

I returned his smile with a warm one of my own. "Just calling it how I see it." I looked down at my empty glass.

"Another round?"

He drained his pint down to the last inch. "Why not?" I got up to go to the bar.

When I sat back down with our fresh drinks, I gathered my courage to ask him the question I was most curious about. "So, how are things on the personal front?" I'd had my eyes fixed on my glass as I asked him, but when I raised them, he looked amused.

"You mean the news hasn't made its way to Jenna via the rumour mill that I'm currently single?"

I hoped the slight blush tingling my cheeks didn't show through my foundation. "She might have mentioned that was her assessment of the current situation, yes." I fixed him with a slightly scolding look. "But you must admit that you do tend to play those particular cards close to your chest, so I couldn't be sure her information was a hundred percent reliable."

His eyes twinkled. "Fair enough. Although in this instance, she is correct. I am not currently dating anyone." He shrugged. "I'm not really in the mood for it. And, to be honest, having zero money isn't exactly conducive to an eventful personal life."

I raised an eyebrow. I was entirely sure that his limited access to cash would not be a serious impediment to his getting dates if he so chose.

"And," he looked at me appreciatively, "I'm not sure that many girls would want to spend their time listening to me moan and tell my tale of woe."

"Oh, I think you might be surprised about that." I was equally sure that there were many girls who would be quite happy to spend at least some of their time listening to such tales, even if only for the privilege of watching him tell them. I crinkled my brow, pretending to try and remember a name. "What happened with… Felicity, was it?"

He nodded. "Yeah. We broke up just after graduation. She went to do a post-grad course in Paris."

I raised my eyebrows. "Fancy!"

He nodded again, resigned.

"But you were together for a while?"

"Yes." His eyes were wistful. "She was great." He fixed an impenetrable gaze on me. "I'm not sure she was 'the one' or anything, though. We parted on good terms, and I didn't miss her that much after she'd gone."

I pulled a face. "Ouch!"

He held my eyes for a few moments too long, and something indefinable passed between us. "Anyway, yeah, after that I dated a few waitresses, very casually, until I came back here." He decided I was not to be let off the hook. "What about you? What happened with Charlie?" I noticed that he didn't even pretend to forget the name.

"Actually, we broke up a few months after I last saw you." I paused. "You were right, he wasn't a good fit for me. A little too 'clinical' and 'black and white' in his views of the world."

Jonny grimaced and drew in air over his teeth.

"I dated a guy from my English course for a while in my third year." I smiled. "Suddenly all the boys got very keen to get a girlfriend, AKA someone to have sex with, in their final year. I think they were all terrified of having to leave university a virgin."

Jonny burst out laughing. "No doubt."

"But he was only convenient, really. And we had shared experiences to talk about, of course." I shrugged. "No one since I moved to London. I've met some men via work, but no one I've found particularly attractive, and I'm too tired most of the time to make the effort just for the sake of it."

He was assessing me with one of his soft, fathomless looks. "Good. I mean, you deserve much better than just settling for someone."

I returned his gaze evenly. "So do you."

We were both silent for a moment, connected by that invisible string that always made itself evident when we were together.

He took a deep breath and sat back in his chair, looking out the window. "Jesus! How is it still raining?"

I followed his gaze outside. "I've no idea. I don't think it's stopped since I got down here." I took a beat. "I was hoping we might get one of our walks in after this drink, but I guess that's not going to happen." I didn't even try to keep the disappointment out of my voice.

He turned back to me. "You can come and hang out at mine for a bit, if you like?"

I perked up. "Yes? Your parents would be okay with that?"

"I'm sure they would be, even if they were here. But they're not."

I furrowed my brow in confusion. "They're away at Christmas?" I realised as I thought about it that I hadn't seen Barbara or Harry at my parents' Christmas party.

"Yes. After the endless rain we've had this year, my mother declared that she couldn't go another month without seeing the sun or she'd do something drastic to herself, so she booked them two weeks in the Caribbean. They're back in the new year."

"And you didn't get to go?"

"I wasn't asked. But I wouldn't have wanted to go anyway. I can think of very little more miserable than being trapped in some resort with nothing to do all day except swim and sunbathe."

I rolled my eyes at him. "Yes, that does sound quite dreadful."

He laughed. "Seriously, I would hate it. Not my scene at all. I've been much happier here on my own. I've even been inspired to paint for the first time in ages. Turns out that even grey, stormy skies over Crantock Bay can be interesting."

"That's fantastic! I'm so pleased."

He smiled. "Well, let's wait and see if I produce anything worthwhile first, then you have permission to get excited."

I shook my head. "Disagree. The fact that you're excited about your work again is plenty of reason for me to be happy about it."

He gave me a look that almost took my breath away, and I pushed back my chair and stood up, picking up my coat and starting to put it on. "Shall we go to yours, then?"

He pushed back and stood up as well. "Sure. You know the way."

Fifteen minutes later I was holding a glass of red wine, looking through a shelf of DVDs in Jonny's living room. His – or rather, of course, his parents' – house was much newer and more modern than my parents'. It was all sleek and muted tones and wood flooring and open plan. A tall, extremely tasteful Christmas tree, dressed entirely in white, was the only decorative concession to the festive season.

"What are you in the mood for?" I asked.

"I don't mind. You pick."

I looked over to where Jonny was watching me, his

butt resting against the counter edge of the island which bordered the kitchen and living areas, his own glass of wine in hand. I was feeling a little heated by his tall, slender body casually taking up space in my immediate vicinity. In the pub, this aspect of him had been fairly easy to ignore, but now, coat off and in his own environment, his long legs in great fitting jeans, and torso in snug T-shirt, I was finding his physical presence distinctly distracting. Even the sight of his feet in socks was somewhat erotic to me. I was fighting a severe assault on my self-control that I wasn't quite sure wasn't purposeful on his part.

I took a sip of my wine. "Give me some idea what you'd prefer, or I can't be held responsible for making a choice you're unhappy with."

He came up behind me, and I swore I could feel the heat radiating from his body. "Honestly, I don't mind. I've seen most of them at least once, anyway."

He was being exasperating. "So would you rather not watch a movie, then?"

"I told you, I'm perfectly okay with watching whatever you want." He took a beat. "I'm just happy to be hanging out with you."

There was a little explosion somewhere deep inside my chest. Oh, good Lord.

I pulled out a DVD. "This is a great film. Have you seen it?"

He took it from me. "'Out of Sight'," he read. He turned it over. "George Clooney?" he said with a touch of disgust. "Summer, I'm disappointed in you. So obvious! What do women see in him anyway?"

I took the DVD back from him. "You know perfectly well what they see in him. But that's not the point of this movie. It's just a great film. From a book by Elmore Leonard. Steven Soderbergh directs. And George and JLo have epic chemistry. Seriously, it's good. And, as you say you've seen most everything else here, what've you got to lose?"

He held up a hand. "Okay, okay, you've convinced me. Let's go put it on."

His parents had the largest, fanciest TV I'd ever seen set up as part of an entertainment centre in a designated area of the living room, with an extremely comfortable looking sofa positioned directly in front of it. Jonny slid the DVD into one of the slim black boxes beneath the TV and did something with one of the remotes. He topped up our wine glasses and set the bottle down on the side table next to him. Then he sat and relaxed back into the sofa, indicating to me to do the same. Once we were both comfortably seated, he stretched out his legs and rested his feet on the large square footstool in front of us. Clearly, everything possible had been done to maximise the comfort and convenience of TV viewing in this house.

The movie started and George walked into a bank to rob it, looking about as devastatingly handsome as he'd ever done in his life. The girl playing the teller behind the counter looked appropriately dazzled. I shimmied down a bit deeper into the squishy sofa cushions and took a sip of my wine. This day was turning out much better than I'd ever envisioned.

By the time George and JLo were meeting in the hotel bar, with snow falling outside, in my favourite scene of the movie, I'd somehow moved so that I was resting my head on Jonny's shoulder, and he didn't seem to mind.

"Well, does this make any sense to you?" JLo asked George.

"It doesn't have to," George replied. "It's just something that happens... And you always remember it because it was there, and you let it go. And you think to yourself, what if I had said something? What if? What if...? It may only happen a few times in your life."

"Or once," JLo said.

"Or once," George agreed.

Neither Jonny nor I moved a muscle, or dared hardly breathe, as the love scene played out, the two beautiful movie stars at the height of their powers, the writing and direction perfect.

Finally, as the credits began to roll and the transport van turned right, Jonny let out a deep breath and turned to me. I sat up and freed him to move.

"Okay, I'll never doubt your movie recommendations again. That was great."

I beamed at him. "Told you!"

He tipped the last of the red wine out into my glass. "Shall I open another?"

I nodded.

"And there's a fairly decent pizza in the freezer I can put in the oven. Pepperoni okay?"

I smiled and looked at my watch. "Lovely. I'd better text my mother and tell her I'm going to be home late." I got up and walked to the window, peering out into the darkness. I sighed. "Good grief. It's still raining."

"Um..." Jonny walked back over from the kitchen, carrying a fresh bottle of wine. "You can stay here tonight if you like. The spare bedroom is made up."

I gave him a careful look. But the thing was with Jonny, he wouldn't be a shit. He wouldn't pull anything weird or make me feel uncomfortable, of this I was sure. The thought of staying here with him, in this beautiful, warm house for the evening, and then not having to walk home through the cold and rain, but be able to go straight to a lovely, comfortable bed and fresh sheets, was just too tempting.

"If you're sure," I said.

He nodded. "Absolutely. You'd be doing me a favour, actually. I don't mind my own company, but two weeks of it is a bit much, even for me."

I smiled. "Then I graciously accept. Thank you."

I found my phone in my jacket pocket and texted my mother: 'Staying at Jonny's for the evening and sleeping over in spare room. See you tomorrow. x'. I wasn't entirely sure why I felt the need to clarify about the spare room, but I did. Better not to give her any ideas.

Jonny switched the TV over to live viewing, and we took turns scrolling through the channels, looking in vain for something to watch. We sat through a truly excruciating dating show while we ate the pizza, taking turns to toss playful insults at the show and its participants. By the time we'd almost finished the second bottle of wine, and I was giving serious consideration to going in search of a glass of water, my TV Guide scrolling advised me that *The Notebook* was about to start in a few minutes.

I looked at Jonny doubtfully. "Have you ever seen it?"

He shook his head.

"It's seriously schmaltzy and entirely intent on the emotional manipulation of its audience, but it's also pretty entertaining and kind of a classic of its romantic genre." I could see I was amusing him.

"Put it on if you want to watch it."

I chewed my lip. "If you're sure. I'm not sure it would be up your street."

"Guests' prerogative," he said.

I selected the channel and sat back into the sofa.

"Okay, but say if you hate it and we'll find something else."

He got up and picked up my empty wine glass. "Do you want anything else? Coffee? Tea?"

I looked up at him. "I'd love a glass of water."

"Coming right up."

He went to the kitchen and came back with a large bottle of Evian and two glasses. He poured water for both of us and settled back down onto the sofa.

Two hours later, tears were trickling down my face as Noah visited Allie's room for the last time. I attempted to discreetly wipe them away with my fingers, but it was no good. I was busted. Jonny put his arm around me and pulled me against him, which just made my tears fall faster.

He kissed the top of my head. "I had no idea you were such a big old softie."

I gave a quiet, somewhat snotty laugh against his chest. "I don't know, some films just really get to me. And with this one... The whole 'love through the ages' thing. And of course the ending. Peak Nicholas Sparks." I sat up and wiped my cheek with my sleeve. "It's all so impossibly romantic."

He looked at me with one of his intense, unforgettable looks. His voice was soft and deep. "Romantic, yes, impossibly so, no."

I managed to hold his gaze without looking away. I had no idea what to do with him. I wanted to kiss him and never stop. I wanted to hold him and never let go. I wanted to watch him fly and have everything he wanted from life. None of these things were remotely possible with where I was in my own life right now. Giving into the temptation he stirred in me wouldn't do anything but hurt him, and there was no one on earth I wanted to hurt less.

I gave him a lop-sided smile. "Now who's the big softie?"

He laughed and held up his hands. "Guilty as charged."

Suddenly a wave of fatigue washed over me, and I yawned extravagantly. "Oh my God!" I said, covering my mouth, "I'm sorry."

He laughed. "I'll attempt to take that as a reflection on this evening's wine consumption and the lateness of the hour, not as a comment on your opinion of me as a host."

"Oh, God! Please do! And actually, more than that, please take it as a compliment. I'm just feeling so relaxed." I met his eyes. "I haven't enjoyed myself so much in ages." I took a beat. "Thank you for a lovely evening."

His eyes on mine were like liquid chocolate. "You're most welcome, Summer. The same for me, of course. Honestly, you've saved my Christmas."

Another yawn threatened, and I stood up. "I'd better go to bed before I completely disgrace myself."

"You remember where you're going?"

I nodded. "As long as everything's in the same place."

"Yes. I put a T-shirt on the bed if you want to change out of your clothes."

I smiled at him, so happy that the thoughtful boy I'd known had lost none of his consideration as the years had passed. "Thank you!" I bent down and kissed him on the cheek. "Goodnight, then."

He brushed my hair briefly with his hand. "Goodnight, Summer."

I woke the following morning and wriggled happily in the Rawlings' extremely comfortable guest bed. I stretched and sighed. I hadn't slept so well for as long as

I could remember. As soon as my head had hit the pillow, I'd fallen asleep and slept undisturbed through the night. I rolled over and picked up my watch off the bedside table. I was shocked to see that it was coming up to a quarter to nine. I levered myself out of bed and drew back the curtains. Yep! Still raining. We'd need an ark soon.

I reluctantly pulled off the T-shirt of Jonny's that I'd worn in bed – plain grey, soft with age and much too big for me, but all the better for that – and pulled on my own clothes from yesterday. I used the bathroom then made my way downstairs.

I found him in the kitchen, sitting on a stool at the island, reading a newspaper. The scent of real coffee was drifting up from a nearby cafetière. Some kind of melodic acoustic guitar music I didn't recognise was playing quietly from a speaker on the bookshelves. He clearly knew how to make the most of his parents' absence.

He looked up as I came in and smiled, apparently amused and charmed by my appearance. I knew I had panda eyes and dishevelled hair, and I shot him a self-effacing eye roll.

"Good morning," he said. "Help yourself to coffee."

"Thanks." I picked up the mug that had been left for me next to the cafetière and poured myself a cup. I helped myself to milk from the fridge and sat down one stool away from him.

"There's cereal in the cupboard or bread, if you want toast. I was going to go to the shop in a minute to get bacon for sandwiches, if you don't mind waiting."

I looked him up and down: sexy jeans, fresh black T-shirt, hair still slightly damp from the shower, bare feet. So, this was what it was like when a man was perfect in every way? Interesting.

I took a sip of my coffee. "Thanks, but I need to go home. I need to shower, and..." I made a circling gesture at my face, "sort this out."

A flash of disappointment showed in his eyes before he rallied. "Why don't you shower here? You can use my parents' ensuite. My mother has the contents of the entire skin care aisle in her bathroom, I'm sure you can find what you need. There's probably even a new toothbrush in a drawer somewhere."

"And she wouldn't mind that?"

"Even if she notices, which is doubtful, I'll just say I was in there looking for something."

Jonny would clearly make the best kidnapper ever. His captives would be positively begging not to be rescued, he made it so impossible to want to leave. I could feel the pull of a hot shower before I had to trudge through the rain with a 'walk of shame' appearance I hadn't even properly earned.

I slid down off the stool. "Well, if you're sure?"

He just gave me an amused smile, not even bothering to answer. "There are plenty of towels, help yourself."

"Thanks." I picked up my coffee and made for the stairs.

The ensuite bathroom was as fabulous as I'd frankly expected. There was no bath but rather a huge rain shower; two basins were set into a marble countertop; warm, fluffy white towels were stuffed onto a chrome towel radiator. It was clear that some items were missing which had been taken on holiday, but, as promised, I opened a large, mirrored cabinet to find it brimming with luxury skincare brands: Kiehl's, Sisley and Clarins were all amply represented, along with a few brands I didn't even recognise. I rooted around and found a bottle of cleanser that promised to also remove eye makeup, and I went to work.

After showering, guiltily luxuriating in Barbara's Aveda shampoo and conditioner, and the Molton Brown shower gel that had been *just right there*, I towelled off, pulled a brush through my hair and cleaned my teeth (new toothbrush in a drawer – check!). I made my way back downstairs with damp hair and bare face, feeling like a new woman.

The smell of bacon frying hit me before I'd even reached the bottom of the stairs. I found Jonny at the hob, supervising a sizzling pan. He looked up at me, and his eyes popped out of his head. My cheeks began to tingle.

"Sorry," I said, setting down my empty coffee mug. "I know it's a shock. You haven't seen me without makeup in a million years."

"No, no..." He was clearly struggling. "You look..." He conceded defeat. "You look beautiful."

My blush stepped into high gear, and I turned away from him to pretend to examine the newspaper.

He came up behind me and set down a clean mug next to me, pouring out fresh coffee. "The bacon's about done."

I took the mug from him without meeting his eyes. "Thanks."

We ate our sandwiches in comfortable silence, sharing the paper. As he was putting the dirty plates in the dishwasher, I stood up. "I still need to go home for a bit," I said. "I need fresh clothes and... underwear."

His eyes widened and shot to my crotch in my jeans. I could practically see his mind working, wondering if I was wearing panties. Until he realised what he was doing and looked back at my face.

"But if it's okay, I'd like to come back again afterwards?"

He smiled, pleased. "Of course."

I rubbed the countertop with my fingertips nervously. "And I actually have another favour to ask of you, although I'm aware that it's ridiculously cheeky."

"Go on…"

"It's just… Well, it's been so great being here, away from the chaos of the house in London, or, frankly, my parents' well-meaning combination of concern and judgement at home. It's felt like a proper break, the first I've had in ages. So I was wondering what you'd think about me staying here again tonight? In the spare room." I bit my tongue at the final bit of unnecessary clarification, but he didn't seem to notice it.

"Of course. Stay as long as you like." He took a beat. "When are you going back to London?"

"Um… day after tomorrow. The quarter past nine train. I only have to change once with that one." I was already dreading the moment we passed over the Tamar bridge and out of Cornwall.

He nodded. "Well, you're welcome here whenever you like until then."

I smiled. "Thanks, Jonny."

I let myself into our house and called out for my parents. "Mum? Dad?" Silence. The house was empty. I walked through into the kitchen, my legs buffeted by the dogs as I opened the door. I shut it behind me to prevent any escapes and walked over to the kitchen table. A note from my mother was propped up against the fruit bowl: *Hope you had a nice time with Jonny. We've gone to visit Mary and Graham in Truro. Leftovers in the fridge. Help yourself. x*

I grabbed a biro from the junk drawer and sat down to

write a reply under my mother's note: *Staying at Jonny's again tonight. See you tomorrow. x*

My phone buzzed in my pocket, and I took it out. There was another text from Jenna, the third she'd sent today. The first one, sent just after nine this morning, had said: 'Let's catch up. Call me. x'. The second, sent an hour later, said: 'Where are you? Call me!!!' This latest one simply said: 'Are you dead?'

I rolled amused eyes at the phone and texted her back: 'Not dead. How about a drink tomorrow night?'

I got up and fetched one of my mother's big hessian shopping totes out of the larder. I took a couple of bottles of my father's claret out of the kitchen wine rack (there were plenty more in the dining room) and stowed them inside the bag. Then I opened the fridge and surveyed the contents. There were various tupperware containers of leftovers, as promised. I selected one of coronation chicken, one of potato salad, one of Waldorf salad and one containing a bunch of mini quiches which had somehow survived the Christmas Eve party. I added a four pack of Peroni for good measure. I was just finishing stacking my haul into the shopping bag when my phone buzzed again. A text from Jenna: 'On for tomorrow night. Text in morning re time and place?' I texted back 'Yes' and put the phone back in my pocket.

I made my way upstairs and changed into fresh underwear and clothes and put on some light makeup. I packed myself a proper overnight bag – including clean pants! – and went back downstairs. Necessary supplies in hand, I let myself out and walked back through the drizzle to Jonny's house.

I let myself in via the kitchen, put my jacket on a peg and carried my spoils over to the fridge. I stacked them inside, all except for the wine and two of the beers. I put the wine bottles on the counter, rooted around in the utensils drawer, located a bottle opener and popped the beer caps. I took a drink from one of the bottles and took both in search of Jonny. I found him at the far end of the living room, in a large wing-back armchair by the bi-fold doors to the patio. He was sketching in an A4 notebook. I realised he'd purposely located himself where there was the most natural light.

He looked up as I approached and closed his notebook. "Thanks," he said, taking the offered beer. "All sorted now?" His eyes twinkled with amusement.

I gave him a grin. "Yes, thank you. I've brought leftovers from home which I thought we could have for lunch? And a couple of bottles of my dad's wine."

"You didn't have to, but thanks. That all sounds like a treat."

I eyed his notebook. "What are you drawing?"

He looked a bit shifty. "Nothing really, just doodles."

I nodded. I wasn't going to push him. "Anything you're ready to show me?"

"Not yet, but I'm feeling more hopeful than I've been in a long time. My artistic muse seems to have returned to me." He gave me a penetrating look, but I just returned it with a smile.

"Well, don't let me disturb you. I can keep myself entertained, if you don't mind me making use of your TV."

"All the house's facilities are at your command."

I gave him a happy smile and took my beer over to the TV couch. I scrolled through the on-screen guide and noticed that *Four Weddings and a Funeral* was about to start in ten minutes. You had to love Christmas holidays film season.

Later that afternoon, we were lounging on the sofa, watching *How the Grinch Stole Christmas*. I was pleasantly stuffed and lightly buzzed. I'd made sandwiches with the coronation chicken, and we'd laid that plate, and the rest of my mother's food, out on a tablecloth on the big footstool, picnic style. We'd polished off the beers with the sandwiches and had now moved on to the wine. All was feeling very right in my world.

Jonny stood and picked up some plates to start clearing up. I made to get up to help him, but he shook his head at me. "No, stay put. You've done enough today. Guests don't clear."

I smiled up at him and settled back into the sofa. I wasn't going to argue.

After he'd tidied everything away, refilled our wine glasses and set down a large glass of cold water next to me without me even having to ask, he sat down on the sofa and looked at me tentatively. "Summer...?"

I removed my attention from the Grinch's antics and looked at him. "Yes?"

"Since we're doing favours for one another today, I wondered if I could ask one of you?"

"Fire away."

"Um... would you mind if I drew you?"

"Er..." I shifted myself to sit up. "Sure, I don't see why not. If you want to. What do I have to do?"

"Oh, nothing really. I mean, you need to stay kind of still, but nothing too onerous. If you're watching TV, that would be fine. Are you sure you're okay with it?"

I crinkled my brow. "Why wouldn't I be?"

"Well, it'll mean my attention being on you without any kind of break for... well, an extended period. I don't want you to find it creepy."

"I don't find it creepy when your attention is on me," I said quietly.

He looked relieved. "Okay, good. The only other thing is… that sweater isn't great for this. Do you have a top on underneath it? Or I could give you one of my mother's T-shirts?"

I looked down at my thick polo neck jumper. "I have a strappy top on under it. Would that work?"

He looked a bit awkward. "That would be perfect, if you're comfortable wearing only that."

I shrugged. "It's fine. Nothing I wouldn't wear on a hot summer's day."

He smiled, clearly very pleased. "Great. So… if you want to find your most comfortable position, I can arrange the lighting, and then all you need to do is stay as still as you can manage. Move if you need to or get uncomfortable, of course."

I smiled at him fussing. "So it's okay if I just stay right here?"

He nodded. "Fine."

He got up while I pulled off my sweater and re-arranged my hair to what I hoped was best effect. I turned my attention back to the film, as he moved lamps around and generally arranged the lighting to his liking. I tried, and failed, not to feel extremely flattered by this whole idea. Once he was happy with lamp placement, he carried the wing-back armchair over to a spot to the side of me, so that he could draw me in semi-profile as I watched TV.

The Grinch finished and the next film up was *Out of Africa*, which was extremely convenient as it was one of my favourites.

I kept my wine glass in my hand to sip from it as Jonny sat, quietly sketching. I couldn't remember ever feeling so relaxed or at peace. As the film progressed, I started to become more and more drowsy, and by the time Karen and Denys were starting their affair, I could hardly hold my head up.

"Do you mind if I lie down for a minute?" I said. "I don't want to spoil your drawing."

"It's fine. Make yourself comfortable."

I arranged a pillow on the arm of the sofa and lay my head on it. Just five minutes...

I woke up again as Karen was reading the A. E. Housman poem that always made me cry. The movie was almost over. It was now completely dark outside, and the house was lit only by the couple of lamps which Jonny had positioned around me and the light from the TV. I blinked slightly sticky eyes and sat up. Jonny was still in his chair, sketchbook in hand.

"Oh, God! I'm so sorry," I said. "I'm a rubbish model."

"Not at all. Your nap was perfect for sketching purposes."

I pushed myself further upright. "Oh, thank goodness for that."

He stopped working with his pencil and looked at me. "Would you like to see?"

"Of course!"

He came and sat down next to me and handed me the sketchbook. There were two drawings of me, one from when I'd been sitting up, and another of me sleeping peacefully on the cushion. A sense of wonder washed over me. I remembered Jonny being good at drawing at school, but these were on a whole other level: clearly extremely skilful. I'd expected he would have improved his abilities a lot during his time at art school, but I hadn't been prepared for this at all. They reminded me of Renaissance sketches I'd seen in museums. The woman in the drawings definitely looked like me, but she was much more beautiful. He'd made me perfect. I wondered if he'd purposefully corrected my flaws, or if that was simply how he saw me. Maybe we all see the people we love as more perfect than they really are.

I gazed at the drawings, hardly knowing what to say. "They're absolutely beautiful," I managed. I looked up at him. "But you've been much too kind to me. I don't really look like this."

His eyes on me were turning my insides to liquid. "Yes, you do," he said, clearly not willing to brook any argument.

I held his gaze, unable to tear myself away. I could see all his love for me in his eyes, the same as ever. And he broke me. The walls I'd erected around myself since seeing him again dissolved like a sandcastle under the influence of the incoming tide, and I leaned forward and kissed him.

He put his hands on my arms as I moved closer, sliding my hands up his sides. He opened his mouth to mine, and I felt myself become molten from head to toe. I deepened the kiss and he responded, taking his lead from me. I moved to straddle his lap, my hands in his hair, my kisses becoming increasingly fevered. I was here now, no point in holding back. He ran his hands over my back, pressing me against him, matching every escalation of my desire with his own.

I ran a hand down over his chest, then his belly to his jeans. He bucked a little against my touch. My head was spinning and all self-control had deserted me. I moved my fingers to his fly, but he put a hand over mine. I froze, holding my breath, terrified he was going to stop things.

"Do you want to go upstairs?" he whispered into my hair.

I let out a relieved breath. "God, yes!"

I felt him smile, and he shifted himself forwards on the sofa and stood up, still holding me wrapped around him. The way he seemed to find me as light as a feather was almost unbearably sexy to me.

He carried me towards the staircase and I wasted no time, my arms wrapped around his neck as I kissed his face, mouth, eyelids, ears. He laughed with delight – a low, velvety rumble – at my enthusiasm as we went up the stairs, apparently only mildly encumbered by his troublesome passenger.

He walked us into his bedroom and laid me down on the bed, briefly disentangling himself from me to turn on a bedside lamp. He returned to providing his share of the kisses, while I curled my fingers into the back of his T-shirt and pulled it off over his head. I thought I might expire with lust; I couldn't believe I was finally going to get to ravish this gorgeous body.

He pulled my top over my head and tossed it to one side, before burying his face in the crook of my neck and pressing soft, urgent kisses against my skin, moving down over my breastbone to the edge of my bra. I wriggled around to remove it for him, gasping as his mouth took advantage, and I wrapped my arms around his head to encourage the attention. He moved down my body, tracing kisses over my ribs and belly until his progress was impeded by the waistband of my jeans. His nimble fingers unbuttoned and unzipped them then pulled them off with what I noted was a pretty expert flourish. While down at my feet, he whipped off my socks, meeting my eyes with a mischievous grin as he did so, causing me to burst into giggles.

He gave my panties a heated look, but I decided it was time to even things up a bit. I beckoned him to lie back down over me. He indicated his intention to comply with a lop-sided smile, but before he did, he reached over and scrabbled in his bedside table, fortunately finding the protection he was looking for without too much trouble. I decided just to be grateful for it rather than be concerned about why he had it so easily to hand.

He returned to me, and our mouths met again as I finally got my way with his fly and freed him from his jeans, allowing my eager hands to roam. I stroked and caressed, drawing low moans of pleasure from deep in his chest and expletives through gritted teeth as he fought for control. Every utterance was music to my ears.

Somehow he managed to shed his jeans, underwear and socks without leaving my body, and then my panties disappeared as if in a puff of smoke. I opened myself up to him, he did the necessary with a smooth efficiency, and then he was inside me and I thought I'd died and gone to heaven. He was just the right fit. We began to move together, the skilful motions of his body pushing mine relentlessly towards an orgasm I knew was inescapable. I looked up at him, and his eyes were closed, his bottom lip caught between his teeth as he focused on putting my pleasure before his own. Our bodies moved together, each of us seeming to know just what the other needed in each moment.

Our tempo increased and I knew that my climax was imminent. I reached up desperately and placed my hand at the base of his throat to encourage him to look at me. He opened his eyes and met mine as the ultimate pleasure took hold. I cried out loudly as the wave of orgasm erupted and unfurled through my body, pulling me apart, making me boneless. He surrendered to his climax and I took my own enjoyment from his. Our bodies finally parted, limp and spent.

I lay next to him, my skin cooling. I pushed my hand over my hair, gathering damp, sweaty tendrils into the dry ones. "Holy shit," I breathed.

I could hear him still catching his breath next to me. "No fucking kidding," he managed.

I manoeuvred my way under the duvet and turned over to watch him as he did the same. I put out a hand and settled it on his chest, caressing the hair with my fingers. He covered my hand gently with his own, his breathing now steady. I watched his chest rise and fall, my heart full of a love I'd only imagined existed up until that time. He lifted my hand briefly to his lips to kiss my fingers before settling it back on his chest. I snuggled into him and slipped into sleep.

The next time I awoke, I realised I'd turned over in my sleep. The light of the moon was streaming in through the window, and I saw that Jonny was standing beside me next to the bed. He was holding two glasses of water, one of which he set down on the bedside table next to me. He was quite naked, illuminated by soft, pale light. I ran my eyes over his body, absolutely dazzled by him. He realised that I was awake.

"Just getting a drink of water," he said, his voice barely above a whisper.

"Thank you."

"Are you comfortable otherwise?"

I nodded, feeling sleep tugging at me. "Mm-hmm."

I lifted myself up to take a sip of water, watching him as he walked away from me around to the other side of the bed. He climbed in, and I put my glass back on the table and turned over towards him. He set down his own glass and snuggled under the duvet, turning onto his side to face me. We looked at one another; the light was dim but sufficient. I reached under the covers and found his hand. I wrapped my fingers around his and lifted them to my lips to press a kiss against them. He curled his fingers into mine, and I felt my eyes closing. I fell asleep holding his hand.

When I woke up the next morning, it was daylight, and it looked like the rain had finally stopped and things were brightening up. I turned over, but Jonny's side of the bed was empty. I'd just taken a drink of water to freshen my dry mouth when he returned, carrying two mugs. He set one down on his side and walked the other around to me, where he put it on my table next to the water glass.

"Thought you might like a cup of tea," he said.

He sat down by me on the bed. He was wearing boxer briefs and a grey T-shirt. I eyed the T-shirt with dissatisfaction. "You're wearing a lot of clothing."

He gave me a mischievous smile. "That situation can be corrected if you'd like."

I shifted myself to sit up a bit, not bothering too much to cover myself up with the duvet. He gave my body a lingering, appreciative look.

"I very much would." I picked up the mug of tea and took a sip. It was too hot; I'd have to wait for it to cool down. "Give me a few minutes in the bathroom, and then we'll see about this whole overdressed situation."

He grinned at me. "Right you are."

I sat up properly and leaned in to press a quick kiss against his mouth before getting out of bed and making my way to the door. I turned around when I reached it, knowing that he'd be watching me, and gave him a little twirl before stepping out into the hallway. I could hear him laughing as I walked down to his parents' bedroom. I went through to their ensuite, where I'd left the toothbrush I'd used yesterday. I peed, washed my hands and brushed my teeth. I was pretty confident he wouldn't mind my messy hair and smudged eye makeup in the least.

I returned to his bedroom, where he was back in his side of the bed, the T-shirt now discarded. I got in my side and lifted the duvet to check the status of his shorts. Also gone. I made a playful sad face.

"Aww! I was looking forward to removing those myself."

He laughed. "Sorry to spoil your fun." He propped himself on his elbow, looking at me. "Can I make it up to you?"

I shuffled as close to him as possible and lay back in the centre of the bed. I raised my arms above my head and arched my back slightly, shamelessly offering myself to him. "You can certainly try."

Our lovemaking then was different to the night before, slower, less urgent – at least until we were chasing our orgasms – but no less satisfying. I hadn't been able to resist spending significant hours over past years fantasising about going to bed with him, but I was not a little astonished to find the actual experience matching, even exceeding, my dreams and fantasies. Of course we had our great, natural connection – that chemistry, that spark – but I also think that how we'd come back to one another after all these years, in spite of everything, had reaffirmed our bond, instilling in us some kind of belief that we were somehow 'meant to be'. So now that we'd finally come together physically, there was no holding back. Each of us took from the other, and gave to the other, completely, in the absolute certainty that we would be there to catch one another if we fell. We could laugh at the ridiculous bits of sex without embarrassment and fully indulge our desire for one another without worrying that we were some-how giving the other person too much power over us. It was utterly wonderful.

Fully sated again, we drifted off to sleep in the morn-ing light.

I was the first to awaken this time. I opened my eyes to Jonny sleeping next to me, his chest rising and falling steadily. The dread of my impending departure began to creep in, slowly but surely building beneath my ribcage. I let my eyes feast on him, feeling that I could quite hap-pily spend many hours over the course of the rest of my life just watching him sleep. But a lump was solidifying in my chest, and I could already start to feel the longing and missing him that I knew would consume my coming days. This before I had even left.

I tore my eyes away from him, got up and went back to his parents' bathroom, where I showered and fixed my ap-pearance as best I could for my return home. I went back to the guest room for fresh underwear and a T-shirt, then back down the hall to his bedroom. He was still sleeping, although he'd turned over to lie on his stomach, and I crept around, gathering up my discarded clothing from the night before and putting on my jeans. I took every-thing to my room and packed up, the lump in my chest be-coming more and more unbearable.

I steeled myself and made my way back to his bed-room. I sat down on the edge of the bed next to his sleep-ing body. I hadn't had much chance to enjoy the sight of his naked back, so I took a minute or two to indulge myself, then I reached out and stroked a hand over his shoulder. He stirred and, realising that I was sitting next to him, he levered himself up onto his elbows, turned over and sat up.

He took in my state of readiness and a sliver of pain passed across his face, before he got a hold of himself and managed to hide it.

"Are you leaving?" He was unable to keep the disappointment out of his voice.

"I think I'd better. If I stay any longer, I might never be able to."

He took my hand and caressed it with his thumb. "Would that be such a bad thing?"

I looked at his hand holding mine. "Probably not. But my life's in London, and I'm not sure how that can change any time soon."

"You don't think you'll be able to make it down here more often?"

I shook my head. "I've racked my brains and I don't see how. Both time and money are against it." I met his eyes. "I wish things were different. Do you think you'll be able to come up to London to visit me?"

"I can try." He sighed. "Probably not." His fingers tightened around my hand. "I just... I don't want this to be it for us." He looked down, for once the one unable to meet my gaze. "I'm not sure I could handle that."

I moved my hand to his shoulder, leaning in to kiss him on the mouth. "It doesn't have to be. But I don't know what's going to happen, and I can't ask you to wait for me indefinitely."

He looked up at me. "What if I choose to?"

"I can't make your choices for you, but I don't want

you to live your life pining. I want you to be happy. That's all I've ever wanted." I bit back a smile. "Well, that and you between my thighs, obviously."

He laughed. "Well, you know that's always on offer."

I became serious again. "I won't hold you to that. If you find someone else you can love and I'm not here, don't feel that you have to wait for me. That wouldn't be fair to you."

He focused his most intense, questioning gaze on me. "And you'd be okay hearing that I was with someone else?"

"Right now? It would probably kill me. But neither of us knows what the future will bring. Perhaps you'll meet someone else and fall madly in love with them. Maybe I will." As I said the words, I didn't believe them for a moment to be true in my heart, but my head told me they had to be said; perhaps one day I'd even be able to feel them to be true.

He shifted himself to sit up straighter. I treated myself to another lingering look at his body before I had to leave. "Well, if you're decided," he said.

"Honestly? This isn't a decision. Right now, I have no realistic choice. The world is not working particularly well to my plan at the moment. Perhaps one day it will be. But right now, it's got me over a barrel and is kicking my arse."

He reached out to me. "I'm sorry. Although," his little lop-sided smile, "I'm not going to lie. I'm a bit pleased you're suffering along with me right now." He looked at me through thick, dark lashes. "I'm not sure that's always been the case."

"Trust me, it kinda has." I let out a deep sigh. "Anyway, I'd better get going. I'm meeting Jenna tonight for a drink."

"Oh, God!" he said. "The whole of the greater Newquay area will know all about this within the next 24 hours!"

I laughed. "I'll swear her to discretion on pain of death. Which will give you 48 hours, at least."

He laughed, a rumble deep in his chest that I knew I would always find irresistibly sexy. "Gee, thanks."

He got out of bed, and I watched shamelessly as he pulled on his boxer briefs and T-shirt. I was certain I would never want a man more. My best luck would be to find his equal, but he would never be surpassed for me.

I collected my bag from the guest room, and he followed me downstairs to the kitchen. I moved about gathering together my mother's tupperware and anything else I needed to take with me, stowing it into the hessian shopper I'd brought from home.

He walked me to the door. "Are you sure you don't want to stay and have something to eat?"

I looked up at him. "I am entirely sure I do. But this isn't going to get any easier. It might even get harder."

"I'm not sure how it could."

I gave a little shake of the head. "Yeah." I set down my bags and stood looking at him for a few moments. I curled my fingers into his T-shirt and pulled him down to me, indulging in a final, long, lingering kiss. I released him and ran my tongue across my bottom lip, savouring the taste of him while I was still able to.

I took my jacket off its peg and put it on, picked up my bags and turned, opened the door and stepped outside. Astonishingly – and entirely inappropriately – the sun was shining brightly in a clear, blue sky. I walked down the path to let myself out onto the lane, a vice tightening around my chest and tears pricking at the back of my eyes. I didn't turn around, even though I could feel him watching me go. If I had, I would never have been able to leave.

A little after seven, my father dropped me outside the cocktail bar Jenna had nominated as that evening's venue. I thanked him, told him I'd get a cab home and got out of the car. I took a deep breath and made my way inside. I spotted her without too much problem. She'd already secured us a table and was apparently discussing the menu in some depth with a waiter with a generous beard and a large hoop earring in one ear.

As I approached, she caught sight of me and got up, pulling me into a hug as I reached her. The waiter drifted off, and I sat down on the bench seat next to her.

"Oh, my God, you told me about this!" she said, picking up one of my long, red tresses in her hand. "It looks fab!"

"Thanks," I managed. Jesus, I really needed to do something about my low mood. I'd been feeling like a wet weekend ever since I'd left Jonny's earlier.

She noticed my expression and frowned as we sat down. "Babe, what's up?"

I sighed as I shrugged out of my coat and folded it up to store on the seat next to me. "Nothing, I'm fine."

She gave me the beady eye. "You're not. Not even close. What's going on?"

I picked up the cocktails menu and began to peruse it. "What's good here? Any recommendations?"

She narrowed her eyes at me. "What happened?"

I was aware that I was looking shifty, and Jenna, of course, was far too perceptive.

"Did you see Jonny?" she said.

"Why would you say that?" I concentrated on the description for the Margarita.

"Because you were asking if I'd seen him, and I'd heard he was down here, and now it looks like there's been trouble."

I looked at her, doing my best to keep my expression neutral. "Why would Jonny being down here mean trouble? Jonny's lovely."

She boggled at me. "Holy shit! What happened?"

I feigned ignorance. "I don't know what you mean." Back to the menu.

She put a hand on my arm, insisting I turn to look at her. "You've never called Jonny 'lovely' in your life."

I met her gaze defiantly. "Well, you've always told me how great he is, how hot, et cetera."

"Yes, but he's not in love with me, so I can say that without it meaning anything. I mean, when I say it, it's just a statement of fact. When you say it..." Her voice was quieter. "Well, there's emotional resonance behind it."

I raised my eyebrows at her. "Emotional resonance?"

"What? I can be articulate, bitch."

I grinned at her. "Of course."

"Anyway, stop changing the subject. What happened?"

I sighed. "Look, if I tell you, will you promise not to spread it about as gossip?"

"If it means something real to you, then of course I promise."

I blew out a deep breath. "Okay... We slept together."

"Fuck. Off." Jenna screamed. She banged the table with her hand. "Just! Fuck! Off! At fucking last!"

People were looking, and I made a desperate calming gesture and urgently shushed her.

"Okay, okay," she said. "Sorry. But I've only been waiting my entire adult life – and, actually, a few years before that too – for this, so I think I'm entitled to a little bit of a reaction."

I tipped my head. "That's fair enough, but we're not telling the whole of Newquay, remember?"

She rolled her eyes. "Fine, fine. But... Oh, my God, Summer! How was it?"

My cheeks started to burn a little, both at the question and the memory. I gave her a look. "How do you think it was?"

She considered me closely. "Well, my thoughts on that are strictly Triple X rated, so just tell me if it was as good as I know that you – and, yes, me – have imagined."

I met her eyes and nodded.

"Holy crap," she said. "Seriously? Cos, you know, these things usually aren't. I mean, when fantasy becomes reality, it's often not all that."

"Well, this was."

She raised her eyebrows, fully impressed. "Well, *damn!*"

I nodded solemnly. "Yes."

"Christ, we need a drink!" She motioned to the waiter to come over. "Moscow Mule, please."

I nodded at him. "Make that two."

"So, what happens now?"

"Nothing. Nothing happens now," I said miserably. "I'm going back to London, he's going to be living down here for the foreseeable. Neither of us has the money to travel up and down more than once in a blue moon, so... Yeah, it utterly sucks. I've no idea what else to say."

"What does he say about it?"

"He doesn't like it, but he doesn't have a solution either."

Jenna shook her head. "I can't believe it. I can't believe you two, honestly. If there was ever a couple that was 'meant to be', it's you. You can positively *see* the electricity sparking the minute you're in the same room. You can't just give up on that, Summer. Honestly, you can't!"

Our cocktails arrived and we both took good, long sips through our straws.

"What would you suggest?" I asked. "I'm open to all sensible options. The only obvious solution that springs to mind is that one of us wins the lottery so we can give up all requirements to earn a living, or struggles to maintain a roof over our heads, and live in trouble-free bliss for the rest of our lives. But I'm honestly not seeing that as a realistic outcome right now."

"Why don't you move down here? I'm sure you could get a decent job with your qualifications. And you've now got a couple of years' experience in a proper job, so that would help too."

"I couldn't get any kind of equivalent job down here at the moment. All the companies that do what I do are tiny, with only a few people. The market for large corporate events is the big cities. Even Bristol doesn't have a big market for that kind of thing. There's nowhere I could move to that would be any better or easier to get here from than London."

She looked at me. "Wow, you've really thought about this."

"I really have."

"And he can't move up there?"

I shrugged. "Well, if he did, he'd have to take some sort of 'proper' job that wouldn't use his degree or his talent and would probably end up killing his soul within a year. So, no, I don't think I could ask him to do that." I sighed.

"Honestly, Jen, I'm not being obtuse here. If I could find a way to be with him, I would."

"God, I'm sorry. I've teased you about him all these years, and now you've really fallen for him and there's no way for you to be together. That really sucks hairy balls." She paused. "And not in the good way."

I looked at her, slightly appalled, and then burst out laughing.

"What?" she said, joining in my laughter. "It does!"

I laughed some more, and so did she, and suddenly we couldn't stop. By the time we calmed down, I had tears streaming down my face.

"Oh, my God!" I said. "Thank you, I really needed that. I mean, tomorrow's gonna suck arse. And so is the next day, and the one after that. But you've really cheered me up tonight, Jenna. I love you."

She made an exaggerated comedy bowing gesture. "And I thank you!"

I leaned in and gave her a hug, which she returned.

I suddenly remembered something I wanted to say to her. "By the way, I have a bone to pick with you. When I asked you if Jonny was down here, you completely failed to mention that he now has a beard."

Her eyebrows flew up. "He what?"

"Has a beard."

She giggled. "I had no idea he did. I haven't seen him. I only had the information I did have about him from Mike, who's seen him a few times and distinctly failed to mention any beardage. I get the impression Jonny's been a bit of a hermit since he came back down here. He seems to have gone very 'artistic temperament'."

"I think he's just feeling poor."

"Hmm... Still, little Jonny Rawlings with a beard, eh?"

She shook her head in wonderment at the idea. "I still remember when he was five and a half feet tall and skinny as a rail. Although, admittedly, he hasn't looked like that for quite some time." She looked at me. "Tell me, is it hot? I mean, some people can pull off a beard and some can't. I bet he can, right?" She fanned herself dramatically. "How hot, exactly, does he look with it?"

I took a long sip of cocktail. "Pretty hot, not gonna lie."

Jenna gave me a mischievous grin. "Certainly had the desired effect on you."

I shot her an admonishing look. "I didn't have sex with him because of his beard!"

"But it didn't hurt, right?" she teased. She eyed my hair. "Clearly the Julia Roberts 'do' you're currently sporting didn't do any harm where he was concerned, either."

I allowed myself a little bit of a smug smile. "Apparently not." I finished my cocktail and gestured to the waiter for two more of the same. "Anyway, that's enough about me, what's going on with you?"

"Hmm." She tipped her head from side to side. "Not much. I'm training to be a nail technician. Did I tell you that?"

I shook my head. "No."

"Well, I am. And once I've done that, I'm planning on taking other beauty courses. I've always been interested in that kind of thing, as you know." I nodded. "And the market for those services has really increased around here recently. I mean, particularly in the summer, there are loads of people who want their nails done, and pedicures and that sort of thing. And even when it's mostly just the locals... Well, there are plenty of people who're happy to pay for that kind of upkeep. And if I add other strings to my bow, like brow threading et cetera, I might one day be able to open my own salon. Which I think I'd like." She took a sip of her drink. "I quite fancy myself as a successful businesswoman."

"That's fantastic, Jenna! I'm so pleased you've found something you're interested in. I'm sure you'll do great at it."

She smiled at me, pleased with the support.

"Any news on what's going on with Mike?" I asked. "Has he moved on from lifeguarding yet?"

Jenna shook her head. "No. Although he's working regularly in an artisanal deli near the surf school now. He definitely seems to be settling down a bit."

"Cool." The waiter appeared with our second round. "So how about your love life? Any news? Stories? Tales of success or woe?"

"Well, I'm still hooking up with Paul the Hot Lifeguard from time to time, mostly cos he's, you know, hot, but still no serious prospects." She eyed me. "Although no heartbreak either, so there's that."

I sipped my cocktail and wondered how many of these I was going to need in order to be able to sleep tonight. "That's always a positive."

A couple of hours later, and a few more cocktails down, I was feeling much less pain than when I'd walked in earlier that evening. We paid the bill and ordered a taxi and sat back to wait.

"Jenna, my love, you are nothing less than an absolute tonic." I wasn't entirely able to disguise the fact that I was, by now, really quite drunk.

"I do wish you lived down here." She was holding her own a little better than me, but not by much. "Seriously, Sum, come back here. Bugger having a 'career'." She made air quotes with her fingers. "That's all bullshit anyway. You could spend your time having amazing sex with Jonny and we could all live together in a house somewhere. I'm sure we could swing it if we all pitched in."

At this point of the evening, I had to admit, it didn't sound like a totally horrible or ridiculous idea. I particularly liked the bit about lots of sex with Jonny.

"I'll think about it," I said, genuinely meaning that I would.

"Good! Screw London and its crappy, dirty air and over-priced shitboxes."

I hooted with laughter. "Yeah, screw London!" We both collapsed in giggles again.

"Excuse me, ladies, your taxi is here." A waiter, who'd clearly seen it all before, gestured smoothly towards the door.

We clambered to our feet, gathered our bags and coats and lurched towards the exit and out onto the pavement. A cab sat patiently in what looked like an illegal parking zone, with its hazards flashing. We both piled in as quickly as possible and gave him Jenna's address. Outside her house, we said a quick, but emotional, goodbye, then I sat quietly as the driver took me at speed back to Crantock village. As the dark shadows of fields and hedgerows passed by my window, I did my best to swallow down the threatening storm of Jonny-less grief.

I paid the cab driver, let myself into the house and shouted out the briefest of greetings to my parents, before climbing the stairs to my room and collapsing onto the bed, welcoming the oblivion of sleep. I didn't even risk waking myself up at all by brushing my teeth. There would be plenty of pain for me to deal with tomorrow. For now, I would sleep right through it.

I climbed onto the train at Newquay Station the following morning with only a couple of minutes to spare. I'd woken up early enough, suffering the inevitable after-effects of the previous night's drinking, but I'd felt so miserable, and had done so little preparation for my departure the day before, that I was slow to get going and then everything was a rush. My mother saw me off with a tight hug, a kiss, a wave and a generous supply of leftovers for the journey, and my father did some serious speeding to get me to the station on time. I kissed him on the cheek and made him promise to come up and see me in London as soon as he could, knowing that he'd sooner swallow razor blades than willingly set foot in the nation's capital.

I found myself a seat, stowed my luggage and sat down, looking miserably out the window, dreaming of Jonny appearing at the last minute to beg me to stay, promising to do whatever it took for us to be together. So far, so foolish. He didn't appear, but just as the train started moving, my phone buzzed and I pulled it out to find a text from him: 'Have a safe journey. Text me when you're home safely. Love, J x'. My heart swelled that he'd remembered what time my train was leaving and had bothered to send me a lovely text. He really would be the best boyfriend. I swallowed hard and sat back in my seat, entirely inclined to spend the journey feeling sorry for myself. As the train pulled out of the station and started its journey across the Cornish countryside, I felt like my insides had been scooped out and left raw and shredded on the platform at Newquay Station.

Part Eight

Present Day

Christmas Day

I was awoken on Christmas Morning by the clinks and bangs of my bedroom radiator stirring to life as hot water hit cold pipes. I vaguely remembered hearing earlier, through the semi-consciousness of winter pre-dawn darkness, creaks on the stairs and a car starting and leaving beneath my window: Jenna. My mouth felt like sandpaper, and I urgently needed to pee, but the warmth and comfort of my bed were too tempting and I snuggled down for another ten minutes.

The demands of my bladder, and light beginning to peek under the curtains, finally persuaded me to move, and I levered myself up and out of bed. I made a quick dash to the bathroom and brushed the cotton wool out of my mouth, then pulled on my old woollen dressing gown, dropped my phone in a pocket and padded downstairs.

I looked in the dining room. There was not a single trace of the consequences of last night's party; it was if it had never been. Everything was completely clean and tidy, all furniture returned to its proper place. Shaking my head a little in wonder, I wandered through to the living room. The same. I hadn't heard a thing. I gave serious consideration to whether my mother employed people to do this or elves.

I walked over to the French windows and looked out onto the patio. The garden was covered in a light layer of snow. Snow in Cornwall on Christmas morning! Maybe this really would be a Christmas for miracles.

I noticed that the blanket I'd wrapped myself and Jonny in last night was still puddled on the sofa. Apparently my mother's magical elves had missed it, or decided that getting up at dawn to clear up inside a warm house was one thing but stepping outside into frigid, frosty, snow-tinged air was quite another.

At least this one thing out of place provided some evidence that the party *had* actually happened. If I hadn't seen the blanket, I'd almost have believed the whole thing had been a dream. Then I remembered I should have additional evidence on my phone. I sat down on the sofa, drew it out of my pocket and pulled up the Photos app. There were the pictures of last night! The ones of me and Jonny, and then Jenna and Mike, standing in front of the Christmas tree, and the ones of the four of us taken by my father. I scrolled back and looked at the three that Jenna had taken of me and Jonny. They'd been taken pretty quickly, one after the other, and were all very similar, the only real difference being how wide I was smiling. (Jenna had kept insisting I increase my efforts on that front – "No, give me a *bigger* smile, Summer!") But there was something about them I hadn't realised last night and couldn't have seen until I looked at them this morning: In all of them, Jonny wasn't looking at the camera, he was looking at me.

I smiled fondly at the images: his head turned down

towards me as I snuggled into him, him a good half a foot taller than me, even in my heels, his eyes looking at me with love. My heart squeezed. I could hardly believe he was finally really mine, that we were each other's.

My phone binged. A text from Jenna: 'Thanks so much for GREAT party last night *party horn streamers* emoji, *Christmas tree* emoji, *Spanish lady dancing* emoji, *champagne popping* emoji. Feeling a bit ruff this morning *green sick face* emoji. Hope we can get together again before you go back *clinking wine glasses* emoji. Happy Christmas! *Santa* emoji'.

I laughed and typed a reply: 'You are most welcome, ofc! Feeling v rough also. Def re getting together before I go back. Happy Christmas! *Christmas tree* emoji, *Santa* emoji, *wrapped present* emoji, *red heart* emoji'.

I was indulging in another little swoon over the photos of Jonny, when I heard my mother's footsteps on the stairs. I heard her go into the dining room (presumably for the same inspection I'd done), then she appeared in the living room doorway. She surveyed the room with a sweeping, practised gaze for anything out of place and smiled at me. "Happy Christmas, darling."

I smiled back. "Happy Christmas, Mum!" I looked towards the garden. "Did you see, it snowed?"

My mother's eyes followed my gaze. "I did. Very pretty. It'll melt as soon as the sun starts warming things up, though."

I rolled my eyes at her. "So practical. I'm going to enjoy it being magical for a minute."

"Very well, darling. Tea and toast?"

I followed her out into the hallway and through into the kitchen, where she filled and switched on the kettle and started moving about organising the breakfast things.

"Are we still going to church at ten?" I asked.

"Well, your father and I are, and of course we'd love you to come along if you'd like."

I pulled up text messaging on my phone. "Okay if Jonny comes with us?"

She looked at me over her shoulder, not entirely able to hide her surprise. "My goodness! Of course, if he wants to."

I typed a text: 'Church at 10. Still want to join? x'. I pressed 'Send'.

I poured myself a glass of water from the fridge and sat down at the table to wait for the promised delivery of tea and toast. My phone binged. A reply from Jonny: 'Yes, meet you by the gate. Text me when you're leaving x'. I smiled at the phone and put it back in my pocket.

My mother put a plate, knife and napkin down in front of me. "So, Jonny's coming to Church?"

I smiled up at her. "Yes. He asked last night about getting together today, and I invited him."

She poured hot water into the teapot, transferred the pot to the table and turned to the toaster. "You two certainly looked very cosy last night."

I smiled happily. "Did we? I guess we did."

She set a plate of toast down on the table and sat down. "So, it looks like you've made your choice." She fixed an eye on me. "No more messing that boy about, now, Summer. If you change your mind after last night's little display it would both hurt him terribly and make him look like a fool."

I couldn't help a little chuckle. "We don't live in a Jane Austen novel, Mum. A kiss is no longer a binding social contract." I took a slice of toast and began to butter it. "But anyway, you don't need to worry. I'm not intending to change my mind again. We just have some details to sort out, that's all."

My mother raised an eyebrow. "Did nobody ever tell you? The Devil is in the details."

I took a bite of toast. "Well, hopefully this time the Devil's on my side."

That afternoon, after Christmas lunch had been eaten and I'd helped my mother clear away, I folded up a tea towel while she finished washing up the last of the saucepans.

"Okay, if I go out for a walk? I'm supposed to be meeting Jonny. I'll take the dogs out if they want."

My mother looked at me fondly. She was in an extremely good mood with Jonny currently, after his attendance with us at Church, looking very clean and handsome (a razor clearly having been taken to his face that morning), and his presentation to her of a large box of Leonidas chocolates in a Christmas gift bag. "Of course, darling. Off you go."

I texted Jonny to meet me by the lychgate and checked to see if I was going to be honoured by any canine company. Douglas bounced around happily, keen to join, but Lucy was lying comfortably ensconced in her bed by the radiator, and when I looked at her she just raised a brow at me, distinctly unenthused. "Okay, girl," I said, "you stay put."

I fastened the Yorkshire terrier's little winter coat around him as it was so cold out, stuffed myself into jacket and boots, wrapped a scarf around my neck twice and pulled open the door to icy air. I let Douglas out in front of me, tugged the door closed and set off down the path, under an azure sky, hurriedly pulling on my gloves.

As my mother had predicted, the sliver of snow that had covered the ground at dawn had largely melted by lunchtime, but the cold had barely abated.

As promised, Jonny was standing in the shelter of the lychgate, his arms crossed tightly against the chill. I started smiling before he'd even seen me, my heart dancing. He returned my wide smile when he spotted me and fell in step as we made our way down towards the beach.

"Not getting any warmer," he remarked.

"Possibly even colder," I agreed.

He looked at the Yorkshire terrier excitedly sniffing his way down the lane in his little tartan coat. "Donald is much hardier than Daisy. She wouldn't move off the couch." Daisy was his parents' latest Dalmatian.

I laughed. "And Lucy. She made it very clear she wasn't interested in vacating her warm spot in the kitchen."

We reached the car park and turned up the coastal path towards the beach. I was striding so fast Jonny almost didn't have to slow his usual pace to enable us to walk together. I made directly for the sea. I reached the base of the sand dunes which ran along the back of the beach and began to climb. This entailed negotiating very narrow paths, which twisted through the grass and vegetation that clung to the dunes, and was not particularly easy or safe, as each step could find the sand giving way and shifting beneath your feet. But I had one goal today: I wanted to reach the top of the highest of the dunes. My heart demanded it.

Jonny followed my every step without a word. He knew where I was going and what I needed, and his support for my quest was automatic and absolute, as it had been so often when we were young. It was exhilarating to me that, after all these years, we'd found our way back to that place in our friendship, although now it was also so much more.

I finally crested the tallest of the dunes, the beach now a hundred feet or more below, and reached out to take Jonny's hand as he joined me. We curled our arms around one another's backs and stood to take in the spectacular view of sea and coastline peeling away from us to the horizon.

I took the deepest of breaths, feeling my spirit lifted to fly with the gulls above. The bay was still about half-full as the tide receded, the water pale blue under a clear sky. I knew for sure I'd never been happier in my life. I manoeuvred myself to sit, my legs dangling over the edge of the sand cliffs. I knew this wasn't particularly sensible, dangerous even, but on this one day I wanted to take the risk. I was preparing to draw a line under my old, safe life.

Jonny sat down beside me, and we curled our gloved fingers together. Douglas, who was completely untroubled by our little adventure with his featherlight weight and four legs, came and sat down on my other side. I pulled him to me and tucked him in against my thigh.

I let out a deep breath. "I can't believe I'm here with you. It feels so wonderful, it must be a dream."

Jonny moved his hand to rest it on my back and nuzzled his nose into my neck. "I'm very real, I assure you."

I turned a mischievous gaze to him. "I shall have to thoroughly examine you later to make sure of that fact." I laughed, and he kissed me.

"Speaking of..." he said. "Do you fancy coming and seeing the cottage at Gwithian in the next couple of days? I thought we could spend some time there together, just us, while you're here. You can give it a thorough going over and tell me what you want done to the place." He added an amused smile. "And you can give me a thorough going over at the same time."

I felt a rush of blood to all the best places, and I gave him another deep kiss. "That sounds like a most excellent plan."

"When do you want to come? We can go tomorrow, or the next day, if you want to spend Boxing Day with your parents."

I looked into his eyes, carried away again by his beauty and how much I loved him. Since I'd seen him again yesterday, for the first time in almost a year, I'd been able to think of very little else other than how much I wanted to go to bed with him. What had been a fervent desire while I was up in London had become a searing ache since I'd laid eyes on him again. I didn't want to wait a single second longer than necessary to quench what was now a severe and intense thirst. I was feeling like a parched, dying man in the desert, and Jonny was a fresh-water pool under the shade of palm trees. I would have crawled over broken glass to get to him if necessary.

"Tomorrow," I said, firmly. "Let's go tomorrow."

He gave me a slow, heated smile and another kiss. "That'll also give me a chance to give you your Christmas present."

"Oooh!" My eyes lit up. "Exciting! Any clues?"

He shook his head firmly. "Nope. You'll have to wait until tomorrow."

"Shall I wait until tomorrow to give you yours as well, then? I was going to suggest you came back to the house after our walk to get it, but if it's easier I can just give it to you tomorrow."

"Yes, do that. Then we can exchange at the same time."

"Okay."

I looked out towards the ocean, and he put his arm around my shoulders and pulled me against him. "So, can we talk about how often you're going to be able to come down here? I know that was one of the things you said you wanted to discuss, and I have some thoughts on the subject."

"Actually, I did want to talk to you about that."

He looked at me, a trace of alarm in his eyes.

"No, no," I said, "nothing bad. Well, I hope not. It's just... I've actually been thinking of moving back down here, not just increasing the number and length of my visits."

His eyes met mine, and they were full of hope. "Really? Oh, my God, Summer, that would be great!"

"It's just... What I'm thinking of involves setting up my own business, not trying to find another job. I'm not going to be able to find an equivalent job down here to the one I have in London. My best bet is to set up on my own."

"And you're good with that?"

I nodded. "I think it's time. I'm ready."

He gave me a huge, wide smile. "That's fantastic!"

"The only thing is... and this is why we both have to be on board with the plan... it'll mean I have hardly any money coming in for a while. Possibly none at first. And it's a risk, as all these things are. I might fail altogether and have nothing to contribute towards the cost of our lives together." I bit my lip. "I'm not sure how viable that is."

His eyes on mine weren't worried at all. He looked full of confidence. "There's no need to worry about that. I can support us both if need be."

"Are you sure?"

He nodded firmly. "I'm absolutely sure."

"It may be worse than that, though," I continued. "I'll have to use all my savings to set up the new company, but I'll probably also have to borrow some money for additional capital. I may not simply be bringing in no money, I might end up bringing *less* than no money."

The thought of telling him this had been preying on my mind for months, ever since I'd started considering this idea seriously. I knew that Jonny loved me, but what I was telling him now seemed to be asking a lot of him, years of devotion to me or not.

"You don't have to take a loan out. I've got money," he said.

I looked at him. "What?"

He was smiling happily. "I have money. My paintings have been selling really well over the past couple of years. And I spend money on hardly anything other than materials. So I have plenty."

I eyed him cautiously. "Jonny, baby, I'm not just talking a few thousand to set up this business, you know."

He laughed. "I know. Summer. I've got about thirty thousand in the bank, and deposits for three new large canvases for five thousand each. You don't have to worry about money. If that's what's concerning you, move here tomorrow."

I looked at him, agog. "Damn! I knew you were doing well, but I had no idea how well. That's amazing, Jonny! Congratulations!" I pulled him into a tight hug. "I am so proud of you."

He looked at me, his eyes shining. "You know, you're a big part of why I kept on going, kept on trying to make it as an artist after I got back from Bristol."

"I am?"

He nodded. "Yes. You always said you thought I could make it. And I know that you were just being a good friend, encouraging me to do what I loved, but your faith in me and your positive words... Well, they were something I always held on to, through everything." He looked down at my hand in his. "Your support of me in that was one of the reasons I've always loved you. And the fact that I loved you meant that support meant more than anything."

I wasn't sure if my heart could take any more. I was beginning to think I might need to go and make an offering to the gods before they noticed how perfect everything was and decided to whisk it away.

I pressed my lips to his cheek and snuggled into him. "My love."

The winter sun began to nestle a little too close to the horizon, and we got up and climbed back down the dunes and made our way out to the road and back up to the village. I kissed Jonny goodbye near the church, with a promise to firm up a time tomorrow morning for him to drive us to Gwithian.

That night, tucked up in bed, with Douglas snuggled against me, I thought back to the one and only previous time I'd seen Jonny's cottage at Gwithian. It wasn't an occasion I liked to spend much time dwelling on, but the memory of it came back to me now.

Part Nine

4 Years Ago

I rested my head against the passenger window of the Jaguar as my father swore under his breath at the slow-moving tractor that was blocking his speedy progress down the lane towards the village.

"Christ! Get a move on, son!" he grumbled. He turned to me. "Fair warning, your mother is not happy that I've had to come and fetch you from the station on Christmas Eve, what with her party this evening. Tell me again why you weren't able to come down yesterday?"

I sighed. "Work, Dad. I told you, I'm working all the hours that God sends at the moment. We're both incredibly busy and simultaneously short staffed. I practically had to threaten to resign to get the time off to stay until the 29th."

"Hmm..." He made grumbling noises under his breath. "I'm assuming all this dedication is worth it on your part?"

I sighed. I had no idea anymore. I felt like a lab rat on a wheel which had to keep the wheel turning in order to be rewarded with sufficient food for survival. My mood about the situation was not great. I'd been living for this brief respite in Cornwall for months now. And my main goal for the coming week was to see Jonny again.

After our incredible couple of days together two Christmases ago, things had drifted between us, and I principally blamed myself for that. After I'd returned to London, I'd missed him at least as much as I'd feared I would, but the distraction of work, along with the inevitable passing of time, slowly did its job of easing the strain on my heart. At first we'd been good about staying in touch, texting daily and talking on the phone at least once a week. But then one of the women in the chain of command a level above me had gone on maternity leave, which, of course, meant that the company didn't replace her, and I suddenly found myself doing both her job and mine. My hours became crazy, and my exhaustion level increased exponentially. Jonny's daily texts would mount up, and I'd find myself replying to them as a bundle after a few days or more. Inevitably he stopped sending them so regularly. With this decrease in contact, our phone calls dwindled to once every couple of weeks, then every few weeks. By the time the summer of that year arrived, we were talking maybe once a month.

Then he moved out of his parents' house to a place in Gwithian with no landline and horrible mobile service, and our phone calls stopped altogether. We kept in touch by occasional emailing, but when the following Christmas rolled around, I realised that we hadn't emailed one another for at least a couple of months.

I'd meant to arrange to see him at Christmas time, but ended up only being able to get the time off to arrive in Cornwall on the afternoon of Christmas Eve, and leave on the morning after Boxing Day. I'd managed to email him the week before Christmas to see if he'd be around and able to meet up on either of those two days, but I hadn't received a reply by the time I came down, and though I'd checked my email religiously, and even called his mobile and left a voicemail, during the couple of days I was at my parents' house, I heard nothing from him. I finally received a reply to my pre-Christmas email in the first week of January, with an apology saying that he hadn't seen my email or heard my voicemail until after Christmas when I'd already left, but he hoped I'd had a nice Christmas.

Things had gone from bad to worse with Jonny the following year. All my hard work, effort and long, long hours were finally rewarded with a promotion to Manager. I now had more money and a team of my own to officially supervise, but even more responsibility and no fewer hours demanded of my time. Following my pay bump, I bought my first really nice handbag. Using it gave me genuine pleasure every day, but I was far from sure that its possession was a fair bargain for what was required to be able to afford it. My contact with Jonny dwindled to almost nothing.

After his email to me in January, neither of us contacted the other again until, in June, I received an Instagram Direct Message from Jenna. Insta DMs were the main way I kept in touch with her at this point. She'd sent me a link to a new Instagram account with the message underneath '^^^ !!!!!!!!!!' plus three *heart eyes* emojis. I went to the new account and saw with a jolt that it was Jonny's. There were only three posts, one of them a really very good shot of a dramatic sky over St Ives Bay taken from the Gwithian sand dunes, and two photos of what looked like oil paintings of Cornish seascapes. The paintings were Turner-esque and atmospheric. I 'liked' each of the posts and on the most recent one left a comment: 'So pleased to see you're painting! Welcome to Instagram!

red heart emoji'. Then I'd followed his account, returned to my DMs and replied to Jenna: 'Thanks for the heads up!'

I'd waited, with an impatience that had surprised and even somewhat annoyed me at this point, for a response from Jonny to my Instagram overtures, and finally, a couple of days later, he'd followed me back and replied to my comment: 'Thanks *praying hands emoji*' (the emoji lots of people used to say 'Thank you'). I looked at it in disgust; was that it? A year and a half ago we'd had the best sex of my life – and, I was pretty sure, at least some of the best sex of his – and he couldn't even send me a proper reply to my comment? No 'Hope you're well'? No 'Miss you'? Instead, he'd given me the bare minimum. I was not happy about it.

As the year dragged on, he didn't post often, and when he did it was photos of Gwithian or Godrevy, or his paintings inspired by the area. Then one day in September, as I scrolled my feed, a photo of him rolled onto my screen, and my heart almost stopped. It was a black and white portrait, clearly taken by someone else. It was a great shot, very professional. He still had his beard, but his long hair was now pulled back in a man bun. The bastard was even pulling it off. He was laughing into the camera, and his eyes looked happier than mine had in a long time. For a brief moment, I was really angry with him. I managed to 'like' the post, but I didn't leave a comment. I honestly had no idea what to say.

Of course, my anger passed almost instantly, and I quickly forwarded the post to Jenna with the message: 'Did you see this??? What's going on with him at the moment?'

Jenna's reply had popped up not long afterwards: 'No idea. Haven't seen either Mike or him for ages. But JFC he looks *fire* emoji'.

She wasn't wrong. I'd spent way too much time over the following weeks returning to that photo, wondering how he was, who'd taken the picture, what had prompted such happiness in his eyes. (I didn't like to dwell too closely on the second two questions, but they would keep popping up in my brain with an unwelcome insistence.) I realised how much I missed him; it was physically painful.

So this year, I was determined not to let another Christmas go by without seeing him. I couldn't be sure when he'd be around, so I'd told my manager that I needed to take Christmas Eve to the 29th December off, giving myself a few extra days after Christmas in case his schedule demanded it in order to fit me in. She'd resisted – "I'm sorry, we just can't manage without you for that long at this time of year, Summer" – but, at the end of my rope with the whole place, I'd told her that if that was the case, they would have to manage without me indefinitely. She'd baulked at trying to replace someone who was still doing the jobs of two people (the maternity leaver never having returned or been replaced), and huffed and puffed, but finally agreed to cover the essentials of my work so that I could have my few additional, precious days in Cornwall.

I'd emailed Jonny a week or so before I was due to arrive to let him know the days I was going to be staying with my parents and asking if he wanted to get together, but I'd heard nothing so far. I was just hoping that if I didn't, I'd bump into him somehow in the village or find some other way to casually see him.

The tractor finally pulled into a field, my father put his foot on the accelerator and we sped into Crantock at far too high a speed. We turned down our lane, my father pulled in and parked in front of the house, and we went inside. With only a few hours until the party, my mother was in crisis management mode and didn't even come out of the kitchen, simply smiling a "Hello, darling!" when I popped my head around the door in greeting. I took my bags upstairs and sat down heavily on the bed. I was exhausted, and the night hadn't even begun.

I took my phone out of my bag and checked Instagram. I went to my DMs and typed to Jenna: 'Have reached home! *red heart* emoji, *house* emoji, *Christmas tree* emoji, *red heart* emoji. Please say you're coming to the party tonight! *praying hands* emoji, *heart kiss* emoji'. I pressed 'Send' and tapped back to my Home page, before, unable to stop myself, going to Jonny's page to see if he'd posted any updates since I'd sent him my email. He hadn't. I put my phone down on the dressing table and started to unpack.

Jenna arrived a little before eight, just as I'd been about to text her for an update as to her current location, and I practically collapsed into a hug with her. We held tight for a good few seconds, and when I stood back to take her coat she was looking at me with concern.

"Damn, girl! We clearly need several large wines and a good catch-up!"

I almost choked up. I hadn't seen her in two years, which was much, much too long.

We went into the dining room to fetch ourselves glasses of wine, but when I'd filled two glasses with Sauvignon Blanc, and was preparing to put the bottle back in the ice bucket, she took it from me before I had the chance.

"We're taking this with us. It will be needed. Now, lead

the way to a quiet spot where we can chat."

The only really 'quiet spot' at one of my mother's Christmas Eve parties tended to be outside on the patio, which was often too cold to sit on for long, but fortunately this year Cornwall was having a very mild December, so once we'd moved the gas heaters to toast our heads and wrapped ourselves in the provided blankets, we were able to make ourselves quite comfortable on the patio sofa. We both took substantial sips of our wine.

"So, please tell me you're feeling better than you look right about now?" Jenna said.

I played offended. "Gee, thanks."

"I don't mean it like that. I mean... Well, let's just say you don't seem the happiest I've ever seen you."

I gave her the eye. "How can you tell?"

She gave me a sceptical look. "Tell me I'm wrong."

I sighed. "I guess... No, you're not wrong. I'm not feeling as chipper as I might otherwise like."

She took a sip of wine. "Wanna tell me about it?"

I took a good, long drink myself and launched into my tale of woe from the previous couple of years: the long work hours, the difficult clients, the pain in the arse boss, the wondering whether it was all worth it. She nodded along and made appropriately sympathetic interjections when required, but when I'd finished, she gave me another hard stare.

"And?"

I looked at her blankly. "What? That's not enough moaning for you? You want more?"

She rolled her eyes. "You're only telling me half the story. Or possibly two-thirds of the story. Whatever, you're leaving a big chunk out."

"I am?"

"You know you are."

"And what chunk would that be?"

She looked a bit exasperated. "Summer, last time we saw one another you'd just had the night of your life with a certain Jonny Rawlings and were clearly madly in love with him. Yet you're sitting here now, supposedly updating me on your life, and you don't say a word about him. Or any man, for that matter. What gives?"

I pouted. "My life doesn't have to be all about another man. Or men."

"Of course not, but it's probably an element of some importance, no?"

I sighed. "I guess."

"So?"

I huffed. "I don't know what you want me to say, Jen. It didn't work out. As I told you when I last saw you, there was no way it could. I'm in London, he's down here. The end."

"And you two didn't even try to make it work after what happened?"

"We tried. We failed." I wasn't able to keep the misery out of my voice.

Jenna reached out and pulled me into a hug. We held on for a long moment, and I felt so exhausted and dejected I thought I might cry. She released me, and I took a long draw on my wine to calm myself down.

"And there's no one else up in London?" she asked. She treated me to one of her trademark mischievous looks. "No rich merchant bankers with too much money and an attitude problem to whisk you off to Paris for a few days? No high-powered lawyers with a fast car and a tendency to buy you expensive and slightly inappropriate gifts to jet you to New York for the weekend?"

I rolled my eyes at her. "Exactly what kind of men do you think I meet?"

She pulled a sad face. "Not the interesting kind, then?"

I shook my head firmly. "Nope."

"Shame. Anyway, in that case, any chance of catching up with Jonny while you're down here? You never know, at least you might get some fantastic sex out of it to take the edge off."

"I don't know. I emailed him to see if he was around to meet up but I haven't heard anything back. We just seem to be on the outs at the moment. We never fell out, exactly. Things just... drifted. Like a plant that dies through lack of attention and watering. That's what happened to our relationship. We didn't give it sufficient water."

She squeezed my hand. "But that's happened before with you two. You've drifted apart, but then you see one another again and it's all..." She mimed an explosion.

I managed a small laugh, but another sigh quickly formed in my chest. "I guess I was hoping that might happen again. But... I don't know. It looks from his Instagram like he's building some kind of life for himself as an artist. Perhaps he doesn't want me bursting in and fucking with his head again. I mean, I don't mean to do that, but..."

"You somehow manage to..."

I nodded glumly. "Maybe."

Jenna shook her head. "I don't know. I'm pretty sure that Jonny has always lived for you bursting in and fucking with his head. It's like his crack."

"Gee," I said, tossing her a look, "thanks for comparing me to a highly addictive yet highly damaging street drug that kills people."

She chuckled. "Well, if the cap fits..."

"You're not being helpful."

"Sorry, sorry. I just mean, I'm not sure that he wouldn't want to see you whatever. I would genuinely be astonished if he didn't."

I considered. "Well, he did say he gets really crappy mobile service where he is. Maybe he hasn't even seen my email. He hasn't posted on Instagram in ages, and not since I sent it."

I could see Jenna noting my Instagram stalking and efforts to excuse Jonny's lack of reply, but she decided to let it go.

I looked at her hopefully. "Do you think he might just not have got my message?"

She shrugged. "It's possible."

"Or maybe he finally grew up, got over me and moved on."

Jenna looked at me. "Possible, but less likely."

My mother popped her head through the French doors to the patio. "Oh, Summer, this is where you are! Hello, Jenna."

Jenna gave her a little finger wave.

My mother took in our snuggled appearances and my somewhat glum demeanour and appeared to reconsider what she'd come out to say, which I suspected was about to involve a request to come inside and help with some type of party-hosting. She made a decision. "Okay, well, it looks like you're doing alright out here." She looked at Jenna. "Do come in and help yourself to more wine if you want it." Then at me. "And don't forget to have something to eat." She pulled her head back inside and closed the door.

Jenna turned to me, impressed. "Your mum's really quite alright, isn't she?"

I smiled. "She has her moments." I took a deep breath. "Anyway, tell me your news. It looks like you're really busy."

She nodded. "Yeah. I'm freelancing at a couple of salons doing nails and brows and eyelash extensions. As you can imagine, it's been pretty much non-stop over December for party season."

"That's great."

"Yeah, it's definitely nice to be working so much."

"And how are things going with Jason?" Jason, an attractive sort with long, blond, floppy hair, had been featuring heavily in various lovey-dovey photos on Jenna's Instagram page.

She smiled. "Yeah, good, good. I mean, there's no imminent engagement or anything, but we're doing okay." She tipped her head, considering. "The sex is good."

"Excellent. You didn't want to bring him tonight?"

"Oh, he had a party with his mates to go to, and I wanted to see you." She bumped my arm with hers.

"Awwww! You picked me over Good Sex Jason? You are the best!"

Jenna winked at me. "You'll find no argument here."

"Any Mike updates?" I asked.

"Um… He's now managing that deli he was working at, if you can believe it. And under his management they've expanded the cafe and are now doing delivery as well as take out."

I pulled an impressed face.

"I know, right?" she said. "Just shows, you never can tell with people. And he's got a serious girlfriend called Briony he's talking about moving in with."

I made a shocked face. "Get out!"

"Yep. He'll be married with two kids and a mortgage

before you know it. Of all of us, I never thought it would be Mike who'd end up settling down first."

"Me neither."

"Anyway, I think that's you mainly caught up with what I have to share of interest."

I went to fetch a fresh bottle of wine from the dining room and piled a plate with finger food, and we continued to keep ourselves to ourselves on the patio, with only the occasional smoker to disturb us. Jenna caught me up on new restaurants and businesses that had opened in Newquay and nearby, and others that had closed for whatever reason. She was becoming quite the business analyst.

But by the time it got to eleven, I was seriously fading.

"I'm not sure I'm going to make it to the midnight cracker-pull," I said. "I'm dead on my feet. I've been working flat out for weeks and only travelled down from London today. My mother's going to have to let me off the full party experience this year, I think." I looked at Jenna. "Do you want to stay, or should we call you a cab?"

"Cab," she said. "I'm pretty exhausted myself. Being in bed by midnight will do me no harm at all."

"Okay, let's do it."

We used the phone in the kitchen to summon a taxi from a firm my mother used regularly and had an account with. I knew they'd be reliable and hoped they might bump us up the order waiting for service on Christmas Eve due to my mother's relationship with them. I was right; they promised us a taxi in only twenty minutes. We both sat at the kitchen table drinking Baileys, barely able to move from tiredness, until the taxi turned up. I walked Jenna out into the hallway to fetch her coat and see her out.

"Now, will you promise to tell me what happens with

Jonny?" she said.

I nodded. "If anything does happen."

She gave me a hug. "Don't give up hope. And if you need reinforcements at any point, call me." She made a 'talking on the phone' gesture.

I laughed. "Okay, will do."

We hugged again, I saw her out and safely into the cab and then made my way up to my room without saying goodnight to anyone; I was just done with the day. I shed my clothes, dropping them on the floor where I stood, and crawled into bed. I fell quickly asleep, even the noise of the party unable to keep me awake.

Christmas Day passed without incident. Church was attended, an extremely delicious lunch was eaten and presents were exchanged. It was nice just being able to take things easy and be looked after for a change. My mother didn't even present me with many tasks to do, apparently sensing my need for a break. Christmas Day rolled into Boxing Day. I slept late, but finally managed to get up and make my way downstairs to help my mother cut up Christmas Day lunch leftovers for bubble and squeak to go with the cold turkey.

I was sitting at the kitchen table chopping up veg when she noticed me checking my phone for the second time in half an hour.

She gave me a penetrating look. "I have to ask... what's so important that you keep looking at your phone? You were doing it all day yesterday as well."

I felt a surge of embarrassment and hoped fervently I wouldn't blush. I turned the phone face down decisively. "Sorry, Mum, force of habit, I guess."

"Summer."

I sighed. "Just waiting for an email. Maybe."

"From?"

"Just an old friend."

"Good grief, Summer, I'm not asking you to violate the Official Secrets Act."

I gritted my teeth. "Just waiting to see if Jonny responds to an email I sent him, okay?"

Her eyes softened and flickered with concern. "I do hope that boy isn't giving you trouble."

"Mum!"

She held up her hands. "Okay, okay!" But she poured us a couple of vodka and tonics and sat down opposite me. "Are you sure you don't want to tell me about it? Maybe I can help?"

I looked at her. I must have looked seriously down in the dumps for my mother to be concerned enough to be indulging me with this kind of treatment. I gave her a quick rundown of the latest in the Jonny/Summer saga, leaving out much of how I felt about things, sticking to the bare facts as far as possible.

Once I was done, she took a pull on her drink and proved that, even after a lifetime as her daughter, my mother could still surprise me. "I think you should go and see him while you're here, even if he doesn't reply to your email."

I looked at her, astonished. I'd been fully expecting to be told to get a grip, pull my socks up and not let the antics of any man bother me.

"You said he lives in Gwithian?" she said.

I nodded. "Yes. But I don't have an address."

"Well, I can easily get that from Barbara. I'll send her a text right now."

My mouth dropped open as my mother fetched her phone from the kitchen counter and fired off a message to

Jonny's mother. My mother's reputation as one not to be trifled with had the intended effect, and Barbara replied within a few minutes. My mother picked up her phone again and gave it some instructions. My own buzzed and I picked it up. A forwarded message from Barbara: 'For Summer: Sunset Bay Cottage, Gwithian Towans, Gwithian, Hayle, TR27 5BT. It can be difficult to find, so I'll email you a map. Barb'.

I blinked, a little shell-shocked by how quickly my mother was able to make things happen when she put her mind to it. "Thanks, Mum. Although... Did you have to say you were asking for me?" I was somewhat mortified that, whatever I decided to do now, the chances were high Barbara would tell her son I'd been asking after his address.

My mother poo-pooed me. "I could hardly ask her for myself now, could I?" She had a point.

"Fair enough. Anyway, you think I should go and try and see him?"

Her voice was firm. "I do." I looked at her closely. Had she guessed what had happened between us when I'd stayed over at his house those couple of nights two Christmases ago? Knowing my mother, probably.

"You don't think it would seem a bit desperate when he hasn't replied to my email?"

"Summer, you've known that boy since you were nine years old, and he's always behaved thoroughly decently to you. Carried a bit of a torch for you, even, am I right?"

Damn, she was good. I gave a small nod.

"Well, then, I wouldn't give up on your friendship because you're too proud to go and knock on his door, just in case he hasn't had the time or inclination to reply to an email you sent him. Assuming he's even seen it."

I looked up at her and bit my lip. Sometimes grown-ups really were wise. "Okay."

"Anyway," she got up and pushed her chair back with her usual abrupt energy, "when you've decided what you want to do, let me or your father know if you want a lift."

I looked at the text message again. Somehow, just knowing exactly where Jonny could be found made me feel better. As if, even if the worst came to the worst and the modern world fell apart, and there was no more email or Instagram or electricity, I'd still know where to look for him. "Thanks, Mum," I said.

By that evening, when I still hadn't heard from him, I decided that I'd go the following day and see if I could track him down. It would be the 27th, and if I waited much longer I might run out of time. Although my mother had offered to help with transport, I'd much rather not ask either of my parents, so I texted Jenna for assistance, as I knew she now had a car to help her with work. She called me back almost immediately after I'd sent my text.

"So you're doing it then?"

"I guess so."

"And you've got an address?"

"Mum got it from Barbara, and she emailed a map. Looks like it's one of those chalets on Gwithian Towans. It's called 'Sunset Bay Cottage', apparently."

"So you take the road down to the car park?"

I nodded down the phone. "Yes. Do you have time to drive me tomorrow afternoon?" I was afraid she'd be busy with appointments.

"Yes. I'm taking the days between Christmas and New Year off until New Year's Eve. There are hardly any customers then anyway."

"So, what do you think?"

"Of course I'll drive you. You know I've always had your back for all instalments of Mission Jonny."

I laughed. "I think you've even personally instigated a couple of those missions."

"I admit nothing."

"Anyway, are you okay to pick me up around two? I literally have no idea what would be a good time, so mid-afternoon seems like the best bet."

"Sounds like a plan. I'll see you then."

The following morning I spent far, far too long on my hair and makeup. I still had my red hair, although its upkeep was increasingly annoying me. But I kept colouring those roots. I wasn't entirely sure I wasn't keeping it because it helped me maintain my increasingly tenuous connection to those couple of days with Jonny. I wondered if, after today, I'd feel more like keeping it, or would finally be free to let it go. I toned down the effort I'd made on my appearance by going super casual with jeans and old walking boots, but I couldn't resist snuggling into my favourite grey cashmere sweater. At least it was no longer new and had seen better days, so I figured it wouldn't look like I was trying too hard. I sincerely hoped I wasn't putting in all this effort for no reason; then I really would feel stupid.

I realised I was placing a huge amount of stock in the potential power of Jonny seeing me again in the flesh. When we were apart physically, it was too easy for our emotional connection to diminish, but we'd always been able to connect again quickly as soon as we met in person. I was relying on the hope that nothing would have changed in that regard. Anyway, I would find out soon enough.

Jenna turned up as promised just before two. She was driving a tiny little bright yellow Fiat. The car suited her perfectly.

"Cute ride!" I said, folding myself into the passenger seat.

"Lucia will be very glad to hear you say that," Jenna replied.

I raised an eyebrow. "Lucia?"

"Well, she's Italian and pretty, so I had to give her a pretty Italian name."

I laughed. "Jenna, sometimes you truly are bonkers."

She grinned. "But I am someone who is truly bonkers with a car and a driving licence."

I nodded. "You are. And I will shut up."

She put the Fiat into gear and we tore off up the lane. We made it safely onto the A30, with only a mildly terrifying near miss at the Three Burrows roundabout, and bombed down the dual carriageway, only slowing down to obey the speed limit when we came to the speed cameras. We reached Gwithian in just over half an hour.

Jenna succeeded in making it down the narrow, single-track lane to the Gwithian Towans car park without taking anyone out, and we pulled into a space to discuss tactics. I pulled out the map Barbara had emailed to my mother, which she'd printed out for me that morning, intended to help me navigate my way to Jonny's cottage through the little maze of unpaved tracks which made up the tiny community of chalets built amongst the Gwithian sand dunes. This was seaside living at its closest to nature. The vast majority of the cottages were timber structures, painted white or light blue, mostly used for holiday lets. You stepped out of the door and were instantly among dunes and only a few minutes' walk from the vast Gwithian sands. The views here were unequalled in Cornwall, and the light of St Ives Bay was world famous for its appeal to artists. It was the perfect place for someone with Jonny's artistic talent and ambitions, and I was happy he'd found a way to live here. The skies today were the pale, faded blue of winter, with a few high clouds. A weak sun was doing its best to brighten the day and make the waters of the vast bay sparkle.

"Do you want me to wait for you in case he's not in?" Jenna asked.

I shook my head. "No, I'm not sure how long it'll take me to find him. If he's not in, I'll go and take a walk on the beach in case he's down there. Judging from his Instagram, he spends a lot of time by the sea. If I still can't find him, I'll text you and just wait here until you get back." I looked out at the breathtaking view. "There are worse places to hang out. Did you have anything in mind to do while you're waiting for me?"

"I think I'm going to drive over to St Ives and see what the salon scene is doing over there. I haven't been down this way in ages, so it'll be a good opportunity to do a bit of research."

I nodded. "Okay." I took a deep breath. "Wish me luck!"

Jenna held up both hands with tightly crossed fingers. "Knock him dead!"

I waved goodbye to Jenna and Lucia and walked towards the cottages of Gwithian Towans. Following Barbara's map, I turned right and followed an unpaved track into the little development. I was still unsure about this course of action, my head and my heart presenting me with a split decision, as they so often did where Jonny was concerned, but it was too late to turn back now. I wandered about amidst the higgledy-piggledy collection of chalets until I reached the spot shown on the map. And there it was, at the end of a row: Sunset Bay Cottage.

It was one of the shabbiest of any of the cottages I'd seen: the white paint job had clearly seen better days, and the windows and doors could definitely have done with updating. It occurred to me that this was possibly why Jonny was able to afford it. A couple of cars were parked outside, and I wondered if either of them were Jonny's. There was a dusty, beaten-up old Renault Clio and a smart, shiny little Mini Cooper. My bet would have been on the Renault.

I gathered together every scrap of courage I had in me, walked up the little wooden steps and knocked on the door. Nothing. I knocked again, a little louder, and waited. There was no movement inside for more interminable seconds, and I was just about to give up and head down to the beach to execute Plan B, when the door opened and a pretty girl appeared from behind it. My heart lurched and my stomach clenched.

"Hello?" Her face was smiling and friendly.

"Oh! I'm sorry." I looked again at the sign to the side of the door. Yep, it definitely said 'Sunset Bay Cottage'. "Do I have the right place? I was looking for Jonny Rawlings."

Her smile relaxed. "You have the right place, but Jonny isn't here at the moment. He's gone for a walk." Her eyes grew fonder. "He does that a lot."

I managed to compose my face into a tight smile, desperate to disguise the sense of horror bubbling up inside me. "Oh, okay." I examined her. She was extremely pretty. Slender, about my height, but delicate, with long, dark hair. She was wearing skinny jeans which showed off fantastic legs, and a sloppy sweatshirt with a wide neckline that exposed one slim, smooth shoulder. I could see that men would find her very sexy. I wished she'd never been born.

"Would you like to come in and wait?" she offered. "I can't tell you how long he'll be, but I can make you a tea or coffee if you'd like?"

Of course she would have to be kind and generous, as well.

I took a step back, so desperate to get away I almost fell down the steps behind me. "No, no. I was just passing, so I thought I'd try my luck, but it's fine. I'll catch him another time."

She looked a bit confused by my apparent eagerness to be gone. "Who shall I say came by?"

"Um…" I considered not telling her but realised that he'd find out anyway that it had been me via his mother. To have run away without even leaving my name would seem truly pathetic. "You can just tell him that Summer was passing. I'll call. Or email him, or something…" I trailed off. I had no idea what to do or say.

Her eyes widened with recognition. "Oh! Yes! Summer. He's talked about you." Her expression didn't give away if what he'd said about me was good or bad. "Are you sure you don't want to come in?"

I shook my head firmly. "No. I've got a friend waiting, anyway." Liar, liar, pants on fire. "Just tell him I said hi."

And with that, I turned and practically ran back the way I'd come.

I got free of the development of cottages and began to walk across the dunes towards the beach, my head spinning, my chest so tight I could hardly breathe. I'd considered that Jonny might have found someone else, of course I had, but that had just been a quiet, gently gnawing worry. There had been no actual evidence of a girl-friend: no photos on Instagram, no mention in a post or email, no gossip which had made its way to Jenna or my mother. So, to be faced with her suddenly in the (oh, so very pretty) flesh... Well, it felt like I'd been punched in the stomach. Hard.

I made my way across the dunes, stumbling at times over the uneven ground, desperate to get to the sea and the solace it might offer. I finally reached the track which ran along the cliff edge, found a path over the rocks and made my way down onto the sand. For me, this was the most spectacular beach in Cornwall, and when the tide was out, as it was now, it stretched three miles uninter-rupted from Godrevy to Hayle and beyond. I walked east, still struggling to hold myself together, until I found a suitable rock formation to accommodate me. I climbed up and positioned myself so I could sit and take in the view of the lighthouse, but even the extreme beauty of my surroundings could hardly make a dent in the grief that was beginning to consume me.

I realised that, stupidly, I hadn't truly believed, deep down, that Jonny would be able to move on. A core part of me had always believed that, even if circumstances kept us apart for substantial periods of time, he would wait for me. Even though I'd told him not to. The irony most cer-tainly did not escape me that a large part of the situation I now found myself in was my fault; I'd *told* him that if he found someone else, he had my permission to follow through on it. Hell, I'd pretty much *encouraged* him to do so. But I realised now I'd only felt so generous because I didn't believe he really would. I mean, how could he, after what we'd shared? I'd certainly thought about that night – those two days – every day since. And Jonny was supposed to be the one who was more in love with me than I was with him, wasn't he? So, how the hell had he been able to move on when I hadn't? I realised I was absolutely, and totally unreasonably, furious with him. Righteous anger supported me for a good couple of minutes before the grief of loss swooped in and swallowed me up again.

I was still fighting back the tears which I feared were inevitable, when I noticed a tall figure walking along the beach towards me, from the direction of Godrevy. I realised immediately it was Jonny. I began to panic, wondering if it would be possible to get up and flee and escape in time before he saw me. But I realised that if I was able to recognise him from such a distance, just from the shape and movement of his body, then he'd almost certainly be able to do the same where I was concerned. Having him see me get up and literally run away from him, when he'd also then find out that I'd gone to his house earlier, was an ignominy I wouldn't be able to live down for the rest of my life. I had to stay put.

I could, however, text Jenna to come and get me as soon as possible. I pulled out my phone and typed a message: 'Please come get me. Now!!!' I was relieved to see the phone register the text as sent, and I put it back in my pocket and watched as Jonny made his way towards me.

It wasn't long until I saw him start to walk more quickly in my direction, and I realised he must have spotted me sitting on the rock, my hair being whipped about by the wind as it carried the sea spray inland. I waited, resigned, as he came towards me, still ridiculously happy to see him in spite of what I now knew. My heart was pounding hard in my chest.

Finally he reached the base of the rock I was sitting on, and he looked up at me, smiling, his eyes bright. And as they always did, the years fell away.

"Fancy meeting you here!" he said.

"Well, if the mountain won't come to Muhammad," I replied, finding myself unable not to smile at him.

He reached his hand up to me, his other holding a large, expensive-looking camera. I climbed down towards him, letting him take my hand and help me the final few slippery steps down. His hand was cool and dry around mine, and I wanted him to never let me go.

But he did. As soon as I had both feet safely on the sand, he dropped my hand and took a step back from me, pushing escaped tendrils of long hair out of his face. The rest of his hair was pulled back in the man bun he'd worn in the Instagram shot, and he still had his beard. He looked as beautiful to me as anyone had ever looked in my life.

His eyes met mine, as penetrating and intense as ever. "It's wonderful to see you, Summer."

My mouth was dry, but I managed to say, "It's good to see you too, Jonny." My heart expanded. "Really good."

"I didn't know you were coming."

"Well, when you didn't answer my email, I thought it might be best to surprise you. Not give you the chance to run away." I looked back towards the chalets. "Of course, now I realise perhaps that wasn't the best idea."

He looked confused. "Email?"

"I sent you an email about a week – maybe ten days – ago? Telling you I was going to be down here. Seeing if you wanted to get together."

His confusion dissipated and he looked mildly horrified. "I didn't see any email." Now apologetic. "I'm sorry I haven't checked my emails in a couple of weeks. I've been working non-stop. I've got this commission for a large canvas, and, well, when I'm working on a big project I can kind of end up shutting out the rest of the world." His eyes on mine were sincere. "I really am sorry."

I shrugged. "Okay, well, that explains it."

He looked at me closely. "And why would you ever think I would run away? I would always want to see you."

My throat felt tight and my eyes began to sting with the threat of tears. I blinked them away furiously and looked down at the sand. "I guess... Well, we haven't been in contact so much recently. I wasn't sure..." I trailed off, unable to say what I really wanted to say. Unsure of what to say instead.

"Well, for the record, you can always be sure I'd want to see you." Ten points for Jenna. We started walking back down the beach the way I'd come. "So did you go to the cottage first?" It gave me some comfort to glimpse a hint of uncertainty in his eyes.

"Yes. Your mother gave me the address. I'm sorry I dropped in on you without warning, honestly."

Understanding was beginning to dawn. "So, you met Amber."

"If Amber was the very pretty girl who answered the door, then, yes, I met her. Only briefly," I said quickly. "We didn't sit down for tea and discuss you or anything."

"Phew!" he said with a half-smile. "That's a relief."

"Although I'm sure you would have got rave reviews all round," I said. In spite of everything, I still wanted to be kind to him.

He looked at me. "That's very nice of you to say."

I didn't look back. "Just the truth."

We reached the path back up the cliffs to the dunes and made the climb up in silence. We reached the top and stopped.

Jonny glanced in the direction of his cottage. "So, do you want to come and visit with us properly?"

Us? I felt like I was going to be sick. I shook my head. "When you weren't in, I texted Jenna to come and fetch me. I expect she'll be here soon." And if she's not, I'm just gonna start walking towards her.

He nodded. "Okay, well, if you're sure." He took a beat. "I'm sorry I wasn't there. I'd like us to have had more time after I missed you last Christmas."

"Never enough time," I said. "That seems to have been our story lately." I paused, pulling together every ounce of bravery I had left in me. "There's just something I need to know."

He looked at me, and I could still discern far too much of concern and love in his eyes. "Yes?"

"Amber. Is it serious?"

He had the grace not to answer straight away, but eventually he said, "Yes."

I felt the final floor drop out of my world, but I managed to say, "Okay. Then I hope she makes you happy."

"Thank you. And I hope you're happy too, up in London."

I had nothing honest I could say to him about that, so I didn't. "Goodbye, Jonny."

He bent down and gave me a kiss on the cheek, and it took everything I had not to turn my mouth to his. "Goodbye, Summer."

I turned and started to walk along the track towards the car park, as he set off across the dunes towards home, taking my heart and all my hopes of happiness with him.

I reached the car park and quickly spotted Jenna's little yellow Fiat, in the same spot where she'd dropped me off. I walked over to it and looked inside, but she was nowhere to be seen. I tried the door: locked. I looked around and spotted her walking towards me from the direction of the chalets. What had she been up to?

She reached me, looking displeased.

"Where were you?" I said.

"Well, I sat here for five minutes waiting for you to show, and when you didn't, I texted you, but no reply."

I fished my phone out of my pocket. No text. "God," I said, "Jonny said the mobile service here is rubbish. I guess he wasn't making it up."

"Anyway, I didn't know if you even knew I was waiting, so I went looking for you. I remembered you'd said the name of the cottage was 'Sunset Bay', and I was able to find it." Her mouth set in a grim line. "And Amber."

Misery roiled my stomach. "Yeah."

"Jesus Christ, that must have been the last thing you wanted to find there."

I tipped my head. "Pretty much."

She looked towards the bay. "But you found him?"

I nodded. "Yes. We bumped into each other on the beach."

"And how was he?"

"The usual. No different to how he ever was. Except…"

"Now with someone else."

"Yeah."

"And did you talk about her?"

I shook my head. "Not really. Although I did ask him if it's serious."

Jenna looked impressed. "Well done! Ten out of ten for guts!"

I gave her a wan smile. "Thanks."

"And?"

"He says yes."

"Damn!" She gritted her teeth. "Bloody idiot."

"It's not his fault."

Jenna shot me a look. "It takes two to fuck up a relationship. He didn't do enough watering either."

I shrugged. "Maybe."

"There's no 'maybe' about it."

Jenna beeped Lucia's key fob, and we climbed in. She started the engine, and we drove towards the main road. We reached the junction and Jenna turned to me. "What do you want to do? Do you want to go for a drink? Go home? Drive to London? Whatever it is, I'm prepared to do it."

I looked at her gratefully. "I don't know. I don't feel like facing my mother. I kinda just want to crawl into a hole and never come out."

"Babe," Jenna said, reaching over and squeezing my hand. "How about I drive us the long way home, taking our time? That will give you the chance to think about what you want to do next."

I nodded. "Okay."

So, rather than drive us the direct route back to the A30 and its speedy dual carriageway, Jenna turned left and started driving us along the coast road towards Portreath. She even kept her speed to something less than breakneck.

We'd just passed the entrance to Tehidy Woods when Jenna spoke again. "She looks like you."

I turned to her. "What?"

Jenna kept her eyes on the road. "She looks like you. You didn't notice that?"

I frowned and turned my attention to the passing landscape, trying to catch the blue of the sea when it peeked between the hedgerows. "I must have been too busy getting my heart stomped on."

"I'm serious," Jenna said. "I mean, she's not your twin, obviously, but anyone who didn't know both of you well might have trouble distinguishing between you in a line-up."

I thought about it. "I guess we might have some similarities," I conceded.

"Honestly, you could almost be sisters." She took a beat. "I can't help thinking... Jonny couldn't have the real thing, so he's making do with a cheap knock-off." Jenna warmed to her subject. "It's almost embarrassing for him, really."

I turned to her, frowning. "Jenna! We don't know anything about her. She seemed perfectly nice to me. For all we know, she's an upgrade." I crossed my arms in front of me. "It's not like I'm the catch of the century."

Jenna set her jaw. "You are for Jonny. There is, and never has been, an upgrade for him."

We took a bend at some speed, and I gripped the door handle. "Things change," I said. "*People* change."

"Not that much."

"Anyway, it doesn't matter now. She is, almost quite literally, 'Johnny-on-the-spot'. Unless I want to uproot my entire life and move back down here to stalk him on the off-chance he might want to pick me over her, it's done. He's moved on."

Jenna's expression was grim, but she wasn't willing to concede defeat. "We'll see."

As Jenna had promised, we took our time driving back to Crantock, wending our way home via the 'B' roads that ran closest to the coast. But by the time she pulled her little yellow car into my parents' driveway, the reality of my situation had really begun to hit home, and I was feeling worse, not better.

She put on the handbrake, switched off the engine and turned to me. I couldn't meet her eye.

"Oh, God," I said. "I can't face my mother. She suggested that visit for the best, and it turned out so horribly. I can't bear the thought of having to explain to her what happened."

"Look, how about I deal with it?" Jenna said. "If you want, go straight in and upstairs, and I'll have a word with your mum. Give her the bare bones of the situation. She loves you. It's best she knows."

I looked at her. "Oh, Jen, that would be amazing, thank you!"

She took the key out of the ignition. "Come on, then."

I let us in the front door and immediately headed upstairs without another word. I closed my bedroom door behind me, removed my jacket and boots and lay down on the bed. Misery washed over me like the incoming tide.

A few minutes later there was a soft knock and Jenna let herself in, closing the door quietly behind her, as if I were some kind of invalid that it was important to treat with kid gloves. I turned over to face her, and she sat down on the bed.

"I've filled your mum in on the essentials," she said. "She got it right away, like she does. You won't have to explain anything to her or talk to her about it at all if you don't want to. She said she'll bring you up a cup of tea in a bit, but other than that you can just stay here and rest as long as you like."

"Thanks so much, Jen."

"Do you want me to stay or would you rather be by yourself?"

"It's fine. You can go. I'm not going to be any kind of

company anyway."

"You know you don't have to be."

"Still… There's no point in both of us suffering my misery. You go and see Good Sex Jason. At least one of us should get to enjoy a satisfactory love life."

"Well, if – and only if – you are completely sure."

I nodded. "I am."

"Okay, then." She got up. "Call me tomorrow. Or anytime, actually. Whenever you need. Call me in the middle of the night to rant and rave. I'm here for you."

I sat up. "Thanks. I don't know what I'd do without you, I honestly don't."

She bent down and gave me a tight hug, which I returned. She gave my back a quick final rub and stood up. "Ice cream," she said. "And lots of it. Send your mother out for supplies if necessary."

I managed a small laugh.

"I'm not kidding. It's scientifically proven that all the sugar and fat in ice cream stimulates the production of serotonin, the 'feel good' hormone."

I gave her a wry smile. "I'll keep that in mind."

She went to the door. "Bye, babe." A couple of minutes later, I heard her car start and reverse out of the driveway. I turned over and curled back up on the bed in the fetal position.

A few minutes after that, as promised, there was another soft knock on my bedroom door, and I heard my mother let herself in. I was lying with my back to the door, tears gathering behind my eyes, and wondering if I should just let them fall, worried that if I did, I wouldn't be able to stop them again. I heard her put a mug down on the bedside table behind me, but I didn't turn over. The mattress dipped slightly as she knelt on the bed and reached over to me. She put her hand on my shoulder and gave it a squeeze. Then she stood up and let herself out, closing the door softly behind her.

My mother's kindness and wordless understanding were the straws that broke the camel's back of my self-control. I gave in to the sorrow – the cortisol and adrenaline and other assorted stress hormones coursing through my body – and let the tears come. I shuddered and wept until this round of tears finally dried, and I drifted off into the relief of sleep.

When I woke up later that evening, it was dark out and someone had drawn the curtains. I sat up and rubbed sticky eyes. I reached over and turned on the bedside light. There was a different mug of tea on the bedside table, and a plate of toast, now cold. I took a sip of the tea, which was still lukewarm, and a bite of the cold toast. It tasted like ashes in my mouth and I could hardly swallow it. I put the plate down and fetched my phone from my jacket, which I'd tossed on the chair earlier. I wasn't expecting any particular messages, but my phone addiction was as severe as most people's by now.

There was a text from Jenna, which she'd apparently sent when she got home: 'A reminder I am HFY, any time day or night. Look after yourself. And remember *ice cream* emoji x'.

I managed a smile and texted back: 'Thank you!' followed by three *red heart* emojis.

I noticed an Instagram notification icon at the top of the phone screen and used it to take me to the relevant page. My heart began thumping in my throat when I saw that it was a DM from Jonny. It said: 'Summer, I just wanted to tell you again how lovely it was to see you today. And apologise once more for how little time we had to spend together. As I'm so bad at reading emails, I wanted to suggest that if – or rather, hopefully, WHEN – you want to get hold of me in the future send me a DM on Instagram. I get hardly any messages here, so I've left the IG notification enabled on my phone, so I shouldn't miss it. I hope all is going well for you in London. All the best, J'

I noticed the lack of any 'Love, J' or any 'x' kisses at the end of the message, which I realised was probably reasonable given the situation, however disappointing it might be to me. I reread the message several times, wondering what, if anything, I should read into it, but finally decided I should read nothing more into it than just what it said. Jonny had always been ridiculously thoughtful and considerate. This was not remotely unusual for him in the circumstances.

I put the phone down and stripped off my clothes, wrapped myself in my robe and went to take a shower. The sooner this day was washed off me, the better.

The following morning, I slept late. I'd originally woken as it was getting light, but it took only a few seconds before the pain and horror of what had happened yesterday engulfed me, and I burrowed down under the duvet and escaped back into sleep. This happened a couple more times, me finding myself unable to get up and face the day and its inevitable requirement for consciousness. But by the time the hands of the bedside clock moved past eleven, my stomach was gnawing away at my insides, and I faced the fact that I might have to go downstairs for some food.

I was still attempting to work up the energy and courage to move when I heard a car pull into the driveway beneath my window. I wasn't expecting anyone, so I assumed it must be a friend of my parents. That put paid to any idea of me venturing out of my room for the time being, so I rolled over and closed my eyes again.

I heard the doorbell chime and the front door open, and then low voices in the hallway. This was all a most annoying amount of disturbance for what was surely supposed to be a quiet few days between Christmas and New Year. I'd just buried my head completely under the duvet, when there was a knock at my bedroom door. I pushed the covers down so that I could see who'd come in; it was my mother. She closed the door behind her.

"Summer?" she almost whispered.

"Yes?" I managed, unable to keep the annoyance out of my voice at the intrusion.

"I'm not sure how you're going to feel about this, but... Jonny's downstairs."

A mixture of horror, pain and – goddammit! – a tiny trace of hope bolted through my system. I pushed back the duvet and sat up. I pushed my hair out of my face. "What does he want?"

"He's asked if he can see you. He says he'll understand if you don't want to, but he's asked me to ask, and I said I would."

I let out a heavy sigh. "Okay, I guess. But he'll have to take me as he finds me. I'm not doing any more than getting dressed."

"I'm sure he doesn't care about that," my mother said.

I gave another sigh, threw back the covers and climbed out of bed. "Okay, tell him I'll be down in a few minutes."

"Okay." My mother let herself out and went to deliver the message.

I went to the bathroom and peed and brushed my teeth, but other than that I was determined to make no additional effort. Back in my room, I put on underwear, jeans, socks and a chunky old Fair Isle jumper. I pulled my hair, unbrushed, into a ponytail, pushed my feet into an ancient pair of ballet flats and I was done. I steeled myself and made my way downstairs.

He was standing in the hallway waiting for me. I was sure my mother had offered him more by way of hospitality, but evidently he'd declined it. I felt him watching me as I came down the stairs, but I didn't meet his eyes. I reached the bottom of the staircase, crossed my arms and finally looked up at him.

"Hi," I said. I couldn't manage a smile, no matter how hard I tried.

He was looking down at me, and I decided I'd had just about enough of the intensity of his gaze.

"I didn't like how we left things yesterday, and I was wondering if we could talk," he said.

I ran a weary hand over my head. "I…" I didn't know what to say to him. He was being far too reasonable, while at the same time asking too much from me. "I honestly don't know what we have to talk about." I finally managed to meet his eyes. "I'm sure you've now got better things to do than listen to my stories, and…" I bit the inside of my lip, willing myself with every fibre of my being not to cry, "I'm not sure I can bear to hear yours right now. I'm sorry."

"Okay. Then how about we just go for a walk? We don't have to talk, but I'd be really grateful if you'd give me some time so we can, maybe, be friends in the future. I'm scared that if we leave things like this, we won't ever talk again. At least, not properly."

I looked up at him. "And that would bother you?"

His expression was horrified. "Of course it would!

Wouldn't it bother you?"

I stared at my feet. "I guess."

He took a step towards me, and I took one back. "Look, I know I'm not your favourite person right now, but we've always been friends, right? At least I hope we have…"

I didn't disagree with him.

"Please, just give me an hour… half an hour… to give us a chance of still being friends."

What could I say? He was asking so little of me. And it wasn't as if he'd done anything wrong. He hadn't cheated on me or treated me badly. I'd had no rights of ownership over him. He'd been an entirely free agent, and he'd found a way not to be alone. What he'd done wasn't just reasonable, it was entirely sensible. And I had no right to simply sever our friendship and cause him pain he hadn't earned and didn't deserve.

I sighed. "Okay."

He followed me as I walked through the kitchen – which was happily empty – to the vestibule by the back door. I took my rain jacket from a peg and put it on, while I toed off the ballet flats and swapped them for walking boots. The dogs came and sniffed at my feet as I laced up, but I pushed them away gently, and we let ourselves out through the back door, securing the dogs inside.

We walked to the driveway, and I was about to turn right down the lane when Jonny said, "How about I drive us to Polly Joke? The forecast said it might rain, and I don't want us to get caught out miles from home."

I looked at his car – which was, indeed, the beaten-up old Renault I'd seen in front of his cottage yesterday – and shrugged. "Sure."

We got in, and I pulled on the seatbelt to do it up, but I realised almost immediately that I'd made a mistake. In

A CORNISH WINTER'S TALE

the confines of the car, with us seated only inches apart, our chemistry quickly filled the space, and my heart rate kicked into high gear. I sensed he felt it too, as he looked over at me awkwardly, but of course it was too late for either of us to back out now.

He started the engine, reversed carefully out into the lane and drove us competently towards West Pentire, not too fast, not too slow. Very Jonny.

We parked in the car park next to the Bowgie Inn, overlooking the bay, and walked up towards the wild-flower fields, currently in their dormant winter state, where the landscape rolled gently down towards the sea. We turned right to take the path towards Polly Joke cove, all the time walking in silence. My hands were buried deep in my pockets, my shoulders hunched, my head down. I suspected he'd never seen me with such closed-down body language.

The sky above was grey, threatening the rain he'd mentioned, but it held off for now. We made our way to the edge of the fields and down the steep slope to the cove. We passed through the kissing gate, along the path that edged the beach and over the little bridge across the stream that ran into the cove from the verdant fields above. We followed the South West Coast Path up steep, slippery steps to the Kelseys, the slice of rocky headland that separated Polly Joke from Holywell Bay. We didn't need to talk; we'd made this walk together countless times before, albeit many years ago, but this walk was timeless. The climb up was much easier for Jonny, with his long legs, than it was for me, and he turned around a few times to check if I wanted him to help me with a hand up. But I kept my head down, making it quite clear that I didn't.

191

We followed the path along the edge of the cliffs until we came to a spot above the little mini-cove at the edge of Polly Joke, where several seals had hauled themselves out to rest. I made my way as close as I dared to the cliff edge and sat down to watch them. I always loved watching seals; without the slightest intention, they were hilarious and full of character, often engaging in some kind of amusing drama. I hadn't had the opportunity to sit and watch them in years, and I wasn't going to let this chance pass me by.

Jonny sat down next to me.

"I remember you always loved seal watching," he said. His voice was smooth and deep, like the most delicious dark, melted chocolate, and I could hardly bear the thought that I might never hear it again. "There are often seals hauled out at Mutton Cove by Godrevy, and I always think of you when I see them."

I lifted an eyebrow. "You think I look like a hauled-out seal?"

He risked a small smile. "You know very well I don't mean any such thing."

I couldn't help smiling too, as I looked back down towards the resting animals below.

"I've missed you," he said, his voice quiet, as if unsure he should be saying it.

My chest tightened. "I've missed you, too."

He paused for a moment before continuing. "Is everything going well for you up in London? I really hope it is. That you're finding what you want there."

I gave a little shake of the head. "Jonny, please don't."

I could feel his eyes burning into my cheek as I refused to look at him.

"I'm sorry. I don't know what to do to fix this."

I looked further away from him, pushing a loose strand of hair, that the wind was taking, back with my hand. "I'm not sure it can be fixed."

"Please don't say that." His voice had an edge of desperation.

I sighed deeply. "I'm sorry. I shouldn't have come to see you. I didn't mean to stir... this..." I made a hopeless gesture with my hand, "up again. Although... in my defence, I didn't know about Amber."

"I know. That was my fault. I should have told you. I guess... at first I didn't know if it was anything serious. And then, by the time it was, you and I hadn't been in contact for a while, and you hadn't come down for a proper visit for so long, I wasn't even sure you'd be interested. I figured you had your own thing going on up in London. It seemed kind of self-important of me to 'announce' to you my relationship with Amber as if you'd give a damn." I couldn't miss the edge of bitterness in his final few words, the sting of rebuke.

I turned to him, shocked. "How on earth could you think I wouldn't give a damn? After what happened between us?" I felt tears gathering. Shit! "Jonny! How could you think that?"

His eyes on mine were dark, and it was as if I could see every ounce of pain I'd ever given him in them. "Summer, what would you have thought if you were me?"

I reflected back on the way I'd let our relationship drift after I'd returned to London, the texts unanswered for days, the diminishing number of phone calls, all because I was too busy with a job of the most supreme unimportance. I felt utterly sick. "I'm so sorry," I said. "I don't know what to say. I feel like there's no explanation I could give you that would satisfy either of us."

"And I'm sorry, too. And I didn't mean to accuse you of anything. I know you didn't mean to hurt me."

"I really didn't." I looked at him. "And if it makes you feel any better, I've ended up hurting myself worse than I can say."

"It doesn't make me feel any better. Not even a bit."

I looked back down at the seals. "I do genuinely hope you're happy with Amber." I gave a wry smile. "At least, I do while I'm sitting here next to you. I'm not sure I'm going to be feeling quite so generous when I'm back in London doing 50-hour weeks and dealing with some arsehole reaming me out because the caterer screwed up his wine order."

"Jesus Christ. That sounds grim."

"It's not all bad," I said, trying to cover myself. "But, I've gotta be honest, it's not spending my days walking on the beach at Godrevy, either." I looked at him. "I'm very impressed you're making it work. And yes, even genuinely happy for you. In a way that will not be diminished when I'm not sitting next to you."

He smiled. "Thank you." I could see him deciding whether or not to risk his next question. "Do you think you'll ever come back down here? For good, I mean."

I watched a ship making its slow journey across the distant horizon. "I honestly don't know. I wish the choice were an easy one. But it's not any easier now than it was before." I paused, meeting his eyes, deciding not to let him entirely off the hook. "Maybe it's even harder."

He caught my meaning and had the good grace to look a little uncomfortable for his part in that. "I'm sorry."

I looked back out to sea. "We all just do our best, right? That's all we can do. Some things we get right, much we get wrong, and we just keep trying to move forward, to

A CORNISH WINTER'S TALE

make the best of the circumstances we find ourselves in. Sometimes we're lucky, and sometimes…" I looked back at him, "we're not."

"I really hope you're lucky, Summer. It's one of my greatest wishes."

I felt my heart squeeze. "I wish the same for you, Jonny."

We got up and started to make our way back to his car. When we came to the steep steps down to Polly Joke, I let him help me this time. His hand around mine was everything I wanted from life, and nothing I could have. We walked the rest of the way in silence.

Once we reached the car, he didn't get in but walked down towards the sea, where there was an area of grass with a view out towards Crantock Bay. I followed him. He waited for me to join him until we were both standing looking towards the Pentire headland across the sands.

"So, do you think we can still be friends?" he said.

I looked up at him. "I think we can certainly try. I'll do my best if you will."

He smiled down at me; there was relief in his eyes. "I will. Did you see my Instagram message?"

"I did. Thank you. I'll definitely do that going forward. And you do the same. Whenever you want to contact me."

"I will."

We stood for a few minutes watching the tide slowly making its way inwards.

"Thank you for doing this, Jonny," I said. "I'm not going to lie and say everything's going to be fine tomorrow. Or the day after that, for that matter. But right now, I do feel better. And much more hopeful that we can still be friends. Which might not be what I want right now, but with time…" I ran out of words. A time in the future when

I might be okay being 'just friends' with Jonny seemed entirely too far away to imagine. But at least it was out there. Which was better than the barren, Jonny-less future I'd been facing only a couple of hours ago.

He looked at me. "Well, thank you for letting me try. After you asked me about Amber yesterday, and I saw how you felt, I thought I might have screwed things up between us beyond repair. And I'm not sure I could've lived with that. Not at peace, anyway."

"Jeeze!" I said. "And there was me thinking I'd made such a great job of pretending I was fine with it."

He gave me a look. "I hate to tell you this, but I've always been able to see how you really felt about things in your eyes. It's been both the blessing and the curse of our friendship."

I felt my eyes widen with surprise and realised I was confirming what he'd just said right then and there. "I thought that was just me with you, Captain Obvious!"

We smiled at one another and one of those moments passed between us that made me realise I would always love him. Even if I ended up loving someone else too.

"Shall I drive you back?" he asked.

I nodded. "Better had."

We returned to the car, and this time the atmosphere inside it was much less charged, even approaching comfortable. He dropped me at the entrance to my driveway. "Say thanks to your mum for me."

I smiled. "I'll thank her for both of us."

I stood back as he reversed into the driveway to turn the car around and watched with a heavy heart as he drove away up the lane. I wondered if we'd ever have that kind of conversation again.

The following morning I made the train in good

time. The pain of opportunity lost still wreathed itself around my heart and extended tentacles into every limb, but after my walk with Jonny yesterday I'd been able to resume at least some sort of normal functioning, even managing to have supper with my parents. My mother was clearly incredibly relieved.

I'd called Jenna and given her the highlights of my and Jonny's conversation, and she'd listened and managed to hold her tongue when I knew that what she really wanted to do was tell me to jack in everything in London and come down here and get him back. His mission to ensure that the break in our friendship wasn't permanent had, of course, convinced her that my efforts to bring that about wouldn't have to be long or arduous. The words "with a snap of your fingers" had been uttered, but only once, and had been swiftly followed with an apology.

I found myself a window seat and took out my phone to while away the time until we pulled out and I'd be able to turn my attention to enjoying the journey through the Cornish countryside to Par. I checked the BBC for the headlines and the weather in London, then turned to Instagram for a leisurely scroll. I spent a pleasant few minutes 'liking' photos on the #beautifulcornwall and #lovecornwall tags, before turning to my own feed to check out what was going on with the accounts I followed. I'd 'liked' a few posts from London friends and Jenna's latest from last night of her and Good Sex Jason, when I scrolled down and a photo rolled onto my screen that put a knife through my heart.

It was a black and white photo of Jonny, looking his usual gorgeous self, but in this shot he was not alone. Amber was with him and kissing him delightedly on the cheek as he smiled into the camera, her hand crad-

ling his face. It was a phone selfie; he'd taken it holding his phone up for them both to smile into. I looked
below the photo for tags, wondering what he would have
gone with; maybe #mygirlfriend or #jonnylovesamber
or #lookathishotandgorgeouscouplearentyoujealous. But
there were no tags or description of any kind, just the
photo.

I looked at it in unreserved horror. My mind ran back
over our time together yesterday, and I wondered if it
had even happened or if I'd imagined the whole thing. Because surely, if it had happened, if he'd really said what
he'd said about wanting us to be friends and knowing
how I felt, he would have known how much this would
hurt me and would have left it, oh, I don't know, at least a
couple of weeks before posting it.

With unsteady fingers, I forwarded the post to Jenna:
'In case either of us were unclear, he's made his choice.'

The train shuddered into motion a couple of minutes
later as Jenna's reply popped up on my phone: 'JFC *red
angry face* emoji, *eye roll* emoji, *bull* emoji, *poop*
emoji'.

I managed a small puff of laughter, in spite of myself,
and replied to her with a row of five *blowing heart kisses*
emojis.

Part Ten

Present Day

Boxing Day

J onny was due to pick me up at noon and drive us over to Gwithian, our understanding being that we'd stay there for a day or two, or as long as we wanted if the mood took us to stay longer. I packed a duffle bag with essential toiletries, a spare pair of jeans, a few extra tops and sweaters and underwear to last a few days, but to be quite honest, I wasn't expecting to spend much time anywhere other than bed.

I put his presents in a carrier bag and took that, duffle and handbag down to the hallway to wait for him. I looked in on my mother in the kitchen.

"I'm not sure how long I'm going to be there, so don't worry if I don't turn up or even text for a few days. The mobile service there is spotty at best, and Jonny's house doesn't have a landline, so I'm afraid if there's an emergency, someone might have to come get us."

My mother smiled happily at me. Her daughter being married and back in Cornwall was so close she could taste it, and absolutely nothing must be allowed to interfere. "Have a lovely time, darling, and don't worry about a thing. We'll see you when we see you."

I heard a car horn toot outside, and I gave her a peck on the cheek. "Bye!"

I looked in on my father in the living room, watching a recording of *Countryfile*, and blew him a kiss. "Bye, Dad!"

He raised a hand in acknowledgement. "See you later, sweetheart!"

I opened the front door, expecting to find Jonny's beaten-up old Renault in the driveway, and got a shock. The Renault was no more, instead he was standing there, proudly leaning against a beautiful red, classic MG sports car. The car was obviously old, but in perfect condition, its red paint job gleaming like a new pin.

He was looking so happy with himself, I couldn't help laughing as I carried my bags down the steps.

"What happened to the Renault?" I asked.

He drew his hand across his neck in a slicing motion. "Had to go, I'm afraid. Still, what do you think?" He motioned to the sports car. Admiring comments were clearly both expected and deserved.

"Gorgeous!" I noted the soft top. "And perfect for summer!"

He beamed at me. "I only got it a couple of months ago, so I haven't been able to take advantage on warm, sunny days yet, but should be fun, huh?"

I realised he hadn't bought the car simply for himself, but for *us*. His excitement and thoughtfulness warmed my heart. He took my bags from me and put them in the boot, then held the door open for me to climb in. He walked around and folded himself in on the driver's side, the seat pushed all the way back to accommodate him.

I raised an eyebrow. "Fab as this car is, isn't it a bit of a snug fit for you?"

He grinned at me. "I manage, and Summer, this was always my dream car. Took me a while to be able to afford it, but I made it." He started the engine and looked over at me. "I finally have my dream car and my dream woman. I'm the luckiest fucking guy in the world!"

We sped down the A30 and pulled up in front of his little cottage a shade under forty minutes later. As we parked, I noticed that the exterior had undergone a paint job since I'd last been here, and the timber sidings were now a fresh, bright white. We took our bags out of the car, and he led us inside. I looked around while Jonny moved about turning on the electric radiators in an effort to take the chill off things.

The front door opened directly into the living room, which wasn't large but wasn't tiny either. To the right of it was an open plan kitchen, and behind that, also off the living room, a bathroom. The room off the left side of the living room was a decent-sized double bedroom. The furniture throughout was so basic it made Ikea seem 'haute luxe', but everything was clean, tidy and bright. The white walls looked freshly painted, and the floor was bare wood.

"I just painted the walls and cleaned up the floor," he said. "I thought we could choose new furniture together so you can get what you like."

I gave him a bright smile and a squeeze of his arm. "Thank you!"

"But let me show you the best bit!" He led me excitedly to some patio doors leading off the side of the kitchen. He unlocked them, slid one back and stepped out onto a deck. I followed him, looked around and gave a little gasp. My hand flew to my mouth.

"I know, right?" he said.

Because the deck had a view to die for: The blue waters of St Ives Bay glinted beyond the sand dunes, and if you leaned forward over the wooden balustrade, Godrevy lighthouse was visible in the distance to the east. Jonny had set up two patio chairs around a cast iron fire pit. There was also room for a small dining table and chairs, and I was immediately envisioning meals out here in the summer.

"You can't see the sea from anywhere else in the house because of other chalets in the way, but I think this more than makes up for it."

I looked at him, my eyes shining. "Totally."

We went back inside, and he led me through a door at the rear of the living room to give me another Wow! moment, because it opened into a large conservatory, the width of the entire cottage: Jonny's studio.

One wall attached to the cottage, and three exterior walls were timbered to about his waist height, but everything else, upper walls and roof, was glass. The entire interior wall was covered with paintings, sketches and photographs. More paintings on canvas were stacked all the way around the room against the lower part of the walls. There was a large work table covered in oil paints, brushes, rags and all the other tricks of his trade. A couple of easels, one bearing the canvas of a work in progress, stood furthest from the door.

"Wow!" I said, looking around in wonder. It was like entering Jonny's holy space, and I was suitably awed. I walked around slowly, looking at the paintings. I'd only seen his work in photographs before, but they were so much more beautiful in real life, layers of paint and glaze skilfully applied to create the most exquisite representations of sea and sky, so that the scenes seemed to be illuminated from within.

I was lost for words. "Jonny, I…"

He walked towards me, looking both vulnerable and hopeful.

I looked around. "I hardly know what to say. These are stunning! You are just crazy talented!"

He reached me and laughed, taking me in his arms and kissing me with a passion and commitment that were somehow new. I curled my arms around his neck and kissed him back. I couldn't get enough of him. I felt myself falling, and I never wanted to come up for air.

I pulled his sweater up his back, and he disengaged himself from me for a moment to whip it off and drop it on the floor revealing his T-shirt. I wasn't interested in that hanging around for long either, so I pushed it up his back and ran my hands over his smooth skin. He took the hint and quickly shed that too.

He hooked his hands under my bottom and pulled me up against him. I was more than happy to follow that lead, looping my arms around his neck and wrapping my legs around him so that he could lift me up and I could kiss him face to face.

He walked us through to the bedroom and laid me down, and slowly he began to undress me, taking the greatest care and attention as to every step of the task he had assigned himself. First my boots were unlaced and removed with elegant, dexterous fingers. Then my socks, with him taking the time to caress my ankles and feet as he did so. Jeans came next, eased off gently as if I were made of the finest porcelain. I sat up to allow him to pull off my cashmere sweater, shaking my head back to sex up my hair once he'd done so. He unhooked my bra with a sure hand and removed it, dropping it to one side. He treated my breasts to a look of such boundless desire I almost combusted. Then finally his hands slipped inside my panties and I was entirely naked.

I was also beyond keen to move things along. The leisurely pace at which he was moving was an extreme turn-on, but it was also driving me crazy.

I watched his eyes as they travelled down my body and back up again, drinking in every detail, and met them with my own. "If you're not inside me in the next thirty seconds, I am literally going to burst into flames."

We both laughed, and he saved me from a fiery death by quickly shedding his footwear, jeans and briefs, whipping on a condom from the box he'd placed thoughtfully to hand earlier and slipping inside in just under his allotted thirty seconds.

I gasped with pleasure as he began to work his magic on my body. I held him desperately against me, urging him on. I opened myself up to him, my body arched against him, the feeling of him inside and his hands on my skin setting every atom of my being on fire. I'd been so ready for him, it didn't take long for me to reach a shuddering climax so intense I feared my brain may melt altogether.

He cried out low in his chest as his own orgasm cascaded through his body. We separated and he rolled onto his back beside me.

We both lay still as our chests rose and fell, catching our breath. I felt hollowed out with satisfied desire and completion. I moved a hand over and found his forearm, curled my fingers loosely around it. There was nothing I could say to convey to him what he did to me, how limitless was my desire for him, so I just said, "I'm yours forever."

After we made love, I wriggled under the duvet and drifted off to sleep, and by the time I woke up, the clock on the bedside table showed it was mid-afternoon. Jonny's side of the bed was empty. I pulled an arm out from under the covers to test the temperature and was pleased, and not a little relieved, to discover that the electric radiator beneath the window had done its job of chasing the chill from the air. I eased myself out of bed and peeked into the living room. There was no sign of Jonny; he must be in his studio. I tiptoed naked to fetch my duffle bag from beside the front door and scooted back into the bedroom. I rescued my bra from where Jonny had dropped it earlier, fished fresh pants out of my bag and completed my state of dress with a T-shirt of Jonny's I found in a drawer. I was pretty sure he wouldn't mind me borrowing it.

I padded through into the studio. As I'd suspected, Jonny was there. He was standing at one of the easels, holding a palette in one hand, applying paint to the canvas with a brush held in the other, with a second, longer brush held between his teeth. He was wearing nothing but blue jeans, low on his hips, his torso and feet bare. I'd never seen a sexier sight in my life.

He turned to me and gave me the kind of sexy eyes which swiftly reversed any cooling down my body may have been doing. He removed the paintbrush from his mouth and treated me to his most devastating smile. "Hello, gorgeous."

I went and looped my arms around him from behind, pressing a kiss against his shoulder blade. "Hello, you."

He popped the spare brush back in his mouth and made a few more strokes on the canvas, before apparently deciding he was done for the time being. I released him and he walked over to his work table to set down the palette. He wiped off his brushes with a rag and dropped them in a jar of liquid, which I assumed was some kind of cleaning fluid. He wiped his hands over with another rag and looked at me.

I'd been allowing my eyes to feast on the journey of fly to treasure trail to belly hair to chest hair, and when they reached his face, they found an expression of extreme amusement.

"See anything you like?"

I treated him to a look of undisguised lust. "Everything."

He laughed. "Good grief, woman! Exactly how exhausted are you intending to make me over the next few days?"

"Very," I said, firmly.

"Give me a minute to wash up." He headed to the bathroom. I was continuing my examination of the contents of his display wall when he returned. "Would you like your Christmas present now?" he asked.

I gave him my most affectionate smile. "I can think of little else in the world I'd like more."

He went over to where several canvases were stacked against the wall, each covered in a protective fabric sheet. He picked up the one at the front, which was a medium-sized canvas, about three feet by two, carried it to an empty easel and set it down, without removing the sheet.

"I'm sorry," he said. "I haven't wrapped it, but I hope you won't mind."

I walked over to him, my heart thumping. He was giving me a painting. I stood waiting for him to show me, but rather he put his hand under the sheet to hold it in place on the easel and said to me, "Go ahead, you can look."

I gently tugged on the sheet to pull it away, and it

slipped down, revealing the painting underneath. I gave a soft gasp. It was a portrait of me! He'd used one of the sketches he'd done years before at his parents' house – the one of me watching television – to create a beautiful oil painting. As with the sketch I remembered from all that time ago, the woman he'd painted was definitely me, only more perfect. I was overwhelmed by all the hours, care, skill and love which had undoubtedly gone into its creation.

"Oh, Jonny! I don't know what to say! It's beautiful. Far and away the most amazing present anyone has ever given me." I shot him a grin. "My mother is going to be heartbroken that the 'Disney's Esmerelda' costume she gave me when I was five has now been supplanted, but *C'est la vie!*"

He laughed. "Do you really like it?"

I was still looking at it in wonderment. "'Like' isn't really a sufficient word. 'Love' barely covers it, to be honest." I looked at the painting again. "I'll treasure it always." I examined it closely, marvelling at the skill of the brushwork. Jonny had modified the usual sweeping style he used for his sea and skyscapes to make it suitable for portraiture, bringing to it the necessary attention to detail. Of course, I'd known since I'd seen his sketches of me that he had the ability to create art in different styles and mediums, but once again the extent of his skill and talent had taken me by surprise. "When did you paint it?"

He watched me examining it. "I actually started it not long after I made the sketches of you. Remember that?"

I looked at him, as we both remembered those amazing days. "Of course!"

He let out a puff of laughter. "God, Summer, I was so crazy in love with you. I was obsessed. I spent all my time drawing you from memory and making water colours and small oils from those sketches." Another puff of laughter. "You should see the state of those sketches now. I handled them so often I have to keep them in clear plastic wallets so they don't fall apart. Anyway, I started this then. But..." I looked at him, fearing what was coming. "After things kind of died down between us, I couldn't face working on it anymore." He met the regret in my eyes. "It's a cliche, but it's true; artists need their muses. But of course I always kept it. And after we talked last winter, and then you left Neil and told me you wanted me, I took it out and started working on it again a few months ago. I'm so happy you love it."

I lifted my hands to his face and pulled him down to me so I could kiss him: a soft, loving kiss. "How could I not? And even more now you've told me the story behind it."

"I have to tell you something, though, Summer."

"Yes?"

"I'm giving it to you now because I'm hoping – and believing – that you'll always be with me. I would never have been able to give it to you if we'd stayed just friends, even if I'd ever finished it. I could never have parted with it."

I put my arms around him and laid my head against his chest, looking again at my painting. "You'll never have to part with either it or me."

I stayed there, admiring my present for a little longer, before I remembered. "Oh, my goodness! I need to give you your gifts as well!" I dropped my arms from around him and went into the living room, with him following. "I'm sorry, these don't remotely compare to what you gave me. I promise to try and do better in the future."

He smiled and took the carrier bag from me. He sat

down on the sofa to dive in, and I perched on the armchair next to him to watch. The first present he pulled out was the book I'd bought him. He tore off the festive silver paper and examined it. It was a large, fine art 'coffee table' style book of photographs and paintings of the Cornish coast. I'd had no idea what to get him, as his needs were so simple, but I hoped at least he would enjoy looking at this.

He turned to where I'd written an inscription on one of the front pages: *To Jonny, Maybe one day there will be a book like this full of your paintings and photographs. I hope you find some inspiration in here. Yours, with all my love, Summer.*

He finished reading and looked over at me. "Thank you, it's beautiful."

I smiled. "There are a couple of other things." I gestured for him to continue. "Open the smaller one first."

He did as instructed, with more tearing of wrapping paper. He realised what it was and laughed. "Fantastic! This will be the first in our collection of shared favourite movies."

I beamed at him. "That's what I thought!" It was the DVD of *Out of Sight*, the movie we'd watched together years before and both loved. I was looking forward to watching it with him again, perhaps tonight.

"But I don't have a DVD player…"

"Keep going." I encouraged him onwards.

He pulled the final present out of the bag and grinned over at me. He laughed as he unwrapped it and his suspicions were confirmed. "Summer, you are a rockstar!"

I laughed. "I guessed you might not have a player. And hey, if you had, it's not like anyone ever died from having two DVD players."

He set the box down on the sofa next to him, along

with his other gifts. "I'll set it up in a minute." He cast his eyes towards the medium-sized Sony flatscreen TV sitting on a small bench by the wall. "I have an admission to make: I only bought the TV a couple of weeks ago. I didn't think you'd appreciate the ancient model I'd had since I moved in here."

I sat down next to him on the sofa and kissed him on the cheek. "Aww! Look at you, feathering your nest for your new mate!"

He looked charmingly bashful. "Just made a start." He leaned in and kissed me on the mouth. "Thank you for the lovely presents."

I smiled. "I have some way to go to even approach breaking even with you, but I'll keep at it."

"No need," he said softly. "You're here." He gathered together all the discarded wrapping paper and got up to take it over to the kitchen bin. "Are you hungry?"

I tipped my head. "Getting peckish."

He pulled a couple of wine glasses out of a cupboard and opened a bottle of red which had been standing on the counter. "I thought we could order a pizza for this evening and go do a food shop tomorrow. What do you think?"

"Sounds perfect."

"There's a Lidl by the roundabout which I usually use, but I thought we might treat ourselves to a trip to the M&S. My mother informs me that one of the best things about coming to visit me down here is the excuse to pop into the M&S Foodhall on the retail park and stock up."

I laughed. "I have to be honest, various London M&S Foodhalls have seen far too much of my hard-earned salary over the years."

"So, that's a plan, then?"

I went over and picked up the glass of red wine he'd put on the counter for me. "It very much is."

Later that evening, we sat snuggled up together on the sofa, pleasantly satiated with pizza and wine, watching JLo and Clooney spark off one another in our first joint favourite movie. I'd never felt more content in a state of domesticity than at that very moment. I wondered if tomorrow we might discuss when we could get a dog.

I woke the next morning, feeling thoroughly satisfied in every conceivable way, stretched and rolled over. No Jonny. I pricked up my ears and made out the sound of a shower running in the bathroom. I tiptoed to the window and peeked around a curtain to ascertain the state of the weather: another brilliant blue sky. I touched the windowpane: yep, another extremely cold day. Still, if the cold air was the price we needed to pay for all this beautiful sunshine, I was more than willing to pay it.

I hopped back into bed and snuggled down under the duvet. I heard the shower stop, and a few minutes later Jonny walked into the bedroom, a white towel fastened low around his hips, another being used to towel dry his hair. I sighed happily and enjoyed the show. I was quickly becoming very keen on this whole 'living with Jonny' idea.

He caught me watching him and shot me a mischievous grin and a wink.

I propped myself up on an elbow. "All these years…" I said.

He finished towel-drying his hair and began to brush it out with a vent brush. "What?"

"All these years… you must have thought I was the biggest idiot."

He laughed. "What? Why?"

"Well, if I'd been you, that's what I'd have thought. I mean... years! For years I could've woken up every morning to this..." I gestured up and down towards him, "coming out of the shower and sashaying..."

He raised an eyebrow. "Sashaying?"

I nodded. "Sashaying in here and blessing my eyeballs with, well... this!" More wild gesturing. I threw myself back on the bed in – not entirely faux – exasperation at myself.

He put down his hairbrush and climbed onto the bed. He manoeuvred himself on top of me, settled himself between my thighs and lowered his head to kiss me. I curled my arms around his neck to do my part.

"Well, at least you finally came to your senses," he said.

I smiled up at him. "Thank you for your patience."

After we'd finished, I managed not to fall back to sleep again but went to take my own shower. I put on light makeup, jeans and a warm sweater and tied my hair up in a ponytail. I came out of the bedroom and found Jonny at the kitchen breakfast bar doing something incomprehensible with his incomprehensibly fancy camera. He looked up as I came in and treated me to one of his adoring smiles.

"I made coffee," he said, nodding towards a steaming French press next to him. I couldn't help but be amused by the fact that he barely had furniture, but he had a French press. I guess if you liked good coffee, you had to put in the extra effort. "Did you want anything to eat? I'm afraid I only have toast and cereal at the moment."

I poured myself coffee and shook my head. "I'm fine, thanks." All this amazing sex was distracting my brain so that it kept forgetting to ask me to eat.

"I was going to go out for a walk up to Godrevy before we go shopping. Wanna join?"

I walked over and wrapped my arms around him from behind, laying my cheek against his back. The wool of his sweater was soft against my skin, and he smelled absolutely divine: a base note of masculinity with top notes of a woody sweetness. I breathed in deeply. "Very much yes."

We made our way across the dunes and down onto the beach and started walking at a leisurely pace towards the lighthouse. I slipped my arm around his waist and snuggled into him, and he put his around me. I couldn't seem to stop touching him, as if I could feel the weight of all the time I'd missed and was urgently trying to make up for it. I was very much enjoying our time together away from the world; no one else's opinions to care about, and no one to please but ourselves. It was heady stuff.

The tide was out, so we were able to walk all the way along the beach to Godrevy. Incredibly to me, there were still some surfers in the water in spite of the extreme chill. When we reached the rocky headland, we climbed up the steps from the beach to join the coastal path that led to Godrevy Point. We took one of the minor paths and found a spot on the cliffs to sit and admire the spectacular view out over St Ives Bay and the lighthouse, standing on its island warning ships away from the Stones reef. The wind was brisk and bitter, but the brightness of the sunshine, causing the bay to glitter beyond the frothing waves below, suited my mood perfectly. And besides, snuggled into Jonny, I didn't feel the cold.

"I was thinking of painting an azure blue series," Jonny said. "I've been so influenced by the truly dramatic skies here – stormy greys, and the brilliant pinks and reds of the sunsets – but I'm feeling a renewed appreciation for the blues of a calmer day."

"I'd love to see that. Obviously dramatic skies can create art which stimulates passionate responses, but I think the type of blue paintings you're talking about could also provoke strong emotions, such as the pleasure of remembering happy days. And blue can be very soothing." I smiled at him. "If you decide to do it, will you paint one for me?"

He kissed the top of my head. "Summer, apart from commissions, you may consider anything I paint, or art I create of any kind, yours for the asking."

I nuzzled my nose against his cheek and breathed him in. "Love of my life," I mouthed soundlessly against his skin.

"Chocolate with fudgy bits, or..." Jonny looked at the other tub of ice cream he was holding up, "vanilla with honeycomb bits?"

I was amused. "I don't mind, you choose."

"Um... okay, both." He tossed the two tubs into the already groaning little M&S shopping trolley.

I wasn't sure when I'd ever seen Jonny enjoying himself so much. With my visit as an excuse, he'd decided to indulge in a huge M&S Foodhall splurge; he was like a kid in a candy store. We'd come into the shop having decided to get supplies for a few days so we wouldn't have to leave our little love nest if we didn't want to, but I estimated we now had enough food for at least a week, possibly two. I was entirely happy with this prospect.

He added a bag of frozen French fries to the cart, which already contained: a roast chicken, two types of pizza, three different varieties of cheese, various salad foods and vegetables, multiple tubs of potato salad, coleslaw and pasta salad, burgers, herby chicken pieces, a loaf of bread, two types of bread roll, chocolate croissants, strawberry jam, fancy tea bags, Columbian coffee for his cafetière, milk, butter, cream, three different types of fruit, bacon, eggs, a quiche, sausages and two tubs of fancy pasta sauces with accompanying fresh pasta. I was just relieved some of it was freezable; there was no way we were getting through all this. But watching him enjoying this shopping trip was one of the best things I'd ever seen.

We reached the wine aisle and he assessed the packed cart. "Are we going to need another trolley?"

I started moving things around and arranging them more efficiently. "No, it'll be fine." He started surveying the shelves of red. "I'm not sure we're not going to need a little trailer to get all this home with your tiny car, though," I teased him. "Do you *have* a tow bar?"

He grinned at me. "Don't be silly, Summer. I've already arranged for an airlift."

I giggled, and he held up a Californian Cabernet Sauvignon for my approval. I nodded.

Having somehow found room for six assorted bottles of wine and four beers for good measure, he tossed some chocolate chip cookies and crisps on top of the pile and announced himself done. "Is there anything you want to add?" he asked.

"If it's not already in there, I'm pretty sure I can live without it." We made our way to the checkouts.

We were rolling our purchases across the car park towards the MG when my phone binged with a text, apparently encouraged to do so by the retail park's reliable mobile signal. I took it out of my pocket: Jenna. I pulled up the text, which was just a photo. I touched the image file and it enlarged itself on the screen. It was a selfie of Jenna, in a red lacy bra, with sexy tousled hair, standing by a large window, through which you could see the sea in the distance. She was pulling an 'Oh my God! Can you believe this!' face.

We reached the car, and Jonny started to load shopping bags into the boot. I peered closely at the screen, examining the photo. I quickly recognised the view through the window as Crantock Bay, and I frowned, trying to work out where the photo had been taken. Then I realised: it must have been taken from a room in Richard Schofield's big new house in the dunes, the one my father so highly disapproved of.

I started giggling, and Jonny looked over at me. "What?" he said.

I was shaking with laughter. "Jenna." I showed him the photo.

He rolled his eyes and gave a little shake of the head, but he was smiling.

I minimised the photo and typed a reply: 'So, what type of trollop *are* you, exactly? Please report back!' I added a *boggling eyes* emoji and a *crying laughing* emoji and pressed 'Send'.

Early evening, pleasantly surfeit of roast chicken, potato salad, green salad and vanilla honeycomb ice cream, we were finishing the washing up. He was washing and I was drying.

"What do you think we should do with the kitchen?" he said. "Cheryl said I can either fix up what's here or put in new units, and anything I spend she'll take off the rent."

"Cheryl?" I said.

"My landlord."

"Ah, okay." I looked at him. "What's the story with that anyway?"

"Oh, well, you remember back when I was stuck living with my parents?"

I nodded.

"Well, I was in this gallery in St Ives talking to the owner. I'd taken in a few small oils to show him to see if he thought he could sell them. He was being pretty decent about it, said he'd put them on display and see if there was any interest. Anyway, Cheryl was in there looking for some art for a couple of her holiday lets – she owns four or five – and she overheard me asking him if he knew of any cheap flats for rent in the area. She came over and said she had this place in Gwithian. She couldn't let it out as a holiday home because it was too basic for what people are looking for now in Cornwall, and she couldn't afford to do the necessary upgrades at the time. So she asked me if I wanted to live in it for a minimal rent, as it would be better for her to have it occupied, and at least that way she'd get some income for it while she was waiting to do it up."

"Makes sense."

"She also looked at my paintings and said she really liked them and would enjoy giving a break to a new artist. She even bought one of them."

"What fabulous luck!" I said.

"Yeah. Anyway, as you can imagine, I couldn't believe it when I looked at the place and saw the deck and the studio space out back. It was like the universe was really on my side for once. I moved in right away, and well, you know the rest."

"And she's never raised the rent or asked you to move out?"

He shook his head. "I pay her more rent now that I can

afford it, of course, but she's basically left me alone. She comes by from time to time to say hello and check out my latest work – she's bought a few more paintings from me – but otherwise she's never given me any indication she wants me to leave, and, frankly, I'm not looking to examine the teeth of this particular gift horse."

I folded my lips to suppress a smile. I was entirely sure that Cheryl was an art lover and undoubtedly enjoyed Jonny's work, but I couldn't help suspecting that the work of art she admired the most was the living, breathing one standing in front of me. "I'm so happy this place has worked out so well for you."

He handed me the last wet plate with a soft smile chaser. "Thank you, me too."

Over the next couple of days, we spent our hours exactly as we pleased: walking the nearby beaches and coastal paths, indulging in our favourite foods, drinking wine and doing our best to make up for lost time in bed. Jonny reinstated me as his muse-in-residence, and I'd wake to find him sitting nearby, pencil in hand and sketch pad on his knees, his focus on his subject absolute. I'd smile and meet his eyes and I could see the happiness – and even a hint of relief – in his own to finally have what he'd desired for so long safely within reach. And in turn, it made me happier than I could have ever imagined to give him what he'd longed for.

By the evening of the 29th, though, I was facing up to the fact that the real world was going to have to be interacted with again soon, extremely regrettable as that was. I wanted more clothes from home and to pick up other assorted belongings from my parents' house. It was now taken as read that Jonny's cottage would be my home base in Cornwall going forward.

"Can you drive me back to Crantock tomorrow?" I asked. "I want to pick up some things, and I really should say hello to my parents."

Jonny put the cream he'd used for our coffee back in the fridge. "Of course."

I was sitting at the breakfast bar waiting for my coffee to cool. "And tell me about this New Year's Eve party you mentioned. What do I need to wear?"

He took a cautious sip from his own mug. "It's at the Tate St Ives. They're throwing a party for various members of the Cornwall 'great and good' who are art lovers. I think fundraising will be encouraged. A number of local artists were asked to provide works to be shown on the evening, and I'm one of those, so I've also been invited."

I boggled at him and then laughed. "Oh, my God! I love how you just casually mention this now."

He looked at me, confused. "I told you we'd been invited to a New Year's Eve party."

"Yes, but you didn't tell me it was some big shindig for rich people at the Tate, with you being one of the main attractions."

"My *art* possibly being one of the minor attractions," he corrected me.

"You say potato, I say potahto."

He grinned at me.

"Anyway, do you think the dress I wore at the Christmas party would be okay?" I frowned. "I just hope I can get away without having it cleaned."

He was far too amused by my state of discombobulation. "I'm sure it'll be fine."

"Will it be too much, though? What does the invitation say?"

"I've no idea, I haven't seen one. I just know it starts at

eight."

I rolled my eyes and huffed at him. "What are you wearing?"

"I have a dark navy suit I wear for these types of things, with a white shirt. I was going to wear that."

"Hmm… okay. I'll talk to my mother and see what she thinks I should do."

"Good idea. But I honestly think whatever you decide will be fine. This isn't London. No one will mind unless you turn up completely naked." His mouth spread into a slow smile. "Although…"

I raised an eyebrow. "I'm afraid my nakedness is off-limits to anyone but you for the foreseeable."

He twinkled at me. "Happy to hear it."

"Anyway, yes, I'll sort something out tomorrow. Can you drive us back in the morning? I want to try and fit in another meet-up with Jenna before I go back to London." I thought about the red bra photo. My phone hadn't been able to pick up a sufficient mobile signal to receive a reply from her since I'd sent my text outside Marks. I was dying to hear what had happened with Richard, and to update her on the situation with me and Jonny. I was frankly astounded at how well that was going and feeling even more of an idiot for how long it had taken me to pursue a serious relationship with him. Jenna was going to be treated to a really spectacular opportunity for many 'I Told You So's, and I didn't want to deprive her of it; I was ready to take my medicine.

"Sure," Jonny said. "No problem." He took a beat. "Summer…?"

"Yes?"

"As our little break is coming to an end, I wanted to ask you… did I pass the test?"

I looked at him. "Test?"

His eyes on mine were soft and sexy, and I just kind of wanted him to kiss me. "Yes, the test to see whether you want to come live with me and be my love."

I smiled at his reference to the Marlowe love poem. "There wasn't a test."

"Eh…" he tipped his head, "it kind of feels like there was."

"A test from me for you?" I wasn't entirely sure I liked where this was going.

"Maybe."

I shook my head. "No test. I just wanted us to be able to take some time and see if we could stand to live together in the same house." I fixed an eye on him. "But it wasn't a test for you. It was just a little try-out for both of us. I mean, I could've loved being here with you while I drove you nuts. Maybe you'd hate that I took too long in the shower and used up most of the hot water, or left drool on the pillow, or forgot to put the milk back in the fridge. I mean, you can love the idea of someone, but the reality of them taking up space in your daily life can irritate you. So it seemed important to test that out before making any irreversible decisions."

He was laughing. "I knew I wouldn't care about any of that crap."

"Well, you say that now…"

He became serious. "Summer, I knew I wanted you to live with me… for us to live together. I never had even the slightest doubt about it. It's always been you for me. So, yes, in reality, I needed to pass your test."

I gave another little huff. "I still maintain 'test' is too harsh a term. I mean, how much time have we really spent together as adults? Not that much. It's true that the connection between us has never been severed, even if it has ebbed and flowed, but neither of us could know how much of the affection we still felt for one another was based on our friendship when we were younger, and our unproven ideas and wishes for what we could be to one another in the future. So it was important we spend some quality time together to assess whether we thought our relationship would be able to stand up to reality."

He looked at me fondly. "So sensible."

I smiled. "Well, I'm not the artist."

"For the record, I never had any uncertainty. I was sure that, for my part, I'd always want you." He took a beat. "Did you really have doubts?"

I met his gaze, enjoying that its intensity never frightened me now, that my feelings for him could go toe to toe with his for me and hold their own. "Not in my heart."

He smiled. "So I passed the… assessment."

I laughed. "With flying colours. A+, eleven out of ten, first class honours degree."

"Is that my answer? Are you letting me off the wait until midnight on New Year's Eve?"

I gave him a twinkle. "Now where would the fun be in that?"

As we snuggled together in bed that night, drifting off to sleep, I reflected back over the past few days and felt a wave of disbelief about how much a person's life could change in the space of a relatively short time. A year ago I would have had difficulty believing that only a year later I would be lying here, in Jonny's arms, with all my worries and concerns mere memories, my future almost settled, completely happy with the direction my life was now taking. Back then, everything had seemed so impossibly complicated.

Part Eleven

1 Year Ago

We turned right off the main road onto the lane down towards Crantock, and almost immediately had to slow down behind a caravan. I bit back a smile. It was two years since I'd been in Cornwall, and I was as excited to be back as a 5-year-old on Christmas morning. And there was really nothing more 'Cornwall' than getting stuck behind a slow-moving caravan on a narrow lane, unable to get past.

While turning down this road towards home just before Christmas was something I'd done many times before, there was a significant difference this time to any of my previous journeys. Rather than my father in the driver's seat, it was my boyfriend, Neil. And I wasn't sitting in the passenger seat of my father's Jaguar saloon, but rather the equally comfortable seat of Neil's Audi.

Neil was being patient behind the caravan. Neil was always calm and patient. We'd just driven the almost 300 miles from Islington to Newquay, stopping only twice, at services outside Bristol and Exeter, and, even when cars had slowed to a crawl for a while on the M5 outside Bristol, he'd not shown a flicker of annoyance. He just took it all in his stride, using the opportunity of stop/start traffic to look over and check on me and squeeze my hand encouragingly when I'd started talking excitedly again about Cornwall.

Following my direction, Neil pulled the Audi into my parents' driveway and parked behind my father's car. As if she'd been waiting in the hallway, my mother opened the front door and came skipping down the steps towards us, followed, at a distinctly more leisurely pace, by my father. Fond greetings were exchanged on all sides. Neil had met my parents twice before. Somehow or other, by means which escaped me as I'd never managed to do it, he'd persuaded them to come up and visit us in London during both the previous summers. Although I suspected the five-star hotel he paid for them to stay in for two nights each time might have had something to do with it.

Bags and presents were removed from the boot, and everyone traipsed into the house. My father and Neil took our luggage up to my room, and I followed my mother into the kitchen.

"Good journey?" she said.

"Fine. Comfortable. I have to admit, it was nice to be driven down rather than have to deal with the train."

My mother filled and flicked on the kettle. "And a very nice car to be driven in."

I smiled, picking up on her point. "Yes. I'm very lucky."

"So you're here until the 30th?"

"Yes. I'm supposed to be seeing Jenna tonight for a catch-up, then your Christmas Eve party tomorrow, of course. Christmas Day and Boxing Day with you and Dad. Then I thought I'd show Neil around Cornwall over the following few days. Incredibly, he's never been here before. Then driving home to London on the 30th. We have a New Year's Eve party to go to in London, some bash at Coq d'Argent with views over the City. Then a friend of Neil's with a flat overlooking the Thames is having a drinks party for people to watch the fireworks."

"Well, that all sounds extremely glamorous."

I laughed. "It does, doesn't it!"

"I'm glad you were able to fit us in down here in little old Cornwall for Christmas."

"Oh, Mum!" I said. "You know I love it here."

My mother gave me a scolding look. "Well, you didn't make it last year. And the year before you were only here for two days before you had to go back!"

"Well, the year before last was a hellish work year when I couldn't get any more time off. And last year I had to go to Neil's parents with him, as you very well know. And he's here with you this year, so everything's now fair and square, is it not?"

My mother conceded the point. "Well, alright. I'm not sure I like the idea of seeing you only every other Christmas, though. I'm sure I don't need to tell you that you were very much missed last year."

I gave her a hug. "You don't have to, but it's still nice to hear."

"Your father, particularly, was quite bereft."

"And I'm sorry for that. But you know that most families split their time over Christmas between the two sides. It's just unfortunate that with his parents in Cambridgeshire and you down here, it's not possible to be with one of you on Christmas Day and one on Boxing Day. So we're going to have to even things up year on year."

My mother raised an eyebrow. "So things are still all very settled and serious, then?"

"Yes. We've been living together for eight months now, and we haven't had a major falling out once. And of course, his flat is lovely."

In April I'd moved out of the flat I was sharing with a workmate in Chiswick into Neil's gorgeous, perfectly decorated, luxury apartment on one of the better squares in Islington. It was an immeasurable step up from anywhere else I'd lived in London, and I absolutely loved it. It was true that it was already entirely decorated and furnished to Neil's taste, but his taste *was* excellent and he'd been perfectly happy for me to add my own photos (in appropriately coordinating frames, obviously) to various surfaces, and my own books to his shelves, even some of the tattier paperbacks. And he'd scrupulously cleared out half the wardrobe and drawer space for my possessions. He paid the mortgage and all the bills (which he said was perfectly reasonable considering how much more he earned than I did, as a partner in his architecture firm), and I bought food and flowers and paid my half of the council tax. So, although it might have been argued that I was simply a very pampered guest who made generous contributions to the household by way of recompense, the flat still felt sufficiently like home.

"Any sign your father will be needing to pay for any large parties in the near future?"

I rolled my eyes at her. "If by 'large parties' you mean a wedding reception, he hasn't asked me yet."

"And there haven't been any signs? He's not been pulling you over to peer in jewellers' windows as you pass by, or anything of that nature?"

I couldn't help smiling at her. "No, nothing of that nature."

My mother pursed her lips and poured hot water into the teapot. "And you're okay with that?"

"Mum! I'm fine with it. Work is going well, and we're

both busy. My life is finally good. Don't worry about me!"

"Okay, okay." She pulled plates and mugs out of the cupboard and moved about the kitchen, laying things out. "So, you're seeing Jenna tonight?"

"Yes. She can't come to your party tomorrow because she has to go to a thing with Tom..." My mother looked at me inquiringly. "The latest boyfriend." My mother nodded. "She sends her regrets and apologies, by the way. I got the distinct impression she'd rather have come here. But anyway, I'm going to hers to catch up with her this evening to make sure I don't miss her. We stay in touch online but I haven't seen her in two years."

My mother got a Christmas cake out of the larder and set it down on the kitchen table. "You've definitely been away too long, Summer," she said.

Just before eight that evening, Neil pulled up outside the block of flats Jenna was now living in on the outskirts of Newquay. The flats were new, modern and very nice, and I knew – because she'd made it clear with both commentary and many posts on her Instagram – that she was extremely excited to be living here. She shared with a girl she'd met through work, who was away staying with her parents in Devon for Christmas, so, rather than our spending money in a crowded bar for our much-anticipated reunion, she'd invited me to come and visit her home of only two months, promising there'd be no shortage of wine and that she'd have raided Sainsbury's for multiple food options.

I put my hand on the car door handle. "Ready?" I said to him.

He smiled at me. "As I'll ever be."

I was under strict instructions to bring Neil up to say hello when he dropped me off, a request he was happy to comply with. He was not a little curious about "the infamous Jenna" himself.

I pressed her flat's number on the intercom, and the main door buzzed open without any interrogation. Clearly the security concerns governing entrance to flats' communal areas were not the same in Cornwall as they were in London. We climbed the stairs to her second-floor apartment, and she was already holding the front door open as we arrived.

"Jesus Christ, Summer! Are you a sight for sore eyes!" She pulled me into a long, tight hug, which I returned with equal enthusiasm. When I was finally able to extricate myself, and had handed over the bottle of Pinot Grigio I'd pinched from my parents' kitchen, I turned to introduce Neil.

Her eyes popped slightly as I did so, and I could see her Having An Opinion. But she just said a very friendly "Hello! Great to meet you at last!" and asked if she could get us a glass of wine.

Neil was a bit fussy about the wine he drank, so I was relieved when she took a nice New Zealand Sauvignon Blanc out of the fridge. She filled three glasses a very civilised halfway and handed them over.

"Come and look at the balcony," she said.

It was a bit chilly to be drinking outside in December, but as we followed her out onto the really quite decent-sized space with its glass balustrade, I could see why she wanted to show it off. It had fantastic views over the tops of the houses below to Fistral Beach and the bay beyond. In the summer, this would be a stunning spot for alfresco drinking and dining. No wonder she was delighted with her new home.

"Wow!" I said. "This is fab!"

"I know! Isn't it?"

I was very happy for her that her excitement in the place didn't seem to be diminishing with time.

"I'm trying to make sure I get on friendly terms with all the neighbours so I don't get any complaints if we hold plenty of parties in the summer. Although a bunch of the flats here are holiday lets, so I'm not really bothered about them." She looked at Neil. "Did you have a good drive down?"

Wow, Jenna doing small talk. We were all so grown up now.

Neil smiled. "Yes, thank you. No problems. And it's good to let the Audi's engine stretch its legs from time to time. It spends far too much time sitting on the street not moving, to be honest."

Jenna nodded seriously, as if she completely understood the problem.

"Do you still have Lucia?" I asked. "Lucia's Jenna's pretty little Fiat," I explained to Neil.

Jenna nodded. "I do. She hasn't let me down yet, so we're still good friends."

I laughed. "I'm glad to hear it."

Neil finished his wine and decided to make himself scarce. "Well, thanks so much, Jenna. It was very nice to meet you. But I think I'll let you ladies catch up now." He looked at me. "Do call me to come and get you if you can't get a taxi easily."

"Thanks, hon." We followed him inside to the door, and I reached up to give him a quick kiss. "See you later."

Jenna said, "Goodbye," and we both gave him a wave as he walked back towards the stairs. Jenna shut the door, and I followed her back to the kitchen, where she retrieved the wine from the fridge and topped up both our glasses to a good three-quarters full.

I hitched myself up onto a stool at the breakfast bar and watched while she moved about the kitchen preparing snacks. She tipped a large bag of Kettle Chips into a bowl and spooned out onion dip into another smaller one. Then she switched on the oven to preheat for... well, I wasn't quite sure what yet, but it would undoubtedly help with wine consumption.

She gave me the dip to carry and picked up the crisps and her glass of wine and led us over to the sofa. She put the crisps down on the coffee table and I did the same with the dip.

"So," she said, "Jesus Christ, I can't even believe how good it is to see you! How is it two years – two years! – since you were last down here?"

I shook my head but smiled. "Just, don't! I've already had a ticking-off from my mother about the length of time I've been away."

She raised an eyebrow at me. "Well, too long away from Cornwall is not good for anyone's health, let alone someone who loves it like you do."

"I know, I know. If there was any invention I really wish the scientists would sort out it would be a teleportation device, so I'd be able to pop down here every weekend. Or every other weekend, at least."

She looked at me doubtfully. "And work really keeps you that busy?"

"Well, work's not as bad as it was. Since my move to the new company and promotion to Senior Manager at the beginning of the year..."

"Oh, yeah! Congrats on that, by the way!"

"Thanks. Anyway, since then, I've got five more holiday days a year, and I'm much more able to control the demands on my time. That's how I was able to get so much time off for Christmas this year. But now, of course, I also have to include time with Neil in my plans. So... Yeah, it's still difficult to get down here."

Jenna nodded. "He seems very nice, by the way."

I smiled. "Thanks. I'm glad you were able to meet him at last. And he was looking forward to meeting 'the famous Jenna'."

"Oh, God! What did you tell him about me?"

"Nothing you wouldn't be happy I told him."

"I'm not sure what that would include. But I trust your judgement. And he didn't seem afraid of me, or anything, so I guess you did a decent job."

I laughed. "Thanks. Although, to be fair, Neil isn't really afraid of anyone. He's always pretty confident and self-assured, whoever we're meeting."

Jenna looked at me, considering. "Yeah, he seems like a pretty smooth type."

I raised an eyebrow. "Is that a good thing or a bad thing?"

"Oh, good, I'm sure."

"But...?"

Jenna shook her head. "No, no 'But'. He's just very... London."

"Very 'London'?"

Jenna nodded. "Yes. You know. Very urbane. Sophisticated. Sure of himself. We don't really grow them like that down here."

I considered. "You're probably right. I hadn't really noticed."

"Had you not?"

I shrugged. "I guess there are a lot of people like that up there. So it's not like he's particularly different in that way or anything."

Jenna nodded, and I could see her trying to decide what to say next.

"What?" I said. I couldn't help but sense a sort of distance developing between us that I'd never felt before, and I didn't like it one bit.

Jenna plunged in. "So, are you happy with him?"

I nodded and said firmly. "Yes, I am. He's kind and considerate, and great in bed." I looked at Jenna to make sure she was taking that point on board. "And we love to do the same things – museums and the theatre and movies. And he's really intelligent – he doesn't just view things in black and white terms, but he sees all the complexities and nuances in a situation."

"You sound like you're writing a recommendation for him for TripAdvisor."

I frowned at her. "Jenna!"

"Sorry, that's honestly not intended to sound mean. He sounds very nice, and I really am glad you get along so well with him, I guess what I'm asking – and I feel that as, possibly, your oldest friend I should be allowed to do this – is… do you love him?"

I looked at her, and I was terribly afraid I took a beat too long to answer when I said, "Yes."

I could tell I'd failed some sort of test with the extra microsecond I took to reply, because she looked at me unconvinced. "Really?"

I was ready for her this time, so I immediately said more firmly, "Yes!"

"So, what is it you love about him, exactly?"

I crinkled my brow. "What does any woman love about any man? There are the things I told you about…"

"Which, apart from the 'great in bed' bit – regarding

which, congrats! – is the kind of thing you'd say about any good friend. What I'm asking, Summer – and again, I appreciate I'm leaning pretty heavily on old friend privileges here – is: Does he set your heart racing when you see him and your loins aflame when he kisses you?"

I set my jaw. "I love spending time with him and having sex with him, and I'm always really happy to see him."

She wasn't backing down. "Not what I asked."

I let out a substantial huff of irritation. "Okay, I know what you want to know, and since you're apparently not going to let it go until I tell you, I will." I gave her some stink eye. "You're lucky I do love you so much and don't want to lose you as a friend, because you're on seriously thin ice here."

Jenna's expression was neutral. "I am aware."

"Okay then. I know what you want to know is whether I love him like I loved Jonny."

Jenna nodded. "Pretty much."

I sighed. "Honestly, Jenna? No, I don't think I do." I took a large sip of my wine. "But I'm not sure that's such a bad thing. Neil might not set me on fire like Jonny did, but he won't destroy me either. And just because the love I have for Neil is different, I don't think that means it's in some way a lesser thing. It's just... different. Neil treats me really well. He's thoughtful and kind, and we have a really nice life together. We live in a lovely flat and don't have to worry about money. And we go to interesting places. And even have a few decent, worthwhile friends." I wasn't entirely sure my eyes weren't pleading for understanding. "I've waited a really long time to be living this kind of life, and I'm happy with it, okay? Not everyone – in fact, hardly anyone at all – gets to live some spectacular life with someone who sets them alight every time they walk in the room. I've come to terms with the fact I'm not going to have that, and that's okay. What I have is pretty great." I looked at her. "And I hope you can be happy for me about that."

Jenna looked a bit taken back by the force of my little speech. "God, Summer! *Of course* I'm happy for you if you're happy. I guess it's just that… Well, as you say, most people don't get to live their life with someone who sets them alight whenever they walk in the room. Most of us never even *meet* anyone who can do that for us. But you did. And not only that, but he loved you back. And not just for five minutes. But for years. I know you think I'm a pain about Jonny, it's just… Well, in a way I've always thought that what you had with him was what I always wanted for myself with someone. And not in the way that I was jealous of you, of course, but, well, I love you and wanted you to have it. Have him. And perhaps there was something of, well… if you two could work it out, maybe there was hope for the rest of us. But if you couldn't, then, what hope really is there for the rest of us? Plus, it's just annoying to see two people so clearly meant for one another, like you and Jonny, not make it work. I'm sorry, but it just is. It's like… You've been given this incredible gift, something that most of us never even get to experience, and you've just chucked it away. I've gotta be honest, Summer, it's pretty fucking heartbreaking to think you've done that."

I looked at her, hardly knowing what to say. I shook my head. "I'm not sure whether to be insulted, or overwhelmed by your concern for me." I tried to sort through her words in my head. "I do realise that what you just said comes from a place of love for me."

Jenna looked slightly apologetic. "Then can we focus

on that?"

I gave her a wry smile. "Sure. But there's something else you need to know about me and Jonny..."

"Yes?"

"After the last time I saw him, you remember, that time we went to his house in Gwithian and Amber was there. And then he came to see me and we went to Polly Joke?"

Jenna nodded.

"Well, do you remember he posted that photo on Instagram of him and her just the next day? The super lovey-dovey one?"

Jenna rolled her eyes. "Jesus Christ! How could I forget? I mean, as you know, I'm usually a Jonny supporter, but that was one major dick move."

"It was. Well, anyway, I know you know I was upset about him moving on with Amber. Even though I was in London and had said he should... blah, blah, blah." I waved my hand dismissively.

Jenna nodded.

"But the thing is, Jen, I know on an intellectual level it wasn't reasonable, and I hadn't expected to feel that way before it happened, but... it almost destroyed me."

Jenna looked at me, her eyes wide.

"It wasn't like I was upset for a bit, and then I got on with it and started dating other people, and I was fine a few months later. For the first few weeks after that, I could hardly function. It felt like the greatest loss of my life. And then for months afterwards I felt awful. All the time. The pain of it filled my chest every day. I got through my work days, but otherwise I had barely any life. I just ate and watched TV in the evenings, and did housework and chores at the weekend, before going back to work on Mondays. It took a good six months before I even began to come out from under. I didn't Unfollow Jonny on Instagram, but I muted his account so I never had to risk seeing anything like that post with Amber. I only really began to live again after I met Neil in November that year and we started going out. We got on so well, and we went lots of great places, and he made me feel loved and wanted again. And since then, my life has been going better and better until I'm where I am now. So, can you see why I want to hold on to what I have with Neil? Why I don't want to risk it for the significant chance of pain and misery that might – and, given our history, probably would – be the result of any further dealings with Jonny Rawlings?"

"Jesus, Summer," Jenna said.

"Not to mention, as far as I'm aware, Jonny's still with Amber. Isn't that your information?"

Jenna nodded, looking awkward.

"I think you'd have heard on the grapevine if they'd split. So, much as you might want me to give up my London life and come back down here to try and peel him away from Amber, I'm not sure it'd be quite as easy for me to do that as you think it would. Even if I wanted to do it. Which I don't."

Jenna looked at me, shamefaced. "Christ, Summer, I feel like both an idiot and a nosy bitch. I'd no idea it had been so hard for you after finding out about Amber. I guess, because I've always been convinced you could have him back any time you wanted, I assumed you thought the same way." She chewed on her bottom lip. "I didn't realise you didn't."

I sighed. "The thing is, I know the idea of us has always been one of a great romance to you. And, sure, our relationship has had its moments. But it was pretty clear to me that he wanted Amber. And it's not like, after he knew I was upset he was with her, he dropped everything and came running up to London to beg for me back. I mean, he could've done, if he'd really wanted to. But he didn't. So what was I supposed to think?"

Jenna looked a bit sick. "You're right. He totally let you go. I've been way too quick to call you out for not following through with Jonny, but he didn't follow through with you, either." Her eyes were full of disappointment. "He's a fucking idiot."

I shrugged. "Our lives just went in different directions. He's not any more an idiot than I am. He's done his best to build a life for himself and be happy, just as I've done, and I don't blame him for that." I gave her a smile. "I'm just sorry we didn't give you the happy ending you always wanted for us."

She managed to return my smile. "S'okay. I know you would have if you could have."

"I really would've."

She looked at me uncertainly. "Can I just make one more possibly Jonny-related comment before we move on?"

I eyed her cautiously. "Okay..."

"Well, you're aware that Neil looks a bit like him, right?"

I rolled my eyes at her. "Just because Neil also has dark, curly hair does not mean he looks like Jonny."

"Sure, but he's also tall like Jonny."

"Not as tall as Jonny," I corrected her.

"But still tall."

I conceded the point.

"And he's good-looking," said Jenna.

We both smiled at one another and started to crack up. "But not as good-looking as Jonny," we said together, and burst into laughter more suited to a couple of teenage girls.

I calmed down. "Oh, God! You're making me feel horribly disloyal. Stop it!"

Jenna mimed pulling a zip across her mouth.

"And," I said, "to be fair, no one is as good-looking as Jonny. I mean, if I was determined to hold out for that, I'd be dead before I achieved that particular goal. Not to mention, most men that good-looking are serious arseholes. Jonny's a definite aberration in that regard."

"Maybe he took classes for that Instagram stunt with Amber."

I nodded. "I guess that's a possible explanation." I looked at my wine. "Did you spike this or something? Because so far this evening I've spilled my guts about years of emotional pain, been horribly disloyal to the man I love, and you've got me giggling like a schoolgirl about the hotness of another man I should no longer be thinking about in such an inappropriate way. You're a terrible influence!"

Jenna shrugged and just looked smug. "I do my best."

The next couple of days passed very pleasantly. Neil was, naturally, a huge hit at my parents' party, which went off swimmingly, and thus left my mother in an excellent mood. Christmas Day church was lovely and festive, and Neil ingratiated himself further by attending. And further still by offering to help my mother peel vegetables for lunch. She refused to allow it, but the offer was noted. By the morning of Boxing Day, I'd eaten and drunk far too much for three days in a row, and I urgently wanted to stretch my legs and see the sea. The weather was grey and cold, but I knew the dogs wouldn't mind, so I decided to take them out. Neil offered to accompany me, but he did so while looking extremely comfortably tucked up in bed, so I told him to stay put. I wasn't looking for company anyway.

I was in the kitchen, finishing up a cup of tea and preparing to get ready to go out, when my mother came in. I looked up in surprise as she closed the kitchen door to the hallway.

"Summer, there's something I need to make you aware of before you go out."

"Goodness, Mum. Was there a secret toxic spill on Crantock Beach, or something?"

My mother pursed her lips. "Don't be silly. No, I just need to let you know... I was talking to Barbara at the party, and she mentioned that Jonny's staying with them over Christmas."

My heart started pumping like I was running for the last 'copter out of 'Nam. I could see from my mother's expression that my face told her all she needed to know about how I was receiving her news. "Er... what? He doesn't live that far away. And he has a car. Why's he staying with them?"

"Well," my mother couldn't entirely hide her enjoyment that she was about to impart some Grade A gossip. "Apparently Jonny broke up with his girlfriend – Amelia, was it?"

"Amber," I said.

"Okay. Well, apparently he broke up with her about a month ago, and he's been very withdrawn and not really looking after himself properly, just working all the time. Anyway, Barbara's been worried about him, so, it took some effort, but she persuaded him to spend time with them over Christmas."

I couldn't stop myself asking. "Why did they break up?"

My mother was getting into her stride. "Barbara said she thought it was something to do with Jonny's refusal to commit. Apparently... Amber? Amber... had talked to Barbara about it, wondering if she could offer any advice. Which she couldn't, of course. I mean, a man either wants to marry a woman or he doesn't. Anyway, Barbara thinks Amber finally ran out of patience and that was the reason for the split."

I swallowed, feeling like someone had just tossed a grenade in and it was sitting there, ticking – or whatever it is grenades do – threatening to blow up my life. If there was one thing I was sure of, it was that I must not, under any circumstances, bump into Jonny Rawlings while I was in Cornwall.

But neither did I want to become a prisoner in my parents' home. And not taking the dogs out just because Jonny was possibly sleeping, or watching TV, or whatever it was he did on Boxing Day mornings in a house on the other side of the village, was an impingement on my freedom I was unwilling to submit to.

"Okay, Mum. Well, thanks for telling me."

"I just thought you should know."

I raised an eyebrow. "About the split with Amber or him staying in Crantock?"

"Both?"

I couldn't suppress a smile. "Well, okay then." Lucy came up to me wagging her extravagant, golden retriever tail and nuzzled my thigh. "Okay, girl," I said, reaching down to stroke her head. I looked at my mother. "I'm going to take the dogs out. I'm in need of a good walk. I'm not sure exactly how long I'll be, but I'll be back in plenty of time to help with lunch."

"Okay, darling." My mother smiled, evidently feeling she'd fulfilled her duty of care on the Jonny Warning front.

The dogs and I hustled out of the house and set off down the lane. We took our usual route down Beach Road towards the coast path, but when we reached the car park, I stopped. If we went left, as we usually did, we'd either have to walk on the beach or take the path towards West Pentire. If Jonny were out and about by any chance, those were the two most likely locations where he'd be. His paintings were all about the sea and its skies; North Cornwall's beaches and coastal paths were his office. But if we went right, taking the path along the banks of the River Gannel, we had much less chance of bumping into him, even if he wasn't tucked up at home.

I called the dogs to me from where they were sniffing around by the gate to the dunes and surprised them by turning right. We climbed up and joined the path through the high hedgerows that edged the Gannel, mostly bare of foliage at this time of year. I strode quickly, breathing deeply, relieved to be out and about. This stretch of path was quiet even during the summer, and there was no one around now. I realised how much I'd missed having quality time to myself over recent years. It had always been work or social gatherings or chores or Neil. Sometimes I wasn't entirely sure where Summer had got to amongst it all.

The tide was in and the Gannel was flowing. A lone kayaker paddled past, making towards the sea. I looked longingly towards the 'millionaires' row' houses on the opposite bank, with their spectacular views and gardens tumbling steeply down to the river. If I ever won the lottery, a home there would be at the top of my list.

We manoeuvred our way through a kissing gate, crossed an open field and came to where Penpol Creek joined the Gannel. Then through the woods, across another field and out onto the lane. We climbed the gentle slope of Penpol Hill to the stile across the meadow, and I picked up Donald and popped him over. Lucy treated me to longing eyes and I did the same for her. As we started cutting across the field to the lane which would take us back into the village, I realised I'd made a terrible mistake. Because this loop, which we'd started on by turning right rather than left in the car park by the beach, took a route which led inevitably past Jonny's parents' house on our way home. The only way to avoid this would be to take a huge detour, much of which involved walking down the main road into Crantock and West Pentire, which was always populated by fast moving cars at all hours. I'd neither the time to walk that route, nor the inclination to risk the dogs' lives by walking them along a busy road.

I mentally kicked myself for my stupidity, but honestly, I'd been between a rock and a hard place. I would just have to walk as quickly as possible past the house and hope he wasn't waiting by the gate to jump out and surprise me. I honestly thought the chances of that were slim.

We started down the lane, and before we got too far I called the dogs to me and attached them both to their leads. I didn't want either of them finding a particularly interesting smell that had them dawdling outside Jonny's parents' house. We approached the hazard in question walking at a good pace – both dogs were behaving and I thought we were going to make it past without incident – when suddenly Donald caught wind of another dog's scent and tugged me to the side, with Lucy joining in momentarily. Barbara's latest Dalmatian appeared on the other side of their gate, and Lucy and Donald started barking excitedly at her, with her joining in the racket. I was absolutely mortified and started scolding them and trying to tug them away, but it was no good; they were absolutely not having it.

"Daisy! Hush!" Barbara appeared from around the back of the house in Wellington boots and a Barbour.

"Oh, God!" I said, as she saw me and approached the gate. "I'm so sorry. I've no idea what's got into them."

"Oh, hello, Summer!" she said cheerily. "This bunch are quite the friendly clique, I'm afraid. I suspect they won't be happy until they've said a proper hello and sniffed one another's bums sufficiently." She opened the gate, and the dogs pulled me through. "Come in, do!" She closed the gate behind me. "Let them off the lead for a bit. They can all get rid of some energy in the garden."

I did as she said and unclipped the dogs' leads. They tore off towards the back garden in pursuit of Daisy. My heart was pumping so hard in panic that I might see Jonny, I was afraid I might pass out. I kept my eyes deliberately averted from the house, praying that, if indeed he was in, he'd take pity on me and keep himself out of sight.

"Why don't you come in for a coffee? I've just made some fresh," Barbara said.

I eyed the house like it was covered in bees. I managed a weak smile, desperately trying to think of an excuse. "I really should be getting back. I'm supposed to be helping Mum with lunch."

"Oh, I'm sure she won't mind. You've got plenty of time for that."

She was right, of course, on both counts. My mother was far more likely to mind if I offended one of her best friends by using her as an excuse to make a hurried exit and refuse a perfectly civil invitation for no good reason.

My smile tightened. "Okay then, that would be lovely, thanks."

Barbara led me to the side door to the kitchen and went in, removing her boots and jacket on the allocated tiled area. I followed her, not having been so unwilling to step foot inside a building since I'd had to enter the science block to take a second-year chemistry exam I was entirely unprepared for. I wiped my feet by the door but didn't remove my jacket. I looked around the kitchen; it was exactly the same as I remembered from my time spent here with Jonny all those years ago. It even smelled the same. As I stood there, the familiarity of everything enveloped me, and the memory of those days clutched at me like soft paws.

"I'm sorry, you've missed Jonny," Barbara said, apparently completely unaware of the mix of emotions her words provoked in me. "He's out on one of his endless walks." She poured coffee from the cafetière I recognised from years ago into two mugs. "I know he'll be sorry to have missed you. I'm sure he would have loved to say hello."

I wondered how much she knew about my relationship with her son. She knew we'd been friends for a long time, of course, but what else did she know? What had he told her, or what had she guessed? How much had my mother told her? I suspected more than I would be entirely comfortable with.

I took the mug she offered me. "I'm sorry to have missed him, too," I said. And, of course, in spite of everything, I was. "Please tell him I said hello."

I sipped the coffee and we chatted about my mother's party. Barbara said that Neil seemed very nice, and I told her a little bit about my job and my life in London. I wondered how much of what I told her would end up being passed on to Jonny, and if he'd care about any of it.

I drank about half my coffee and decided I needed to make a break for it before my luck ran out. "Thanks so much, Barbara."

I was relieved when she didn't press me to stay longer. "It was lovely to see you, Summer. I hope you'll be able to come and visit us down here more often." She looked at me, and I couldn't help but feel there was some form of deeper meaning behind her words when she said, "You're very much missed here."

I opened the door and stepped outside. I was about to call to the dogs when the front gate opened, and Jonny came through it. I saw him do so with a sense of inevitability that I realised had been hanging over me since I'd got out of Neil's Audi on first arriving back in Cornwall. How on earth could I expect to come down here with my life under some sort of control in London and *not* bump into Jonny Rawlings? The idea that the Fates would let me off so easily was, frankly, preposterous, and I'd been guilty of extreme hubris to even imagine it. It was entirely hopeless; the universe had no intention of letting me off the hook where Jonny was concerned.

He saw me standing by the door at just about the exact same moment I saw him. A brief look of shock and surprise passed across his face, and then he smiled at me, the warmest, most beautiful smile imaginable. And of course I smiled back. He walked towards me and I took only one step away from him.

"Hello, Summer." His voice curled around my heart like warm honey.

"Hello, Jonny." I looked up at him. His hair was still long, but shorter, whipped by the wind into a mass of curls which he pushed back with a slender, sinewy hand. A vision shot through my mind of that hand on my body and I blinked it furiously away. His beard was no more, but his face told the tale of being at least three days unshaven. He looked ridiculously, wildly and irrevocably sexy, and I knew, with the same sense of inevitability that I'd felt when I'd first seen him, that he still had my heart.

"It's good to see you," he said.

"It's good to see you too." And it really was. The sight of him was like Optrex in tired, irritated eyes after a long day in a smoky room.

Daisy came up to him with a wagging tail, followed by my errant pair. He bent down to pet her, and I took the opportunity to drink him in. Seeing him felt like balm on a wound, like calamine lotion on sunburn. I tried to ignore that I'd possibly just mentally compared my life with Neil to sunburn.

He stood up and hitched the little backpack he was carrying onto his shoulder. "How long are you here for?"

"Er... until the 30th. Well, driving back on the morning of the 30th."

He raised his eyebrows. "Driving? Nice. At least, I hope it's nice."

I smiled and nodded. "Very comfortable, thanks." He didn't ask me who was driving, so I assumed Barbara had told him about Neil.

He fixed me with one of his soft, penetrating gazes, and I knew immediately I was in trouble. "How about a walk one day? For old times' sake?"

"Um… I'm supposed to be going out with Neil tomorrow if the weather holds. I said I'd show him some of Cornwall. He's never been down here before."

"Ah, okay." His eyes flashed with disappointment.

I chewed my bottom lip. Oh, what the hell! My peace of mind was shredded for the foreseeable future anyway. "But I might be free the day after, if you're around?"

He looked at me hopefully. "Yeah?"

"Why don't I text you in the morning when we know what the weather's going to do? Your number the same?"

He nodded. "Same as it ever was. Yours?"

"Yes." I called Lucy and Douglas to me and attached their leads.

"Where are you going with Neil?" he asked.

I could see some sort of concern in his eyes and wondered if I knew the reason for it. "I thought we might go and look around Fowey. It's so pretty and different to the north coast. Kind of like a crash course in the other side of Cornwall." Don't worry, I'm not taking him to any of our spots, I thought.

I saw him relax and wondered if I'd been right, and he'd wanted to be sure that I wasn't showing Neil any of the places we'd shared.

"Well, have a nice time," he said. "I hope it stays dry for you."

"Thanks," I moved towards the gate. "See you soon, then, maybe."

"Yes, see you soon."

I felt his eyes on me as I let us all out into the lane and turned towards home. I called the dogs firmly to heel and didn't look back.

The next day treated us to a bright morning with a forecast of a dry afternoon, so Neil and I followed through on my suggested plan and drove to Fowey. Neil was absolutely charmed by the beautiful river, with its banks of fields and trees, and the scenic estuary, with its adornment of boats. And no less so by the pretty town, with its narrow streets and large selection of shops, restaurants and drinking establishments. We did some shopping, and Neil bought me some charming earrings in one of the many tasteful boutiques. We had lunch in an extremely decent burger place with a view of the water and then climbed up winding, shop-lined lanes to wander along the Esplanade and enjoy the views across to Polruan.

There was something about Fowey that just suited Neil. Perhaps it was that his type of civilised urbanity, as noted by Jenna, fitted in so much better here, on the gentler, more sheltered south coast, than on the wild and rugged north. He was certainly feeling the love for the place. He admired the elegant houses lining the Esplanade, and I could see him coveting their views.

"I bet it's beautiful here in the summer," he said.

"Oh, it is. And the water is so blue then, you wouldn't believe."

He looked out over the estuary towards the sea. "Hmm... Maybe we should get a place down here. I've always quite fancied learning to sail. We could buy a boat and spend time exploring the coast. What do you think?"

I looked up at him. I'd very much noticed his generous and encouraging use of the word 'we'. He was interested in discussing plans for us both; he was thinking about his future with me in mind. I thought about the beautiful, sunny future he was offering me, and I could almost taste its possibility. It was the future of so many people's dreams. But then I thought of where we were in the world. It was certainly true that Fowey's pretty charms

were very different in nature from the wild, rugged landscape of the north coast, but that same north coast was
only an hour's drive away. If I lived here, I'd never be
able to escape the call of my beloved Crantock, Polly Joke,
Holywell, St Agnes, Godrevy and Gwithian, and the pull
of the man who inhabited them. I would never live in
Fowey with Neil, of that I was sure. If Neil wanted to buy
a sailboat, I was perfectly happy to support that ambition,
but that boat would have to be moored far, far away. I
wondered if Norfolk would be far enough.

The following day brought with it a gloomy ridge of
low pressure, along with accompanying grey cloud and
drizzle. I was in my dressing gown, looking doubtfully
out the window, while Neil sat propped up in bed with a
mug of tea beside him and *South West Coast Path: Padstow
to Falmouth: National Trail Guide* on his lap. Neil had been
reading Cornwall guide books and was keen to explore
the Lizard. He'd taken a particular fancy to Kynance Cove,
and even though I was expressing uncertainty about the
forecast, he professed himself willing to make the drive.

"The thing is," I said, "it's not just the getting wet from
the rain, and that the place won't look its best in this
weather, it's the fact that the descent down to the cove involves negotiating many, many steps. Steps that are steep
and slippery at the best of times, but, frankly, death traps
in the wet. I'd love to visit Kynance with you, but I'm not
sure that our Christmas would be enhanced by a trip to
A&E."

"Hmm..." He turned his attention back to the guidebook. "Is there anywhere else you suggest?"

"Frankly, any of the coastal paths can be dicey in the
rain. Why don't you take it easy this morning while I take
the dogs out, and then we can drive to St Ives this after-

noon for a look around and something to eat?"

Neil flicked to the relevant part of the guidebook. "It certainly looks like a very attractive town."

"Yes, it's lovely. And much less chance of ending up with a sprained ankle. What do you say?"

"Okay. Let's do that, then."

"Great." I sat down at the dressing table and began to tie my hair up. I'd let go of the red not long after I'd last seen Jonny a few years ago, and now I just had my hairdresser put a brunette tint on it to enhance the natural colour and add condition and gloss. I'd kept the long, layered cut the same, though. It was easy to maintain, and Neil liked it.

I looked at him in the mirror. "I'm just going to take a quick shower, then I'll walk Lucy and Donald. I'm sure my dad would be very happy to entertain you if you get bored." I finished with my hair and slipped my phone into the pocket of my robe.

"I'm sure I'll be fine. You go and enjoy your walk. Your mother said you like time to yourself on the coast path, so I don't want to cramp your style."

I went and dropped a kiss on his cheek. "No need for both of us to get blown to hell and back, anyway."

In the bathroom, I turned on the shower to run hot before I got in. I took my phone out of my pocket and typed a text to Jonny: 'Taking the dogs out this morning if you want to join. Will be by church at 10. Let me know. Summer'. I reread it to check for content and tone and pressed 'Send'.

I put the phone back in my robe pocket and stepped into the shower. Bringing the phone in here to send my text felt both faintly ridiculous and simultaneously absolutely necessary. Of course, I wasn't strictly doing anything *wrong* by meeting Jonny, but I had no good way to explain it to Neil. He wouldn't have been happy that I was going walking with another man without him, even an old friend I'd known since childhood. And he'd have been even less keen if he knew the extent of my and Jonny's history. And he'd be perfectly right not to be. I wouldn't be physically cheating on him in any way, certainly, but I couldn't kid myself that I hadn't been mentally cheating on Neil since I'd seen Jonny on Boxing Day morning. Thoughts of him had been filling my every waking moment. I rarely remembered my dreams, but I was pretty certain that if I did, Jonny would have been filling those too.

I finished with the shower, wrapped a towel around myself and stepped out onto the mat. I made sure my hands were dry and pulled my phone out of my robe pocket. There was a text from Jonny: 'See you there. J'.

My heart rate kicked into a higher gear, and my stomach started to churn out butterflies. I realised I was basically a junkie seeking a fix. My years in London had enabled me to go cold turkey on Jonny, but it had taken just one small dose to make me desperate to shoot up again. The physical effects on my brain chemistry were probably not even too different. I was utterly powerless to resist the addiction.

I rubbed the steam off the bathroom mirror with a towel and examined my face. I just had to get through these next couple of days. The day after tomorrow Neil and I would be gone, back to London and my sanity. I'd see Jonny this morning, get my fix, and then I'd return to the calm, contained safety and security of Neil and our life together. I just needed to get this done without it exploding into some huge drama: no unnecessary explanations to Neil of things which wouldn't matter in another 48 hours, no stupid decisions on my part which would mean anything past today. Just shoot up and get right for now, Summer, then put the pin back in the grenade.

I got ready as I normally would do. Since I always made myself presentable for Neil, this meant light makeup, ponytail, jeans, cashmere sweater and Hermes scarf, with my new Barbour and walking boots donned as I went out the door. My wardrobe had seen something of an upgrade over the past couple of years.

I reached the church with Donald and Lucy just after 10, and Jonny was waiting under the lychgate with Daisy, sheltering from the drizzle. We both knew we'd likely not be taking this walk in this weather if it weren't to see one another. Our wordless recognition of this meant that our greeting involved merely an exchange of glances, a pulling closer of hoods around faces and a tucking of hands into pockets. We set off down the lane towards the beach.

There was equally no conversation regarding what direction to take. Jonny stood back for me to go through the gate that led to the sea, manoeuvred the dogs through and followed me up the steps. We walked, heads down, across the dunes, but this time, rather than take the coastal path towards West Pentire, I veered right. He followed me as I climbed up the high dunes which backed the bay, until we crested the hill and were able to take in the view of a moody, sulky, but still beautiful Crantock Bay. The tide was about halfway out and receding.

I found a path down to the beach and started my descent over the sand. The dogs ran ahead of us, eager to reach their expansive, windswept playground. My whole being was alive with electricity. These surroundings, this man, were all my soul desired. This was my natural frequency, and my body told me so as I reached the beach and turned to walk west.

Jonny came up beside me and fell in step. I slowed down and we walked at a leisurely pace. The breeze had picked up, but the drizzle had stopped, and I lowered my hood. He did the same. We walked for a few more minutes across the sand, the wind whipping us. The sensation of exhilaration, of being here, of seeing Jonny again, of feeling the 'real' world slip further and further away, continued to build in my chest. I gradually changed course, walking towards the sea, following the outgoing tide. All the time, Jonny walked by my side, calmly and quietly, not asking anything of me, his gentle energy soothing my soul, giving me that blissful fix of pure pleasure and comfort that no one else could. The ground could have started to shake beneath our feet and the world collapse around us, and it would have been alright, because Jonny was there and would have held my hand through it.

I veered back towards the base of the cliffs and walked until we came to an area of rock formations exposed by the receding tide. The rocks were still damp from the rain, and their shape not the most conducive for comfort, but I found a spot anyway, tucked the back of my jacket under me and rested my butt against them as if against a high stool. I'd made sure to pick a spot where Jonny would be able to perch next to me, and he did so. I sat, looking out towards the sea, and tried to live in the moment.

We sat for a while, watching the waves and the dogs gambolling about having the time of their lives, when I sensed the heat of Jonny's gaze on me and I turned towards him. The look in his eyes was unmistakable, and my heart swelled with all the love I knew we still felt for one another. The world had fallen away, and it was just us, here, now, no troublesome choices to make, no poor decisions to live with.

I held his eyes, not attempting to keep my feelings from him, and he placed his hand gently over mine.

"I'm sorry, Summer," he said.

I blinked at him. "What for?"

"For everything."

I sighed. "Me too."

I knew that we both wanted to give one another – to give ourselves – a clean slate but felt the hopelessness of that wish. "I'm glad your work's going well," I said. "I saw your website. Your paintings are wonderful."

The pleasure my words gave him illuminated his face. "Thank you! That means... a lot coming from you."

"And you're still living in the cottage in Gwithian?"

He nodded. "Yes. It's basically perfect for me. I'm extremely lucky to have found it."

"I'm happy for you. I'm happy that you're happy."

He looked at me. "I wouldn't say that I'm happy, necessarily." He took a beat. "How could I be?"

I looked out towards the horizon again and shook my head. "I don't know what to say to you, Jonny." His fingers tightened around mine, and I turned my hand so I could hold his.

"That's okay. You don't need to say anything. I'm just happy you're here with me."

My heart squeezed, and I wondered how I was ever going to be able to walk away from him. How was I going to make my legs physically do it?

"I do have some things I want to say to you, if you'll allow it," he said.

I looked up at him. My heart beat high and hard in my chest. "I'll always hear what you want to say to me."

He swallowed, and I could see him steeling himself. "Amber left me."

I nodded. "I know." I saw his eyes widen a little in surprise. "My mother told me," I said, by way of explanation. "Your mother told her."

"Ah, of course. Anyway, she left me. But it had been coming for a long time. Looking back on it now, I'm not sure it wasn't always inevitable. She just wanted something from me I couldn't give her. And she wasn't wrong to want it. I think I even thought for a while that maybe I could give her what she needed. But I couldn't. And I never would've been able to."

He looked down at me, but I didn't look back at him. I would let him speak, and I would listen, but that was all.

"I've always loved you, Summer. I think you've known this in the past, even though I've never actually said it to you. But maybe after Amber... Well, perhaps you think that I stopped loving you. But I didn't. Even when I was trying to love her – and at least partly succeeding – I still loved you. I can't help it; it's part of who I am. I hope you can forgive me for that."

My eyes on his were confused. "Forgive you? Why would I need – or even want – to forgive you for loving me?"

"Because, maybe, my love isn't what you want. Or need. I think, perhaps, I make your life more complicated than you want it to be. More messy. That's never been my intention, of course. I've only ever wanted you to be happy. But I seem to have been able to do almost nothing at all to bring that about."

I sighed. "I'm not sure that's been your failure. I've played my part in that, with my own choices. And the world has had plenty to do with it, with its impossible demands and unending, suffocating requirements."

He squeezed my hand. "I'm sorry. I'm sorry I haven't been able to make life easier for you."

I met his eyes. "That's not your job."

"I feel like it is. I want it to be. I've always wanted it to be."

I rested my head against his shoulder.

Donald trotted by, coming close to my feet, checking that all was okay, before running off back to Lucy and Daisy in the distance.

"And you're wrong," I said. "About me not wanting your love. Maybe once, a long time ago, I was afraid of it. Afraid of what it would do to our friendship, which was so important to me... *Is* so important to me. But that was a long time ago. For many years now, I've wanted little more in life than I've wanted your love." I paused, realising something. "You know... I see now one of the reasons I was so destroyed by you choosing Amber..."

He looked down at me, his eyes full of concern and pain. "Destroyed?"

"That's not important now. Let me continue."

"Sorry."

"One of the reasons that caused me so much pain... I hadn't realised before... possibly even until now... is that a big part of the reason why I felt like the world had shifted beneath my feet then, was that a large part of who I saw myself as – my personal sense of self, of identity, if you like – was as someone who was loved by you. I was a woman who was loved by Jonny Rawlings. Whatever happened, however much time passed, you would love me. Before Amber, even when we were with other people, I felt we were never quite lost to one another. As if we were just waiting for our moment, if that makes any sense.

And that belief sustained me on some deep level that I didn't even recognise or think about most of the time. But it was always there, as something I could hold on to, to trust. That kind of trust, it's an incredibly powerful thing. But then, when I thought you didn't love me anymore, when I thought you'd chosen her over me – something for which I largely blamed myself and my choices – for a long time I didn't know how I could go on. Just breathing in and out... every breath felt like my lungs had to move over sandpaper just to draw in oxygen."

He was looking at me, horrified. Then he looked out to sea, his jaw tight. "Jesus Christ."

"I don't say this to make you feel bad, I honestly don't. I know we've both suffered because of the mess we've made of things. But I want you to know... I didn't not want you to love me."

He looked down at me. "And now?"

I shook my head, hopeless. "I can't tell you I don't want it, because I do. It makes me selfish to say this to you, and... God knows what it makes me towards Neil... but I do want your love. I'm afraid that my life without it is, at its core, ashes. And that terrifies me."

Tears were pricking at the back of my eyes, and I turned and buried my head against his chest. He put his arms around me and pulled me tightly to him.

"What do you want to do?" he said.

I curled my fingers into his jacket. "I don't know!" I looked up at him, and then suddenly, in that moment, everything was crystal clear to me. "Or rather, I do know. I know exactly what I want to do. I want to live here with you, and see you every day, and spend my life making you happy."

His face cracked into the widest smile. "Then do that!

We're both still free! Come and live with me in my little house in the dunes and let me love you and look after you and do everything I can to make you happy! I promise I'll spend every minute of every day doing what I can to make that happen." He looked a little proud. "I can even support us both now. I make enough money. We wouldn't be rich, but we wouldn't starve. Please, Summer! Say you'll do it. Say you'll come back to me!"

I looked up at him. "You make it sound so simple."

"Because it is."

I sat back, taking deep breaths of the sea air. Above us, gulls swooped and cawed, enjoying their God-given ability to ride the currents, their lives a simple cycle of eat, breed, survive. For a moment, I really envied them.

"I wish it were," I said. "But once we leave here, this precious place, I have responsibilities. The world will start kicking my arse again. I've made commitments – perhaps not legal ones, but emotional ones – to Neil most especially. I can't just walk away from them." I looked at him. "And I'm fairly sure, once I'm away from here, I won't even be sure that I should."

His eyes on mine were like the darkest pools, pulling me down into them. But these were depths I wanted to drown in.

"What can I do to help you decide? I'll do anything."

I sighed. "Wait for me."

He nodded, slowly.

"I know I've said in the past not to, but, clearly, that didn't work out so well for either of us. So, if you really want me, wait. And I'll do my best to make my way back to you." I made a decision. "Give me a year. I'll give you an answer in a year. If I can make it sooner, I will, but I'll ask you to wait no longer than that."

He nodded. "Okay."

We got up and started to walk back across the sand. Jonny called Daisy and all the dogs came tearing towards us, circling and barking, thoroughly invigorated by their beach adventures. We walked around the edge of the dunes this time, taking the easy route along the side of the Gannel and into the car park. Our pace was slow, both of us reluctant to return to reality. As we stepped from soft sand onto firm ground, I realised there was something I had to find out.

"I need to ask you something," I said.

"Anything."

"I hope it doesn't sound too petty."

He just looked at me, confused.

"Back when I'd just found out about Amber, and you came to see me, and we sat and watched the seals..."

"Yes..."

"You knew that finding out about her had upset me, and you asked if we could still be friends. Why did you post that photo of the two of you on your Instagram the next day? You must have known it would hurt me."

I saw the memory come back to him, and his jaw tensed with regret. "Shit! I think I hoped you wouldn't see that, at least not right away."

"Then why did you do it?"

He sighed heavily. "It was to do with Amber. After you came to the house, and then I came home having met you on the beach, she picked up on something in my mood she wasn't happy with. I'd told her about you, of course, but when I talked about us when I first became friends with her, I was hurting. I thought you'd chosen your London life over me, and I was angry. I didn't know then that she and I would become anything serious, let alone that you'd ever meet her, so I think I made it pretty clear to her how much I'd loved you. So when you came to Gwithian, and she knew I'd seen you again, she was, understandably, on her guard for fallout. The evening after I saw you at the beach, she asked me if I was okay with seeing you again, and of course I told her yes, we were done, it was nothing. But then I couldn't let it rest the next day and I drove over to see you. Nothing actually happened between us, of course, and I told her that. I told her I'd just wanted to make sure you were okay, and that she didn't need to worry, you were going back to London." He paused. "I could have lied to her and not told her I came to Crantock to see you, I guess, but I couldn't do that."

"Of course not," I said.

"Anyway, after I got back from seeing you here, I went out for a long walk. Seeing you had stirred things up in me," he let out a puff of laughter and shot me an eye roll, "as it always does, and I tried to clear my head. But that evening, when I got home, she kept needling me about you, she wouldn't let it go, really unhappy I'd felt the need to go and talk to you when I'd sworn to her it was over between us. We had our first blow-up row, and I left the house." He gave a little shake of the head. "I actually slept in the car. Anyway, I came back early the next morning and she was all apologies, but I could tell she still wasn't satisfied with my explanations of why I'd done what I'd done. I wanted things to go back to the way they'd been between us, and I felt like I had to find some way to mollify her. She was always very keen on Instagram; she actually set up my account, and she was the one who originally posted to it. She'd always teased me – seriously, I realise now – about how I didn't post any pictures of us together. All the boyfriends of the girls she knew did – as she would point out to me while showing me the pictures – and she felt left out, and, presumably, that my failure to do so said something about our relationship she didn't want to face. But up to that point, she'd let it go. It wasn't as if I posted much of anything, anyway. So I thought that giving into her on this simple ask would be a good way to make her feel sure of me. What she was accusing me of wasn't entirely untrue – although, of course, I couldn't admit that to her. And her wish for some kind of public recognition of our relationship wasn't unreasonable. So that morning I took a selfie of us both and put it on my page. As I said, I was hoping you wouldn't see it. Or that if you did, you wouldn't see it for a while. Or that if you did see it, you'd just roll your eyes at my bullshit and ignore it. I'm sorry it hurt you, I really am."

"Jenna had your preferred reaction, though," I said.

"What?"

"She rolled her eyes at your bullshit." I told him about her DMed emoji message.

"Oh, my God!" He started laughing. "I'm sorry, that is so Jenna. She is such a rockstar!"

I couldn't help joining in with his laughter. "She is."

"Anyway," he said, becoming serious again, "I'm sorry. I was a coward. I should have been honest with Amber and not put up that post. To be honest, I wonder if your visit didn't change things between us from then on. I'm not sure she ever entirely believed afterwards that I was completely over you."

"I'd say I'm sorry to have screwed things up for you with Amber, but that would be a huge lie, obviously." I risked a lop-sided grin in his direction.

He chuckled. "Well, I guess we'll never know if it would have worked out in the long run if you hadn't shown up that day." He considered for a moment. "In all honesty, probably not." He took my hand and gave it a squeeze as we reached the fork in the road where I would go right and he would go left. "I've always been a sucker for the real thing."

We moved to the edge of the road, then a short way up the lane to the church where there was little traffic, either car or foot. The dogs followed, happy to be given longer to explore all those exciting hedgerow smells. We both looked around, and I knew he was checking, as I was, if there was anyone around to see us.

"I'm not sure when I'll be in touch again," I said. "I have a lot of thinking to do. And some very big decisions to make."

He nodded.

"I need you to trust me that I've heard everything you've said today, and I want to do everything I can to be fair to you." I took his hand in mine and lifted it to examine its beauty and masculinity. The vision of him using that hand when making love to me for the rest of my life washed over me, and a wave of desire surged through my body, heating every drop of blood. "The best I can say to you is: I want to find my way back to you. I know what we could be to one another, which is so much more than we've ever been so far, and I don't underestimate the gift that is." I looked up at him. "So, will you wait?"

He curled his hand around mine and raised my fingers to his lips. "I will."

I stood looking at him, unable to move. I put my hands on his chest, feeling hopelessly torn as to my next move, but he made the decision for me, pulling me to him and bending to kiss me. His lips met mine, and I opened my mouth, accepting his kiss, deepening it with my own.

I curled my arms around his neck and poured all my love and longing and desperation for him into it.

At last we separated, and I took a small step back. "I will see you, Jonny Rawlings."

"I will be waiting, Summer Lowell."

And with that, I managed to turn and walk back towards the road. The dogs took note that playtime was over and separated to follow their respective owners. When I reached the corner where I had to go left around the side of a little stone cottage, I turned and looked back. He was standing watching me. I waved and he did the same, and then somehow I made my legs start taking me home. As I walked up the lane, behind me I heard the distinct sound of a grenade going off.

I towelled off the dogs outside and then let us all back into the kitchen. I eyed their grubby paws as they trotted across my mother's clean quarry tiles. I was considering what to do about it when I heard my mother come back into the room from the hallway.

"I think I'm going to have to wash the dogs," I said, my eyes still on Lucy's damp, wagging tail. My mother shut the kitchen door for the second time in three days and I looked up. She walked over and switched the kettle on, but her casualness seemed forced.

"You'll want a hot drink to warm you up after that long walk in the cold and damp," she said.

"Thanks. I'll have a quick hot shower in a minute when I've dealt with the dogs."

My mother retrieved two mugs from the kitchen cupboard. She didn't turn to me when she spoke. "I was just on the phone with Barbara. She mentioned she saw you the other day, that you popped in for coffee."

An alarm bell started ringing at the back of my brain.

"Yes, sorry, did I forget to mention that? It was Boxing Day morning."

My mother continued to busy herself with tea preparations. "She also mentioned that you bumped into Jonny while you were there."

I kept my voice steady. "I did."

"And how was he?"

"Oh, you know, same as always." Hot, sexy, love of my life.

My mother took the milk out of the fridge and poured some into a small, white jug. "And she mentioned that Jonny had gone out for a walk this morning, with Daisy." She looked at me sideways. "At the same time you were out with Lucy and Donald."

Oh, God. So very, very busted. "Yes, we bumped into one another on the way to the beach."

"Bumped into one another as in 'in passing', or...?"

"Well, we decided to walk together. Take the chance to catch up, you know."

My mother sat down at the kitchen table and began to pour the tea. I pulled out a chair to join her. "I see," she said. I realised that the problem was that she probably did. "So, this 'bumping into one another' that you did with Jonny, I'm assuming this is a 'bumping into' that Neil will not be privy to?"

I took a deep breath. "Probably best not."

She looked at me. "Oh, Summer."

I huffed out a sigh. "I haven't made any stupid decisions. It's just probably a good idea if he doesn't know about something from which no good can come."

"No good for whom?"

"For anyone."

"So, what are you going to do?"

I looked at her incredulously. How had she guessed? "Are you a witch?" I said.

She gave me a hard stare. "No, Summer, I just have eyes."

I realised that Jonny's kiss was probably written all over my face. I touched my cheek. I suspected that if I looked in a mirror I'd see a flushed complexion, slightly swollen lips and blown pupils. Realistically, I'd never had any chance of getting past my mother without raising suspicions. The conversation with Barbara had just sealed the deal.

I let out a heavy breath. "I need to think about it."

"So, you're still not clear on the path to take?"

I shook my head. "At this point, I feel like I'm standing at a crossroads with no clue as to the right direction."

My mother's eyes on me were calm. "I think you do know. I think you always have."

"I need to be fair to Neil," I said.

"Yes, you do. But you also need to be fair to yourself. And Jonny."

I looked at her fiercely. "Of course I want to be fair to Jonny." I took a breath. "I've asked him to wait, and he's said he will. I've promised to make a decision as soon as I can."

My mother sighed and took a sip of her tea. "Very well." She looked at me, her eyes softening. "And I want you to know, you can talk to me about anything, at any time, okay?"

"Thanks, Mum."

That afternoon, the worst of the weather had blown through, and Neil and I took my suggested trip to St Ives. We parked at the top of the hill and took the steps down into the main part of town, with Neil admiring the views and professing himself quite astonished that he'd never been to Cornwall before. "I can't believe I've been missing out all these years!"

We wandered around the town, poking our heads into shops and galleries, walked along the edge of the harbour with its small flotilla of pretty little boats and found a well recommended restaurant we liked the look of which served food in a buzzy upstairs room overlooking the bay.

I'd been doing my best not to let the morning's events affect my mood, but as we shared red wine and pizza, he looked at me carefully. "Is everything okay?"

I nodded. "Of course."

"You just seem a little distracted, that's all. Like you've got other things on your mind."

I took a sip of my wine. "I'm sorry. I think I can just feel the return to London looming already. I've got so much to deal with when I get back to the office." I gave him a bright smile. "I'll try to do better."

"Well, we still have a few days until either of us needs to be back at work so let's focus on that, shall we? What were you thinking of doing tomorrow?"

"I was wondering if you'd mind terribly going and exploring with my dad? He's probably a much better guide of the area than I am. Jenna wants to see me before we go back, and as I'm not likely to see her again for a long time, I think I should."

This was a lie, and even as I said the words, I felt thoroughly ashamed of myself. Jenna didn't want to see me; I wanted to see Jenna. I wanted to talk to her about Jonny, and if I didn't see her tomorrow I wasn't going to be able to. A phone call wasn't going to cut it for this kind of conversation. I hadn't even asked her yet; I was hoping she'd be able to make time for me for lunch tomorrow. These thoughts had only coalesced in my mind as we walked around St Ives. Neil was right; I *had* been distracted.

We finished our coffee, and while Neil was paying the bill, I nipped to the loo. I typed a text to Jenna: 'Calling an emergency meeting for tomorrow lunchtime. Please tell me you can join?' I signed off with three *praying hands* emojis.

Her reply buzzed as I was fixing my lipstick: 'Where and when? *popping eyes* emoji and three *ear* emojis'.

I responded: 'C-Bay at noon?'

Her reply came back immediately in the form of three *thumbs up* emojis.

I returned to Neil, and we made our way back up the hill to the car. I noticed him giving me some concerned glances as we climbed. I just hoped that when we got back to London and resumed our normal lives, I'd be able to get some proper perspective on things. And if I decided my life was going to be here, with Jonny, I prayed I would have the strength to deal fairly and honestly with Neil.

The following day, I took a shortcut across the fields from the main road to join the South West Coast Path and followed it around to the western side of Crantock Bay. There I turned left and made my way up towards the C-Bay cafe, a modern, white building with some of the best views for miles around. As I approached, I spotted Jenna's little yellow Fiat already parked, overlooking the bay. I found her easily, settled in at a prime sea view table. The bi-fold doors which opened onto the terrace in good weather were closed today against a brisk wind.

She got up for a hug, and we embraced before sitting back down.

"I've ordered a bottle of Pinot Grigio," she said.

"It'll be needed," I replied.

"So, come on, then! You've dragged me away from my warm bed and an appointment with the latest season of *The Crown* for an emergency meeting. Spill!"

The waitress appeared with the wine, and Jenna told her to just leave the bottle, we'd help ourselves. We both ordered the crab sandwich without looking at the menu, and Jenna filled our wine glasses halfway.

I took a deep breath. "Jonny split from Amber."

Her eyes popped out on stalks. "Oh my God, yes!" She did a little fist pump.

I gave her a pretend severe look. "You shouldn't revel in other people's misery."

"I only revel in the misery of people I don't like," she said, refusing to be admonished.

I shook my head at her but couldn't avoid smiling. "You didn't even know Amber."

"I didn't have to. She pinched my best girl's man. No further knowledge required."

I tossed her a small eye roll, but of course I always enjoyed her fierce and unwavering support of me.

"So, how did you find out? Did he tell you? Have you spoken to him? Has he begged for you back?"

I took a deep draw on my wine. "My mother via Barbara. Yes, yes, and yes."

She put her hand to her mouth to stifle a scream, but she managed a little one anyway. "Halle-fucking-lujah! My prayers, and," she fixed a stern eye on me, "in spite of anything you might say, I know yours, have been answered! God be praised! Let us welcome the blessed Jonny Rawlings back into the fold – and to the breast of the woman who loves him!"

I was laughing hard in spite of myself. "Oh, God, Jenna! What am I to do with you? I've asked you here for a serious conversation to discuss my best course of action, and you've already jumped ahead to the final act."

"Best course of action?" she scoffed. "I would have thought that was obvious. Ditch me immediately, go and find Jonny and get him to take you to bed without delay in that shack he considers home. I expect it's a bit draughty in the winter but I'm sure he'll soon warm you up."

I was laughing so hard, tears were beginning to form. "Will you be serious for one minute!"

"I am perfectly serious. And more to the point, how do you even need me to tell you this? What are you still doing sitting here? Honestly! Go!" She made a shooing motion towards the door.

I shook my head. "Jenna, you know it's not that simple."

She rolled her eyes at me. "It absolutely is that simple. You just have this apparent incomprehensible need to make it complicated."

"Can we discuss this properly, please?"

She huffed out another eye roll as our sandwiches arrived. "Fine, go ahead."

I gave her the heavily edited highlights of recent events and talked through the pros and cons of staying in London and continuing with my life there, versus giving up everything I'd worked for, including my very nice life with Neil, and travel and opportunities still to come, to return to Cornwall and live in a small, run-down cottage with Jonny, with very little money and no (or a pretty poor) job. I also felt duty bound to point out that Jonny was someone with whom I had slept only once (twice if you wanted to be generous with your statistics), who I wasn't at all sure wouldn't quickly get sick of me once he actually had the thing his heart had desired since he was a teenager.

Jenna eyed me reluctantly when I'd finished laying out the case for both sides. "Well, when you put it like that…"

"I'm arguing worst case scenario for if I come back to Cornwall to try and give myself some sort of perspective," I said. "I mean, obviously, coming back could mean the start of a blissful existence with Jonny, who will continue to love and worship me for the rest of my life, and which will involve endless days and nights of spectacular, knee-trembling sex and watching the sun set over the sparkling waters of St Ives Bay."

"Now, you see, *that's* what I'm talking about," Jenna said.

"I know it is, but can you at least *see* my dilemma?"

She nodded seriously. "I can. But honestly? Are you really going to be able to live with yourself if you don't at least try? I mean, what if Scenario Number Two is the right one? The one that turns out to come true? I mean, even if the chances of that are only fifty-fifty… Isn't that a chance worth taking? To live a truly spectacular life?"

I bit my lip.

"Honestly, Summer, I can't help but wonder… Did you really ask me here to discuss the pros and cons in a dispassionate way, or did you want to talk to me because you've already made your decision and you wanted someone to rubber stamp it for you? Because you know what I think. You know what I've always thought. I get there are 'issues'…" she finger painted air quotes, "to be resolved, and arrangements to be made, but you know I think you should just go ahead and resolve them. You and Jonny have been dancing around one another for over a decade, for Chrissakes. It's time to shit or get off the pot."

I shot her a look. "Delicately and poetically put."

"Thank you."

"Look, I do appreciate that it might seem that way – and obviously some of what you say is true. A big part of me wants someone to cheerlead for Jonny, and who better than you to do that? You cheerlead better for Jonny than Jonny does for Jonny, to be quite honest. But I also wanted the chance to talk it through with someone who wouldn't judge me. There's literally no one else in the world I can do that with. The couple of girlfriends I have in London who might lend a friendly ear don't know Jonny – don't know everything he is and what he can offer me – and they'd just think I was utterly mad to even consider jacking everything in with Neil and running off down here to live with an almost-starving artist."

Jenna raised an eyebrow to me. "Perhaps you should invite Jonny up to London for a bit and show him around. Let these friends you speak of meet him. That might clarify things for them somewhat."

I had a vision of introducing Jonny, with his hair and his body and his face, to a select gathering of my female friends and acquaintances in London, and I couldn't help smiling. "I'm sure they'd enjoy that, but I'm not sure about him."

Jenna waved a hand. "I'm just putting it out there. I mean, if you really want another perspective to help you decide. See which option those bitches would pick when they've been exposed to the Jonny Experience. I bet they'd be coming to sit by me in no time."

I laughed. "Maybe."

She gave me a look. "There's no 'maybe' about it. I mean, obviously the odd one might not know what's good for her, but I feel confident I'd be able to gain the majority vote."

We asked for the bill, and I prepared to let Jenna go.

"Has this at least been some help?" she said, serious for a minute.

I smiled at her gratefully. "Oh, definitely. I mean, I'm not going to know how I'll feel once I'm in London until I get there, but talking to you has helped me lay out what I need to think about."

"Just promise me you won't be swayed by bullshit like cars and houses and nice holidays. You and Jonny might not be rich, but if you pooled your resources, you'd definitely be able to get by. And, just think, every morning you'd be waking up in Jonny Central." She made an exaggerated happy face. "Bliss!"

I laughed. "You make a powerful argument."

"Good. Now stop messing about and get your arse back down here. Cornwall misses you!"

Part Twelve

Present Day

The Day Before New Year's Eve

J onny pulled up outside Jenna's apartment in Newquay just after one o'clock.

"Text me when you're ready for me to come get you," he said.

"Will do." I leaned over and kissed him, before climbing out of the car and waving goodbye as he zoomed off down the road. He was taking his camera to the Bedruthan Steps as he hadn't been there in a while, and he liked to visit in the winter when it was quiet.

I pressed Jenna's apartment number and she buzzed me in.

I'd called her that morning from the car to arrange to see her after her reply text to me had finally hit my mobile: 'Trollop Report: Richard was alone on Boxing Day, so how could I say no? Footnote: He's excellent in bed – woo hoo!!! *tongue out* emoji, *huge smile* emoji, *exploding brain* emoji, *sunglasses face* emoji, *thumbs up* emoji'.

"So, when can we meet?" I'd said, without preamble, the minute she picked up. "Are you free for lunch?"

"I am. As I have so much salacious gossip to share,

why don't you come to mine? Colleen is away for Christmas again. I'll order in."

"One o'clock?"

"See you then."

She already had wine poured when I came through the door. I just about succeeded in getting my coat off before she'd put a glass of red in my hand. "I ordered pizza, and I have the bits to make a big salad. I hope that's okay."

I nodded. "Perfect."

"Does Jonny have a new car?"

I noticed that the sliding door to the balcony was slightly open. She must have seen him dropping me off. I took a drink of wine and nodded. "He does. A beautiful little classic MG. It's huge fun. I already can't wait to drive around in it in the summer."

She looked at me, beaming. "So it's all on then? The last few days went well? Are you going to come down here to live with him?"

I laughed at her excitement. "Yes. Yes, very much so, I can't wait to tell you how well. And most probably." I paused. "Honestly, I can't give you a definite yes on the last one yet because I still haven't given one to him, but unless something terrible and unforeseen that no one could have predicted happens between now and New Year's Eve, then yes, I think so. There's a lot to sort out in London, of course, but I want to move back down here to be with him." It suddenly hit me, and I looked at her a little shocked. "Jenna, I'm not sure I could live without him anymore."

Jenna's reaction to my declaration was much less dramatic than I'd expected. She just smiled, looked thoroughly satisfied and said, "Of course you can't, Summer."

We put coats around our shoulders and went to hang

out on the balcony, leaning on the rail as we drank our wine, enjoying the crisp air and view of the sparkling blues of the sea and sky.

"So," I said, "what happened with Richard? Apart from him seeing your fabulous red bra."

Jenna smiled. "Well, as I said in my text, he wasn't busy on Boxing Day. He called me in the morning –" she looked at me for emphasis, "*called me*, mind, none of this texting bullshit – and asked me if I was free, and if I was, would I like to come for lunch. Well, I was supposed to be going to a family thing, but obviously I ditched that and told him I'd love to come for lunch. Anyway, he made some fantastic fish thing – I think he said it was trout with almonds – and plied me with champagne and some really delish white wine, and he was really charming and fun to be with, and we just had the best time."

"I'm so glad."

"And, well... Yeah." She sighed happily. "It was just really working with us, and I'm really comfortable with him." She crinkled her brow. "More comfortable than with anyone else I can ever remember, actually. And evening came, and I didn't want to go home and he didn't seem to want me to, and then he kissed me, and..." Another sigh. "Yeah, it was wonderful. And you know the best bit?"

"What?" I was dying to know.

"Afterwards and the next morning, I actually felt better about myself. Not just the same. And definitely not worse." She pulled a face. "And let me tell you, there's been *far* too much of that in my life. But actually better. And not just happier or on a post-great-sex high. But better about *myself*, who I was as a person. Does that make sense?"

I thought about how I felt about myself being with Jonny now. "It absolutely does."

She looked at me, slightly alarmed. "I've never felt like that before about anyone. Christ! I really hope I don't fuck this up."

"You won't fuck it up. When it's the right person, you can't fuck it up by accident, only on purpose. And I know you won't fuck it up on purpose. You're far too good of a person for that. He'll be lucky to have you. I just hope *he* doesn't fuck it up." I looked at her cautiously. "Has he called you since?"

She smiled at me triumphantly. "Oh, not just called me. He came here yesterday for dinner and brought me wine *and* flowers and stayed the night. And when he left this morning, we arranged to go out for dinner tomorrow night. I've no idea how he's going to get a table anywhere on New Year's Eve, but I've no doubt he'll manage it."

"I've no doubt either. I'm so happy for you, Jenna. I really hope you get your Happy Ever After."

She held her glass up to me for a toast. "I hope we both do!"

I was just clinking my glass with hers when the intercom buzzed and she went inside to let up the pizza delivery guy.

We ate pizza and salad at the breakfast bar, and Jenna opened a second bottle of wine.

"Summer..." she said, topping up my glass, "now that everything's going so well with Jonny, I wanted to ask you something. But it's just to satisfy my curiosity, so you can tell me to fuck off if you like."

"Go on..."

"Well, after last Christmas, why did you take so long to finally get together with Jonny? I mean, I'm sure you had your reasons, but I kept waiting for you to tell me you were coming down here, and, well, it took a while."

I considered. "You know how everything always takes longer and costs more than you think it will?"

She tipped her head.

"Well, it was kind of like that on steroids. After Neil and I returned to London, after I'd had my conversation on the beach with Jonny, I needed to take a bit of time to decompress and see if my feelings stayed the same. I realise you didn't consider Neil when we talked at C-Bay..."

She gave a shrug of admission.

"But I had to. I admit I never felt the way about him I did – and do – about Jonny, but I did still love him and we were really good friends. I had to be quite sure I didn't just act rashly from the results of the surge of lust I always get when I see Jonny. I needed some time to see if my feelings settled down, and whether London gave me a different perspective. I knew that Jonny was free again, and he'd promised to wait for me. Knowing that, I needed to see if I'd continue to yearn to run back to him, or if a few weeks back in London would have me thinking that ditching it all for Jonny and Cornwall was completely mad. It turned out that as time went on, I didn't become less keen on the idea of coming back to Jonny, but more keen. I couldn't think of anything else, and I realised I was no longer in love with Neil. I'm not sure I ever was, really. I mean, I certainly believed I was, but looking back on it… Well, I'm not sure. It was definitely never the same with him as it is with Jonny."

Jenna poured me an additional silent top-up.

"Anyway, of course, once I'd realised that, there was the issue of the fact that I lived in Neil's flat, and my life was really entangled with his. I had to find a place of my own and find a good time to talk to Neil about everything and then move out properly. And… Oh, my God! I've never had to actually leave somebody before! I mean, I've split from boyfriends, but leaving someone you've lived with is a whole other level of traumatic. At one point I was so angry with the unpleasantness of the whole situation, I was almost angry with Jonny for causing it." I took a big slug of wine. "I wasn't really, of course, and it quickly passed, but… well, I just want to give you some idea of how hard it all was."

Jenna nodded sympathetically before continuing, "But you were done with all that by the summer, weren't you?"

I nodded. "But you remember my company then sent me to Amsterdam over the summer to do some training for junior staff?"

"Right, right."

"Well, by the time I got back and sorted out at work after that, it was October. So I arranged with Jonny for him to come up to London to see me for a weekend at the beginning of November. But the Friday he was supposed to come up and had his train ticket booked, there was that massive outage on the GWR that caused all the trains to be cancelled, and Jonny got stuck at Bristol and never made it. After that we just decided that, with me coming for ten days at Christmas anyway to discuss everything and tell him my promised decision, we'd leave it and I'd see him here." I shrugged. "So, there you have it. Everything really does always take so much longer than you think it will."

Jenna nodded. "It really does." She looked at me. "I hope it's not going to take you another year to get back down here?"

"Christ! So do I! No way I'm not coming down here for visits while I'm sorting things out. I'm going to be leaving my job, so I won't worry about taking days off for long weekends, and I'm not going to care much what they think about me being away a lot. I'll do enough to cover my responsibilities, but my days of going the extra mile are over. I'll be focusing on my future down here with Jonny from now on."

She let out a relieved sigh. "I'm so happy, Summer, I can't tell you! So happy for you *and* him. That sweet, beautiful boy deserves to be happy."

Part Thirteen

Present Day

New Year's Eve

T he following day we were back at Jonny's cottage, and I'd even brought some of my paperbacks from home that were now on the bookshelves in his living room. He'd watched me putting them there with such a dopey grin on his face I'd had to go and kiss him, and, well, we'd only made love once the day before so we had some catching up to do.

Following consultation with my mother, and a close examination of it for Christmas Eve party wear and tear, I'd decided to go with my black cocktail dress for this evening's event. I showered and put my hair in rollers, but I left my hair down and my makeup considerably less dramatic than for my parents' party appearance. Jonny's navy blue suit and white shirt were elegant and perfectly cut (he admitted his mother's supervision of the purchase of both), and when he was ready he looked so beautiful and sexy I had to employ significant self-control not to peel his clothes right back off him. As we were preparing to go out the door, I caught him looking at me as if I were a magical thing, and it almost took my breath away.

I hadn't even left the house and I couldn't wait to get back here and let him kiss off my lipstick.

The party was being held in one of the gallery's large, elegant, high-ceilinged exhibition spaces, and there was already a nice buzz about the place when we walked in. We took glasses of bubbly from a proffered tray and moved into the room, Jonny's hand resting lightly on the back of my waist.

This was the first time I'd been out in this kind of public setting with him, and I was startled by how amazing it felt. Somehow, with him by my side, I felt sexier and more confident and just overall more *fabulous* than I'd ever done in my life, like some of his beauty and talent and all-round wonderfulness rubbed off onto me. If he'd wanted to tattoo a brand of ownership on me at that moment, I would have been sorely tempted to comply.

A handsome gentleman in a dark grey Savile Row suit approached us and shook Jonny warmly by the hand, thanking him for coming and for lending two of his paintings. Jonny introduced me, there was some small talk, and then the man led us over to where Jonny's paintings were hanging. He'd provided two large canvases, one of a sunrise and one of a sunset, and they were spectacular, the pinks, reds, golds and blues seeming to shimmer and gleam.

But I was just as keen to watch the reactions of the people looking at them, to ensure they were suitably impressed and admiring, which, happily, most of them were. His work was definitely amongst the more popular pieces on show that evening.

He smiled and small-talked and glad-handed like a trooper for over an hour, with me at his side beaming with pride and happily ignoring any and all envious looks dispatched in my direction. We were enjoying a brief break from fielding Jonny's admirers when he looked at me and said, "Want to get out of here?"

"Are you sure you should?"

His eyes on mine were heated. "Not what I asked."

I looked at his mouth, found myself licking my lips and said, "God, yes!"

We said the briefest of goodbyes where absolutely necessary and made our way back to the car with indecent haste, with me at times actually breaking into a run so as to keep up with him. But I didn't want to slow him down, and I held his hand tight as he strode up the hill. I'd never seen him drive with such fierce speed, and I wondered for a moment if he'd had too much to drink, even though I'd seen him switch to water after his initial glass of sparkling wine, but I realised he wasn't drunk, he was just high on desire for me. I had to stop myself telling him to pull over right then and there so that we could attempt a hot and heavy fast coupling in the confines of the MG.

We almost fell into the house, so eager for kisses and to remove one another's clothes that all semblance of any kind of control was entirely abandoned. My dress wasn't going to be able to avoid a trip to the cleaners this time, as it hit the living room floor, followed swiftly by Jonny's jacket. He picked me up and carried me like a bride over the threshold towards the bedroom. I was impressed we made it without incident since I wouldn't let him stop kissing me. We fell on the bed and quickly shed the rest of our clothes, and then he was inside me and my blood was on fire and my brain was exploding. We came together, and the blissful calm that had evaded me all day finally washed over me.

Just a little later, I was lying on my belly, luxuriating

in the sensation of post-coital bliss enveloping my body, when he sat down beside me on the bed. He swept my hair to one side with a warm hand and dropped a kiss on my shoulder. I gave a soft moan of pleasure and noted the time on the clock. It was just gone half past eleven. Only a little while longer before I'd give Jonny the answer I'd promised him a year ago. The butterflies were gathering in my stomach.

He stroked the back of a finger down my arm and the thrill of his touch scudded through me. "Will you get dressed and come out onto the deck with me? I've lit the fire," he said.

I turned over and reached up to him for a kiss, before pushing back the covers and going over to the dresser. I pulled my jeans, socks and one of his big woolly sweaters out of a drawer and put them on, then pushed my feet into my sweater boots. I followed him outside. He'd made the deck cosy, with cushions on the chairs, and he settled a thick blanket around my shoulders. I leaned back into him, receiving the nuzzle and kiss on my neck I desired. Then I sat down and pulled my chair as close as possible to the fire, crackling brightly in its iron bowl. He handed me a furry hot water bottle for good measure, and I laughed.

"Best. Boyfriend. Ever!" I teased.

He disappeared back inside for a minute, before re-appearing with a bottle of champagne and two glasses.

"Where were you hiding that?" I asked. I hadn't looked in the fridge today, but I definitely hadn't seen it earlier.

He gave me a wink as he started to tackle the foil. "You're going to have to let me keep a few secrets." He opened the bottle with a small pop but no escape of alcohol and poured us each a glass. I took mine and waited for him to sit before I clinked my glass gently against his, and we took sips of the delicious, crisp liquid.

He looked over at me, and I met his eyes. His voice when he spoke was the darkest, honeyed chocolate. "Summer, I wanted to tell you, these past few days have been the happiest of my life."

I swallowed down the lump in my throat and held his gaze. "Mine too." I contemplated him for a moment: so many things I wanted to say to him, so impossible to capture in words how I felt. "I love you, Jonny. So very, very much."

He took my hand and raised my fingers to his lips, pressing his mouth softly against them in a gesture I was now familiar with but which I only appreciated more every time he did it.

I had no idea what the time was, how close or otherwise to midnight, but it didn't matter anymore. I was ready. "My answer is yes," I said. "I will come live with you and be your love. And I'll be forever honoured and grateful that you asked me." In the distance, fireworks began to explode over Carbis Bay. I looked at him, his eyes on mine as intense and loving as I'd ever seen them. "And I promise, I won't ever make you wait for an answer again."

Part Fourteen

Epilogue

So, dear reader, if you're reading this you have most likely read my and Jonny's story. I do hope you enjoyed our little tale. Jenna, however, was worried that our history of ups and downs might leave some concerned that one or other of us (okay, mainly me) might find a way to turn champagne into three-day-old boxed wine and spoil our chances of future happiness. So I have been urged, in the strongest (and not entirely polite) terms, to give you a little glimpse into our future. A request with which I am happy to comply.

I hope you will be pleased to hear that I managed not to make any further silly decisions in my life where Jonny was concerned. We were married only the following summer at St Carantoc church in Crantock. The bride wore ivory, the maid of honour wore lilac and the mother of the bride wore a very relieved smile. We were blessed, a few years later, with the arrival of our first daughter, Lily, and then a couple of years after that with her sister, Rose (or Rosie, as she came to be known to her family). Both girls inherited their father's dark, curly hair and were the height of giraffes by the time they were fifteen. From me they inherited blue eyes and the ability to drive their father crazy whilst not losing an ounce of his unbounded affection.

Christmases were always spent with either my or Jonny's parents in Crantock, and post-Christmas lunch walks on the beach were always taken whatever the weather.

I did set up my events management business in Cornwall, and it did well for a while, but after Rosie was born, I decided that the time it required wasn't worth missing out on any more hours watching my girls grow up, so I sold the business and shifted my efforts into managing Jonny's career full time, giving him the freedom he'd always craved to focus entirely on creating his art (turns out artists *really* don't like admin).

Once I became pregnant with Lily, we bought a house near Hayle, but Jonny always kept his studio at Gwithian, eventually buying the chalet from Cheryl (who, I wasn't surprised to discover, did have a little bit of a crush on him). She wasn't overly keen on letting it go but was eventually persuaded, and she and Jonny stayed friends for many years.

Jenna did get her Happy Ever After with Richard, and, with his investment and her substantial amounts of moxie, she ended up being the owner of no fewer than three nail and beauty salons, one in Newquay, one in Perranporth and one in St Ives. She lived happily with Richard in his big, luxurious home on the dunes. My father never did come to terms with the house.

Mike enjoyed a not-insubstantial fling with the divorcee, but in the end returned to Briony and Claire. He even ended up owning his own little deli-cafe in Perranporth. Sometimes people can surprise you.

So, I hope this has allayed any concerns you may have

had that I didn't learn my lesson where Jonny Rawlings was concerned, because I most assuredly did. We had the occasional blazing row about silly things (he *would* leave oily rags in the most inconvenient places), but I never lost that feeling of amazement and wonder that we found one another, and that he chose and waited for me. I always appreciated I was amongst the luckiest women alive.

(Jonny just popped in to say that he also wants you to know that I made him ridiculously happy, in spite of my habit of forgetting to remove my hair from the shower drain, and that he could never entirely believe how lucky he got that I came back to him, so I am just passing that on.)

We hope that one day you might visit our spots in our most beautiful, beloved Cornwall, and that you will love them as much as we do. We might even pass you on the coastal path, walking our dogs.

A Thank You

Thank you for reading *A Cornish Winter's Tale!* I hope you loved reading it as much as I did writing it.

If you enjoyed it, please be so kind as to leave a brief review on Amazon. By doing so, you're helping others find this story and my work and providing encouragement to this author to continue writing and publishing.

Visit my website to subscribe to my mailing list to be first to hear about new releases and giveaways, and for access to sneak peeks and bonus content. Subscribers will also have the chance to be amongst the first to read my latest books for free before publication.

I'd love to hear from you, so if you'd like to get in touch you can do so via any of the channels below. Please follow me on social media for updates on my writing and to be alerted about new releases.

Twitter: @AnnaRCarlyle

Instagram: @annarcarlyle

Website: annacarlyle.net

Author's Note

I was inspired to write this story by my love of Cornwall and its beautiful coastline. I have made use of locations I know well in its writing and included real details where appropriate, but I must stress that considerable licence with reality has been taken where it benefits the story, and most especially that absolutely none of these people exist in any way in the real world and neither do any of their houses. All of these characters are entirely the result of my imagination, and any specifics as to personal residences are completely fictionalised and bear no resemblance to real places.

Printed in Great Britain
by Amazon